M000199857

conviction

Conviction
Copyright © 2015 Corinne Michaels
All rights reserved.
ISBN 978-1-942834-26-7

No part of this publication may be reproduced, distributed or transmitted in any form or by any means including electronic, mechanical, photocopying, recording or otherwise, without the prior written consent of the author.

This book is a work of fiction. Names, characters, places and incidents either are products of the author's imagination or are used fictitiously. Any resemblance to actual events or locales or persons, living or dead, is entirely coincidental and beyond the intent of the author or publisher.

Editor:
Lisa Christman, Adept Edits

Proofreading:
Ashley Williams, AW Editing

Interior design and formatting:
Christine Borgford, Type A Formatting
www.typeAformatting.com

Cover design:
Okay Creations

Cover photo © Perrywinkle Photography

THE SALVATION SERIES

Beloved

Beholden

Consolation

Conviction

Defenseless

conviction

CORINNE MICHAELS

dedication

To my mother, you always believed in me even when I didn't. Your love, friendship, support, and courage made me the woman I am today. Without you, none of this would be possible.

chapter

one

T

IME ISN'T SOMETHING I ever thought much about. It ebbs and flows, but it never changes. I can't make it stop—no matter how much I want to. There's no way to rewind the clock or halt it. In this moment, all I want is to make the world stop and go back to when I was happy and ready to tackle the world. Just two short minutes ago, there was no worry about how my day would go. I was going away with the man I love, the one who healed me. But time isn't my friend. It slaps me in the face and laughs as I stand here wondering how the hell any of this is happening. I don't want to move forward, and I sure as hell don't want to slow it down.

"Aaron?"

He stands before me—alive. The man who I would've sold my soul to have back again a year ago is here. I take a hesitant step forward. I'm aware of the people around me, but my mind can't focus on anything else but him.

"Hi, baby," he rasps.

"Oh, my God. You're alive?" I ask and step closer. His dark brown eyes glimmer with hope and happiness.

"I'm here," he says, and I rush forward. My arms wrap around his neck while the tears fall. He's alive and here. In my arms, I hold my lost husband as he rubs my back. My heart races as I fully start to process what's happening. Aaron holds the back of my head as I sob into his chest. "I missed you so much," he murmurs and rocks.

"You're alive." My heart stutters while I struggle to catch my breath. I hold him closer and squeeze just to be sure.

He winces, and I step back. Aaron comes forward with a smile, and I place my hand on his face. He has bruises on the side of his cheek and neck, his hair is long, but it's really him. The man I loved for so long and the father of my daughter is home. It's unbelievable.

"I-I thought . . ." I choke on the words, as my breathing grows shallow. "You're . . . I don't know what—"

My mind spins as the last year of grief, sadness, and devastation crashes around me. He was alive and we didn't know. We didn't look. Or maybe it's just a dream?

"Shh." He takes my hand in his. "It's okay now. I'm here, we're going to be fine, baby. I'm home."

The words filter through me and my gaze shifts as I notice movement to the right.

Liam. Oh my God . . . Liam.

I look over to the side where he stands with his head bowed. My heart thumps out of sync. Tears well in my eyes as the enormity of this moment comes down around me. Liam still doesn't look at me. The pain lances through me as I beseech with my eyes for him to turn and look at me.

Please, just see me, I beg him, but he doesn't lift his eyes.

My feet move toward him, but he still doesn't move.

"Liam, please," I plead with tears falling.

His eyes lift, and while his face is stoic, his eyes give it away. He's hurting.

"Natalie?" Aaron's voice breaks through the small moment I was having with Liam.

I turn around and try to get a hold of myself. Jackson and Mark stand to the side, watching the mess unfold. There's so much confusion rolling around within me. I don't know what to do, where to turn, or how any of this is happening. I was packing my car to go to Corolla. I was going to spend time with the man I love. The man I was building a future with. And now my husband is here.

I step back and my body begins to shake. This is too much. No one can endure this and come out on the other side. I'm losing it. Shock rolls through me like waves on the sand. "I can't breathe," I say aloud.

Mark takes a step toward me. "Lee, it's okay."

I laugh sarcastically. "No. None of this is okay. None of this makes any sense!" I scream as my heart implodes. "I can't! I mean, this isn't real."

I feel someone close in behind me and Mark shakes his head. "It is real."

Turning around, Aaron is right there. "I'm here, Lee. I'm home." He sounds so hopeful as if this is everything I could want. Of course I had wanted this for so long. He was my world and now he's back, but what does all this mean? Liam is the man I love. How am I going to do this now?

Aaron's hand reaches out then he touches my arm. My body locks as Liam watches with sadness in his eyes. I look at Aaron, and the past comes down upon me. This isn't my husband I dreamt of. This isn't the man I loved with every part of me. This is the man that a few months ago I found out had an affair. The same man who almost had a baby with someone else. His hands feel foreign, and as he goes to embrace me, my hand rises and I stop him. I'm no better than he is in this moment. "Please, just, I need . . ." I trail off.

Liam is here, watching me go into another man's arms. Five minutes ago, I was relieved Aaron's alive and Liam saw the joy in my face. I'm killing him. I see it.

"No!" I yell and step back. "Please, don't touch me." My hand flies to my mouth as shock locks my body in place.

Aaron's hand drops and his breath hitches. "You're my wife, Lee. I know you're confused and this is a lot to take, but I'm here, baby."

I move toward Liam, his blue eyes meet mine as I rush toward him. I take his hands in mine, but he releases them. My heart shatters as he steps back.

"Don't pull away from me," I demand.

"I think you need some time," his voice cracks. "You need to talk."

"I don't know what I need," I acknowledge.

"Lee," he says and looks at Aaron, but then he returns his gaze to me.

I see it in his eyes, the resolution forming and masking over this pain. "You're going to walk away from me, aren't you?" Tears fall relentlessly as I wait for his answer.

Liam's hand lifts, and he tenderly cups my cheek. "I'm not walking away. I need a minute."

Aaron clears his throat. "I missed a lot more than you filled me in on. I guess I understand why you've been so quiet now."

The loss of Liam's touch registers immediately.

Anger boils within as the hurt and betrayal at Aaron's hand over the last few months comes flooding forward. "You should stop," I demand.

"My wife?" he yells and steps forward. "You've been fucking my wife?"

"You were dead!" I scream, and my legs give out. I fall to the hard ground as the gravel scrapes my skin. Liam's arms are around me in an instant.

"Get your hands off of her! You son of a bitch!" Aaron continues to raise his voice warning Liam. "I'll kill you!"

I look up, and Jackson and Mark are holding on to Aaron,

dragging him to the back of the house.

I turn into Liam's embrace allowing his strong arms to hold me close. "Take me to Corolla. I'll grab Aara, and we can go," I plead. "Please, take me away."

"Lee," he says with regret laced in his voice. "I can't. I wish we could, but we can't."

"No," I reply defiantly. "You and I had plans."

"And now your husband is home."

"My cheating husband?"

Liam sighs while pushing me back slightly. "You both need to talk. I can't be that man."

We both stand looking at each other before I speak. "What man? The man I fell in love with? The man who told me he loved me? Because that's the man I need."

Liam wipes his hand down his face. "He's your fucking husband, Lee! Not to mention he was my best friend. I saw the way you looked at him. It was clear in the second you saw him how much you love him. You ran to him, and I get it," he says despondently. "I get why you would. You loved him. I mean, what the hell do you want me to do?"

"Fight!" I slap his chest and push. "Fight for me. Fight for us. So what, you're going to walk away? Just hand me over like I mean nothing?" The question hangs in the air as I wait for the bomb to drop.

"You want me to fight?" he steps closer. "You think I'm not? You think this is what the hell I wanted? To deliver your husband back to you when I'm so fucking in love with you that I would've rather cut out my own heart? I hate that I brought him home to you."

Anger stirs between us as the weight of the situation descends around us.

"I can't believe this."

Liam's shoulders sag in defeat. "You both have a lot of things to work through. I should leave before this escalates. I won't be that guy."

I huff and look away. Unreal. "I can't believe you think so little of us."

With my pulse beating rapidly in my chest, Liam grips my shoulders pulling me close. Our noses touch while we both breathe heavily. "I would give my life for you. I would go in there and pummel his ass to a pulp if I thought that would help. But it won't. You're married to him. You're his wife. Right this minute, I'm the other man. Do you understand that?"

"I belong to you."

"No, you belong to him."

I need him to understand me. My life changed when Liam came. He made me feel again, loved me like I've never known. I don't know that I'll survive if he leaves me. I close my eyes and press my lips to his. Gripping his shirt, I yank his body against mine.

Kiss me, dammit.

Claim me.

He stands unmoving as I pour myself into him. He doesn't respond, and my anger grows.

Pulling back, I glare at him as his eyes shut. My hand rears back then I slap him across the face. I take pleasure in watching his eyes snap open, hoping this draws him back to me.

"What the hell was that for?"

I slap him again. I see the fight coming to life inside of him.

"Fuck you. If I mean this little to you, then go. Go. Run. Leave! Go be the man you're not because of whatever bullshit you'll feed yourself! Go!" I raise my hand again, but he grabs it.

Liam's control snaps, he grips my arms tighter jerking me against him. I breathe one deep breath before his lips crash against mine. I savor the feel of his mouth pushing against mine. I get lost in the brute force of this kiss. His fingers are a vice around my arms, and I don't care. I want him to bruise me. Leave his mark so I have proof of what we shared. My lips mold to his as I give him back all I am.

I escape the moment we're both drowning in when our tongues touch. His grip loosens as his hands glide to my neck until they cradle my head. The mood shifts to sadness. My fingers thread in his hair as I try to hold him against me. Liam's hands tighten, and he breaks us apart.

"I need a minute. I need a few of them. I love you, but I have to go."

My heart shatters all over again. I've lost him.

"If you leave me, I don't think you're coming back," I say, hoping he'll refute me and give the comfort I'm desperate for.

Liam rests his forehead against mine. "I'm never far. You need to get through this without worrying about me."

"You think I can do that? You think right now as happy as I am he's alive. That I'm not distraught? That I'm not worried about how the hell you and I will survive this? I'll worry every day about you and us." I beg him to stay. I need him to stay.

"Aaron and you had a whole life together. We had a few months."

"Don't you dare downplay what we have!" I fight the urge to slap him again.

Liam runs his fingers the length of my arm. "I need you to see this from my side. I never knew if you'd have chosen him, but now I don't know if you should choose me. I need to get my fucking head on straight. Right now, you have to let me go." Liam's eyes mirror mine with the agony of this moment.

I fight the tears that build. As much as I know he's right, I wish he were wrong. I don't know how to navigate this. It's too much. My heart had healed, and instantly I'm raw all over again. There was a time that Aaron was everything I wanted. Now that he's back in my life, I no longer want him. If any prayer I wish went unanswered, it was this one, only because now I have to endure the pain of breaking a man I love. But my life doesn't work that way.

"I want you to know something before you walk away from me. I need you to know that I want you. You are the man I'm in love with. Yes, he's my husband and Aarabelle's father, but I love you, Liam. I love you so much more than I want to, but God, I love you. Please, hear me. I love you."

"I love you too, but I have to do what's right."

"Right for who?" I scoff.

Liam leans back and waits until I look at him. His blue eyes shimmer with unshed tears. "For you. For Aarabelle. For all of us. I can't be the man who destroys a marriage, and sure as fuck not yours and Aaron's."

There's no convincing him, and all I can hope for at this moment is that he heard me.

Before I can respond, I hear someone approach from behind. Liam looks up, and by the flash in his eyes, I know it's Aaron.

"I hate to break up this touching scene, but I've been gone more than a year and this isn't exactly the reunion I anticipated." Aaron's voice is on the edge. "If I could have my wife, brother."

I don't miss the way he enunciates "wife" or "brother."

Liam doesn't say anything, but his arms fall, as does my heart.

He walks away without a word. I face my husband, my first love, with tears in my eyes as the man I love more than anything leaves me behind.

I want to die.

chapter two

ARON AND I walk toward the back of the house where Jackson and Mark are standing. Jackson shifts, and I smother the urge to punch him in the face. "No one thought a heads up would be a good idea?" I spit the words. "No one thought I should know this? Did your cell phones all die? Because I can't think of any reason why you all wouldn't want to tell me."

"Natalie," Mark steps toward me. "First of all, none of us knew if it was definitely Aaron. Secondly, we couldn't compromise the mission. This all had to happen very secretly and very covertly. And what, did you want us to call on the way over? No one knew how to handle this."

Jackson takes a hesitant footstep. "I know you were getting your life together. I know you were happy, and for that, I'm sorry. No one here would want to hurt you. Least of all me."

"Sure, you're sorry." Anger flows through me, tearing me apart.

His head bows then he turns to Aaron. "We should let you guys talk. Remember what I said about a lot changing in a year. But I'm glad you're home."

Aaron looks at me before turning back to Jackson. "I appreciate it. I'm happy to be back with my girls."

The last few months rush back. I remember how I felt finding out about his transgressions. How he loved another woman. My mind starts to wonder if he means me and Aarabelle, or me and Brittany.

I can't listen to this. I need to get a grip on what the hell is festering inside of me. There are so many things I'm feeling all at once. I walk down onto the beach, the sand burning my feet, and I welcome the pain. I stand still, lifting my head to the sky. *Why?* I ask the clouds. This should be a happy moment. One filled with hugs and tears of joy, but I'm left feeling as if a gaping hole was punched through my chest. Just when I thought my life was on track—boom.

My mind drifts to Liam and how devastated he was. His eyes lost the spark I loved to see. I don't know where my life will go—once again. There are no easy answers in this situation. I have a husband, a baby, a boyfriend, and suddenly a shitload of problems. But I need him to see that I meant what I said. I want him beside me.

"Are we going to talk?" I hear Aaron ask from behind me. The raspy voice that once made me long for him now makes me want to cry.

I turn as he stands still, waiting for something from me. "No, I'd rather not. I feel like I'm about to wake up any moment, so I'm just waiting for it to happen. All of this is so confusing," I reply and wish I could slap myself.

Aaron steps forward. "Lee," his voice trembles, "I'm here."

"You keep saying that. But how? How is this happening?" I take a moment to look over his face. His brown eyes are dull and lifeless, there's a large gash on the side of his neck. My eyes travel down his arms where there are a few scars from what look like burns, and he's missing a finger on his left hand. He looks broken and alone, but then he smiles at me and I try to stop my heart from swelling a little.

"All I could think about was seeing my girls," he steps closer. "I fought to be here for you."

"For me? Really?" I question, not actually wanting an answer. Aaron looks at me with confusion. *Well, I'll be happy to clue him in.* "Are you sure it's me you want, Aaron, or do you want me to call Brittany?" I ask, shooting daggers at him. I stand watching his reactions. I catalog the way he shifts to the side and the way he grips the back of his neck.

I see the fear flare in his eyes, and if I hadn't known him for most of my life, I'd have missed it.

"It's not—"

"Not what I think?"

Aaron takes another step closer as his face pales. "I love you. I've always loved you."

"You love me?" I scoff. "That's rich. You have a funny way of showing it. God, this whole situation is so insane," I say in disbelief. "I mean, you were dead. I buried you. I stood and wept for you. Then I go through hell finding a way to put myself back together. Only to find out you cheated on me for months! Months, Aaron!" I move forward this time allowing him to see the anger on my face. "You betrayed me. The man I married wouldn't have done that. But the man who held my hand and told me he'd die before touching another woman did exactly that."

"And you fucked Liam!" he bellows before sinking into the sand. On his knees in front of me, I see the hurt all over him.

"You have no clue."

Aaron looks at me and tears form in my eyes. "We have a lot to work through, Lee. I know I fucked up. I know I made mistakes and I wish you'd never found out about them. Can we please give ourselves a few days?"

A tear falls and my heart breaks. "And then what?"

"I don't know," he admits. "But I've thought about you every day that I was gone. Every fucking minute of the day, I fought death to come home to you. All I wanted was to see you and the baby." His eyes flood with tears and every part of me aches.

I don't want to hurt him. I don't want to cause him pain. That's not who I am. This is the man I thought I'd spend every day of my life with. The man I struggled to have children with. Agonizing months of shots and treatments because I wanted to give him a child. A part of me is pulled to him, but I don't trust myself. He represents every memory of our twelve years together, and we have a child. It's taking everything inside of me not to collapse.

I sink in the sand beside him. "I'm in love with Liam." My voice is a whisper. The way his hands clench tells me he heard.

Aaron tenderly lifts my chin. "I'm begging you, Lee. I'm on my knees begging you to give us some time. Let's wait a few days before we decide anything. There are a lot of things we have to discuss regardless."

The words catch in my throat as I think of Liam. I don't know how to feel in this moment. Who am I loyal to? Aaron was . . . is . . . my husband. But Liam has my heart. He brought me to life in a way Aaron never did. He's good to me, loyal and faithful. There's no mistrust between us. It's not Aaron's fault he's been gone a year, but it's not Liam's either. Now, all of us have to pay the price.

"I don't know that a few days will change my feelings," I warn.

"I think you should know everything."

His hand drops, and I look back at the house. So much has changed in a matter of a few minutes. I sit here, wishing I could go back in time. I would've made different decisions. Maybe I'd have seen the writing on the wall with Aaron and left him. I don't know that I'd be with Liam if that were the case, but I could've started over.

"I missed you so much, Aaron. So much that it broke me, and now . . ."

He takes my face in his hands. "I'm here now, and I'll fix the broken, baby."

My heart shatters because in this moment, I don't think he can. I'm destroyed by what we've both endured. I'm wrecked for what Liam is feeling. I'm devastated for what's about to come down the road for both of these men—and me. We will all have blood drawn and be left to try to heal after this.

Aaron and I stare at each other as so many emotions flow through me. I'm so happy he's alive, but with that comes sadness. The flame that was once so strong I could feel him in my soul is barely a flicker.

His thumb brushes my cheek, and I try to catch my breath. "I'm so sorry, Lee."

Another tear falls as I start to shut myself off. I have to hold my child right now. I have to have her in my arms because she's real and what I need to focus on. "I need to go get Aarabelle."

"Aarabelle? Is that what you named her?" Aaron's demeanor shifts, and he smiles for the first time. Oh, how I missed his smile. "I thought we decided on Chloe?"

"I wanted her to bare your name always." The pain shoots through me. "I wanted her to know you in some way. I needed her to know how special she is because her father was a hero."

Aaron's body leans closer. "She has you. She was always going to be special. I want to see her."

My throat goes dry as I fight the tears threatening to fall. "I don't want to confuse her. I know she's your daughter, but I don't know what to do."

"I'm your husband too," he reminds me.

"You and I may be married right now, but there's so much

we have to talk about, Aaron. This isn't an easy place for either of us. You haven't been a husband for a long time." I give Aaron my own reminder. We're both victims here. "I'm going to pick her up from the sitter. I need time. There are a lot of things we need to decide on to press forward."

"Where does your boyfriend fit into all of this?" he sneers. He's lucky I don't punch him.

I stand, giving myself the height advantage. He doesn't get to degrade me for something he did. I won't let him taint the love I share with Liam. If he wants to be an asshole, I'll show him how much I've grown.

"I'll let you slide on this. I didn't date Liam behind your back. I didn't betray you. I thought you were *dead*." Aaron looks at me, and I know this is killing him. I didn't fall in love with someone random. I fell in love with his best friend. The immense pain he must feel is something I can't understand. Brittany was bad, but I didn't have to lose two people I care about.

I know this isn't easy for him. I hate that now I'm the one holding the knife to his chest.

"But I'm not gone."

"No, you're not, and I'm so happy you're alive. I'm glad Aarabelle will have her father. But Liam is the reason I smiled again and found a way to muddle through the days. Liam is the reason when I found out about your affair I didn't go off the deep end. So that was the one dig you get. I'm not the liar or the cheater—" I let that hang in the air between us.

Aaron stands then grips my shoulders. "I came back to you. I lived to see your face again. Not hers—yours. Every moment, I thought of you, dreamt of you, needed to touch you again." His hands graze my arms as he speaks. "I need you, Natalie. I need you, and I'm not letting you go without a fight. I lived for you and our daughter. I'll be damned if I'm going to let anyone take that from me again."

I stare into his amber eyes and choke back the sob that threatens to escape. "It's not your choice anymore."

"No one is going to take my family from me. I'm going to win you back. And I'll be sure to let Liam know that as well." Aaron's hands fall, and he heads toward the water.

I stand in shock at the promise he made. My heart races while the nausea bubbles up. I don't have any idea how I'm going to handle this. All I know is right now I want to be wrapped in Liam's arms in Corolla, away from all of this.

chapter

three

"THANKS, PAIGE," I say as I lift Aarabelle into my arms.

"No problem. I hope you have fun in Corolla," she smiles and I nod. I can't say the words because they will break the carefully constructed front I've managed to build.

I buckle Aarabelle in her seat while she smiles at me. "Dada-dada," she babbles and then I fall apart.

My muscles go limp while I lie with my head in her lap and sob. I think about how she called Liam "dada" and how much it made a part of me happy. Now, the sound of her saying it makes me break. I drown in the sea of pain as each sound of my own cries takes me under.

She plays with my hair as I lose it in the back seat of my car. *Breathe and you'll figure this out. You're stronger than this.*

I look at Aarabelle, and brush the side of her face. "So much has changed, baby girl. So much. Mommy's going to be a mess, but I'll do everything I can to protect you from it all. I love you so much," I tell her then close the door.

When I left the house, Aaron was sitting on the deck. He asked if we could talk more tonight and try to find some kind of middle ground. I don't even have a clue as to what kind of agreement we can come to, but I at least have to try. If I want any shot in hell with Liam, I need to know where things stand at home first.

There are so many issues flying through my mind: where he'll sleep, clothing, do I file for divorce, what about all the money from him being declared dead? I sit in the driver's seat and put the music on. I don't want to think about any of this. I want to take a moment.

I pay no mind to where I'm going, because I'm singing as loud as I can with tears streaming down my face. Life is cruel. Love is a joke. And not even death is final.

I'm not ready to head home. I know I should because he's waiting for her. He's waiting for me. I'm being uncaring, but all I want to do is head to Liam and beg him to take me into his arms. Looking back in the rearview mirror, Aarabelle stares out the window, and I wish things could be different, but I'm grateful she'll never remember all of this mess. I turn into my driveway and sit. The turmoil boiling through my veins makes it impossible to move. There's not only the fear of him with Aarabelle, but also me too. I'm a match next to a canteen of gasoline, ready to ignite at any moment. We haven't dealt with anything and I reluctantly agreed to let it rest for a few days.

A few days that I can't go to Liam.

Time to get your shit together.

Aarabelle smiles when I get her from her car seat. I walk slowly with her to the deck where Aaron is standing with his back to me.

He turns slowly and casts his eyes on Aarabelle for the first time. I hold her close as she looks around. Aaron takes a slow step forward and smiles. "She's beautiful."

Words fail me, so I nod.

"She looks just like you, Lee." Aaron's eyes swim with love as he stares at my—our—daughter.

"I always thought she looked like you," I say looking at her while she smiles at me.

"Can I?" he asks, his arms extended.

I shouldn't pull her back, but I do. I can't stop the fear that festers. He's her father, he wanted her, and he will love her, I know all of this. But she's only ever been mine. It makes me harsh and selfish, but I don't really care. She's *my* daughter. I've been through it all with her. Well, me and Liam. He's practically been a parent to her, and I feel as if I'm betraying *him*. Which is insane.

"Lee," my name rolls off his tongue.

Tears pool and one lone bead of moisture escapes. It slowly descends down my face before landing on my lip. "I j-just . . ." I stutter. My hands grip Aarabelle as she squirms to get free. Aaron moves closer, keeping his eyes trained on her as if he can't look away.

This was the culmination of years of heartbreak. Years of both of us feeling inadequate and alone together. She's the beauty in all the heartache. She's the prize from all the desperation we endured. And she's his. Not Liam's.

No matter where Aaron and I land, Aarabelle is the glue that will hold our lives together. Forever we will be tied to each other. I slowly extend her, and his arms meet me halfway. Our hands touch as his eyes fill with tears.

"Hi, Aarabelle," he says adoringly to Aara. The way he looks at her, like she's the air he breathes, makes my chest tighten.

The arms I'd wished would wrap around her, protect her, love her are now holding her. She looks at Aaron with her signature smile. My body goes stiff as it all settles around us.

Aaron somehow lived and is home.

He's holding our baby.

"God, she couldn't be any more perfect," he laughs and looks at me.

I sniff and try to rein myself in. "Yeah, she really is perfect."

"You look just like your mommy." He bounces her and wipes his eyes. "I dreamt of you. I wondered if you were okay," Aaron talks to Aarabelle, and I have to take a few steps back.

Father and daughter are united.

"What's her birthday?" he asks.

"August ninth." She looks at me, and I walk over to them. I place my hand on her back while she touches his face.

Aaron just stares at her. Aarabelle squirms again and begins to fuss.

"She's almost one. She just wants to move around," I explain, reaching for her. "Do you want to go for a walk? She loves the beach." I offer the olive branch to him. The confliction on how to handle this entire thing is too great to make things any harder.

His eyes soften, and he nods. "That would be great."

I lean down, place Aara on the chair, and then remove her shoes. "You'll need to hold her other hand. She's a little unsteady."

Aaron holds his hand out to her, and she wraps her fingers around his. With me on the other side, we begin to head toward the water. Mother, father, and daughter. It's a picture perfect vision of how our lives could've been. My thoughts wander to the man who's been at my side the last year. How would he feel about this?

"Lee?" Aaron asks as we walk along the water line, breaking me from my reflections.

"Yes?"

"I really do love you." Aaron's voice doesn't waver.

"Mama!" Aara yells demanding my attention. I'm grateful for the distraction, because I don't know how to respond. Do I love him? I'll always love him. But because of Liam, my life this last year has been different.

"She's getting hungry."

"Okay," Aaron says then looks away. "I should probably lie down. I'm exhausted."

We start to walk back to our home, but I don't speak. The silence says everything.

After I get Aarabelle to bed, and Aaron hovers watching everything I do, we both head toward the living room. It's the first time we're completely alone. I don't know how I'm going to last days without talking about all the crap between us.

He sits on the couch, but he's not relaxed. The muscles in his arms are coiled tight. His head rests on the back of the seat, but everything in his body shows his distress.

"Aaron? Are you okay?"

Immediately his eyes fly open. "Hey," his voice is like ice. "I'm fine. Just got lost for a moment."

I'm a fairly empathetic person, but how to navigate this is beyond my understanding. I have no idea what it's like to be held captive. I don't know how someone can endure that and resume their old life. Especially one that everyone has spent the last year moving on from, so that it doesn't even exist anymore. "Do you want to talk about it?"

Aaron shakes his head. "I can't yet. I'm trying to figure out a way to make it through this. I came home to a world I don't have a place in. I lost you, my house, my life."

"I know you want to give it a few days. I don't think we can. How are we supposed to sit here and have all this just hanging? It's putting us both on edge."

Aaron shifts forward so that his forearms rest on his knees. "I don't know. I'm in agony, Lee. It feels like you wish I'd stayed gone, and I don't know how to feel about that. I'm your husband."

"You were dead. You were gone. I had to live."

"I fucking know that." Aaron stands while his eyes focus on flag sitting on the mantle. "I see it in your eyes though, baby."

"Don't," I warn. "You told me to move on, you made me promise. You can't hate me or blame me for doing what you asked."

My heartbeat falters as he kneels while gripping my hands. "I can't. I've loved you my whole life. I can't look at you right now and think of my fucking best friend touching you."

I pull my hands back. He's suffered and I know this. I can't begin to imagine what the last year has brought him, and then to add insult to injury, I wasn't here waiting for him. "You ruined me. I trusted you, and then to find out you had an affair . . ."

Aaron's gaze drops, and he sucks in a breath. "I know. It was never like that."

"No?"

He looks back up as I search for the man I once loved. Not because I want to be with him, but because I need to know he's there. I implore him to tell me the truth. If he lies, there will never be a way for us to move forward.

"I was the broken one. I needed you so much, and all you cared about was getting pregnant. We didn't talk if it wasn't surrounding infertility. We didn't touch if it wasn't a part of your schedule. I couldn't have sex with you because it would diminish my counts. I hated coming home. I volunteered to go on missions just because I needed a fucking break."

His words cut me deeper than I ever imagined. They tear through any whole part of me that remained. He and he alone made these decisions for our family. My emotions and my needs were secondary in every way. I had to go through hell because he was too much of a chickenshit to fight. "You volunteered when I was already pregnant?"

"No, the ones before. When I would go on those trips, it reminded me of how it felt to be in charge of *something*. I failed at every fucking turn. Being your husband was exhausting."

"So she was just some way to escape the horrors of being my husband?" I ask with disparagement dripping from my tongue.

"Natalie, it was a way to escape the horrors of not being man enough. It wasn't about you. Don't you get that?" He waits, but I don't say a word. "It was me who wasn't able to give you, my wife, the woman I would've laid my own life down for, a baby. I was inadequate on every level. She didn't see that in me. She saw the strong, virile male who wasn't a failure. I needed her to take the pain away."

"Was she worth it?"

"It wasn't about her."

"Would you go back and do it again?" I ask with raw pain drowning my words.

Aaron looks away and then back again. "She gave me something you weren't willing to give anymore. She looked at me like a man. She looked at me like a hero. In her eyes, I was someone worth loving. I needed that. I deserved that."

"Would you do it again?" I ask again.

"I don't know!"

I look at him, and he knows me well enough to see the hurt, anger, and despair in my eyes. He knows that was the end of any chance he had.

He just lost me.

Completely.

CHAPTER

FOUR

LIAM

"FUCK!" I SCREAM and throw the glass against the wall. It's been forty-eight hours since I last saw her face. Two fucking days. I haven't slept. I can't eat. I want to rush back to her house and take her and Aarabelle. I need her like I need air.

But I have to stay away.

He's my best friend.

He's her husband.

I'm a piece of shit.

"Dempsey, open the fucking door!" I hear someone, but I'm not moving.

"Suck my dick!" I yell back and reach for my glass. Oh, yeah, I broke it. The bottle will be just fine. I grip the neck of the bottle as the vodka pours down my throat. I need the numbness that won't come.

"I'll knock it off the goddamn hinges. Don't think I won't," I hear Quinn on the other side threatening me. He's the last person I want to see. Like I need a talk about why loving her was a bad idea.

"Go away," I reply, taking another swig of what I'm hoping will give me a break from the hell I'm living.

I hear the wood splinter as Quinn kicks the door in. Asshole.

"You're going to pay for that," I inform him.

"If you'd have opened the damn door, I wouldn't have kicked it in." He looks around the room, and I sink into the couch.

"Good to see you're taking it well."

I open my eyes then flip him off. "If you've come here to gloat, you can see yourself out the door. I don't need anyone's shit."

Quinn pushes my leg and sits next to me. He grabs the bottle from my hand and puts it on the table. "No one could've seen this coming, man. You didn't know."

"I brought him to her. I had to sit on that fucking plane and listen to him go on and on about her." I want to throw something again. "He wouldn't shut up about being with her again. I just sat there, and Jackson and Mark didn't know what to say either. None of us could tell him. None of us could talk. How fucked up am I that I wished it hadn't been him?"

Quinn sits there quiet for the first time in his life. I reach for the bottle, but he moves it before I can grab it.

"Give it to me."

"You've had enough, Demps."

"I'm on leave! Give me the goddamn bottle," I growl as I reach again.

Quinn smirks and I stand, ready to fight him.

"You wanna hit me, buddy? Go ahead. I'll have your ass laid out before you get your first hit in," he taunts and sits there lazily.

"Fuck you!"

"Nah, you're not really my type."

"Are you enjoying this?" I ask and head to the kitchen before he can answer me. He may have taken my vodka, but I'll grab the whiskey.

I try to be as quiet as possible while I grab the Jameson. I get the top off and take half a swig before Quinn grabs it from me.

My fist clenches, I go to take a swing, but Quinn's hand goes up and grabs my hand and twists it. "You wanna kill yourself? You want to be a pussy and drink yourself stupid, or do you want to be a man?"

I don't say anything. I'm drunk, angry, and I want my girl back.

My other hand flies up, and before I know it, I'm face down on the ground with Quinn holding my arms behind my back. "Pussy it is," Quinn laughs and uses something to secure my hands behind my back.

"Untie me, you son-of-a-bitch." My voice is borderline murderous. "I'll kill you when I get out of this."

Quinn squats in front of me while I lie on the ground. "I'm not worried." He pats my back and grabs the whiskey. "Now that you can't do anything stupid let's chat."

I lift my head while glaring at him.

"You have two choices here. You can either let Aaron claim his wife back, or you can show her why you're worth her time. It's clear you love her and she loves you."

I look at him incredulously. This was the same guy who told me to stay away. "She's married to *him*. She's not just some guy's wife."

"Did she tell you to leave?"

I close my eyes and see her face. She was so angry and slapped me, but I couldn't be that guy. I can't be the one who breaks up a family. It's not just about Aaron . . . there's Aarabelle to think about too. She may not be mine, but I love her as if she were. I can't be the reason that she doesn't have her father. If Natalie wants me, she'll have to decide that on her own with no influence from me. I'd never stop wondering.

"No, but she was in shock."

"You're clairvoyant now? Wow, okay," he pauses. "What will the winning lottery numbers be? I could use some serious dough."

"Untie me," I demand as I try to move my hands.

"I'm not done talking," he states as if there's no issue in this.

"Quinn, I promise I'll kick the shit out of you if you don't untie me."

He laughs then moves to the chair, making himself comfortable. "You can try, but first you'll need to get out. Here's the deal. I don't think you're capable of making a rational decision right now. You need to sober up and figure out how the hell to claim your balls back. Right now, you're waving a white flag to a man who cheated on his wife. Yeah, he was your friend. I get it. Are you willing to fight for her? If you're not . . . then you don't deserve her."

Quinn stands and places a knife on the floor, clear out of reach. "You better run," I warn him.

"You should be chasing someone else. Think about that and then clean this shit. You're better than this," he says and walks out the room.

I start to slide against the floor toward the knife.

Each inch I get closer, I think about what he said. The alcohol fog I was hoping for is lifting as the anger sobers me. Natalie begged me to take her away and fight for her. And all I wanted was to whisk her away and run. But the part everyone fails to understand is that this isn't my fight. It's hers.

I'll never be able to push her away. I'll wait forever if I have to, but I can't fight this battle.

She has to be the one to choose me.

If she loves me like she says, she knows where to find me.

chapter *five*

NATALIE

"THANKS, REA," I say as I place Aarabelle in the porta crib at her house.

I haven't heard from Liam in two days. I've tried to get a hold of him multiple times, but he doesn't respond. He's starting to worry me.

"No problem. I love waking up at two a.m." She yawns and nudges me.

Aaron was asleep on the couch tossing and turning. I literally snuck out of my own house. Since the first night, we haven't spoken much. There's not much for me to say. He tells me repeatedly that he wants to work on us, but it's two people fighting to have the other let go. He wants me to let go of resisting him, and I want him to let me go. "I just need to see him. I won't be long."

Reanell takes me into her arms and holds tight. "Go. I'm sure he needs you."

"I don't know what to say to him," I admit.

"Just talk to him. How are things at home?"

Reanell and I haven't been able to talk except through text messages. Aaron hasn't left my side except to sleep. "I don't know.

Rocky at best. He's on the couch, which he's not happy about. He keeps saying he's going to prove how much we belong together."

She looks at me with empathy. "I know this is hard. I can't even imagine what you're feeling, but I can say I've seen you with both men. I know the Natalie you were with Aaron and who you are with Liam. Neither was wrong, but one was definitely happier. I'm here no matter what." Rea kisses the side of my cheek and swats my ass. "Now, go."

I turn and head toward the man I'm desperate to see.

As I drive, I debate whether I should let him know I'm on my way. I worry that he won't want to see me. The pain in his eyes haunts me. The need to see Liam as he was before all this is my only goal.

Guilt over leaving Aaron at home chews at my heart. It wraps around and squeezes me tight. My chest hurts, but I keep heading toward Liam. He's who I need right now. I miss him, love him, and long to touch him.

I park and check my reflection, already hating the dark circles forming under my eyes. The red, blotchy marks on my skin from all the tears I've shed. The acid marks on my skin matching my insides.

I knock twice but he doesn't answer. It's the middle of the night and I didn't call. I shouldn't be surprised. Regardless, disappointment swells over me. I rest my head against the door, hoping to feel some sort of connection to him. If he can feel me here, he'll open.

But instead the door shoves forward.

"Liam?" I speak quietly as I enter.

The hinges are broken, but look as if someone rigged the door back up. What the hell happened? I flip the light on in the living room, suddenly unsure if I'm in the right place. It's a mess. Papers, bottles, and shattered glass is everywhere. There's a hole in the wall by the television and a bloody towel lying on the floor.

"Liam?" I call out more loudly, but no answer.

When I reach his bedroom, I'm floored at what I find. Liam is passed out in the bed, wearing only his boxers. "Oh, Liam," I whisper and move toward him. Crouching down by his face, I gently brush his hair back. "I've missed you." He lets out a long, slow breath as if he's been holding it. "Why haven't you called me? I don't want to lose you. I feel so alone, Liam." My eyes prick as a tear falls. He sleeps as I confess my pain. "The tension is so thick, and I can't breathe without you. I close my eyes and pretend you're next to me. I feel your arms wrap around me, but you're not there. I wish I could be with you and not feel like I'm dying inside. We could be away, making love, holding each other, but you're passed out, and I'm sobbing on the floor. How did we get here? How do we go back?" My breathing becomes difficult as I let it all out. My fingers rub the side of his face, letting his beard scratch the pads of my fingers.

I need to be closer to him, so I strip down to my t-shirt and climb next to him. I lift his arm and drape it over me, allowing his warmth to blanket me. Tears continue to fall as I cocoon myself into him. I need to be close to him. Liam adjusts onto his side, and pulls me flush against his chest. He's still asleep, but it's as if he knows I'm here.

"I miss you, sweetheart," his deep voice trembles.

My eyes stay trained on his, but he keeps them closed.

"So fucking much," he says as his hands move down my back. "I need you, Lee."

"You have me. Take me," I murmur and press my lips to his. He kisses me with reverence and tenderness. Liam lets out a moan as his hands glide up my back.

He flips me onto my back while his delicious weight holds me beneath him. I'm where I belong. "Are you real?" he asks then crashes his lips back against mine. Our mouths stay fused as his fingers scrape down my sides. Liam doesn't break, he doesn't stop touching me, as if I'm going to vanish. His eyes stay glued shut as he gives me all of him. I breathe in every touch and every moment that I'm here with him. He brings me back to life.

My heart feels light, and it's as if I'm floating.

He stops and gazes at me with so much emotion in his eyes I can't move. Words fail. My heart stops. And time doesn't move. All that exists in this world is us right now.

Liam's strong hand presses against my face. He gazes lovingly at me as I begin to cry. The connection we share is more than I can explain. It bonds us stronger than ever before. I'm his and he's mine. This one look has cemented our love and forged an unbreakable bond. Even if we will never be together again, I'll never be anyone else's.

His voice is thick and husky as he refuses to break from my eyes. "Tell me you're real."

"I'm real."

"Tell me you're really here."

"I'm here with you." My hand rises, and I press my thumb to his lips. "I'm here for you. I'm here with only you. I need you so much."

His eyes close as I rub my thumb, savoring the rough feel on my skin.

"Stay with me," he pleads.

Liam's hands rest on each side of my face as I drag him down further. "There's nowhere else I want to be." Our lips meet, and I lose myself.

I may be married.

Aaron may be alive.

But my heart belongs to Liam.

My body is his, and I want him to take me.

My hands roam his thick back, memorizing each dip and ridge along his taut muscles. He hovers above me and his tongue brushes with mine over and over. I feel his hardness against my core, and I need him to fill me and bring me back to earth. To him.

My fingers trail his spine and hook in his boxers, dragging them lower. He becomes frantic and pulls me on top of him. Liam rips my shirt off and then discards my bra.

"I don't want to wake up," he says as he squeezes my nipple. I writhe on top of him, wishing I could convince him this is real.

"You are awake. This isn't a dream."

His hands slither down and cup my ass. "You're my dream." His eyes slam closed, and he groans as I grind down. Only the fabric of my underwear separates us. "But in my dream, you'd be fucking me already."

My head falls back as he grips my hips setting the pace. Liam rocks me against him. I feel his length rub against my clit. The friction drives me higher and then he stops. I moan in protest. But he rises and his hands hold my face.

Liam stares at me for one beat.

Then two.

Then three.

I need to feel him. I lean forward and kiss him. Our tongues tangle and he bites my bottom lip, holding it between his teeth as he pulls back. My God. He's killing me. His head drops to my breasts as he runs his tongue along the top of one and then repeats on the other side. My fingers grip his hair, and I tug him closer, needing more. For the first time in two days, my body has come to life. Liam latches on, and I cry out, feeling his teeth, tongue, and the warmth of his mouth.

"Liam, I need you inside of me." I don't recognize my own voice. It's thick and heavy with a need only he can fulfill. "Take me, sweetheart. Take me," I beg.

He responds with a throaty groan and flips me onto my back. He tears my underwear off and stares at me, blinking a few times. I see the moment he realizes this isn't a dream. Awareness registers and his hand travels down my side. "You're here."

I grip his cheeks. "I'm here. I'm yours. Now prove you're mine."

Liam settles between my legs, and our eyes stay locked as he slowly enters me. I refuse to break the connection we share as he fills me. I stretch and savor the feeling of being complete.

We stay together as he glides back and forth. Liam brushes my hair, rubs his thumb across my lips, and keeps his gaze trained on me. My hands gently trail his spine, his shoulders, and down his arms. He sucks in a breath when my nails scratch across the tattoo on his ribs.

Liam thrusts me forward, and the sound of our lovemaking echoes in the room. Our tangled bodies and heavy breathing mixed with the smell of sex and sweat fill my mind. I want to bathe in this moment. Drench myself in the happiness and love I feel, because I know all too soon that it will end.

"Don't," he commands.

Confusion sweeps over me.

"Don't go there. Stay here. Stay right here with me, Natalie."

I crush the thoughts that were chasing me and focus on him. My thoughts only memorize his frame that's covering me, the connection we share right now, soul to soul and body to body.

My orgasm comes out of nowhere and I fall apart in his arms. "Oh, oh my God."

Liam stops moving and watches me burst into pure ecstasy. I wriggle and he reaches between us, putting pressure on my clit, drawing out all pleasure from my body. "I can't," I say, needing him to stop. It's too much.

"You can," his voice is strained.

He milks each ounce of bliss my body holds. It lasts forever. My limbs are limp at my sides when he begins to move again. "I'll never grow tired of watching you come apart." He pounds harder and I slide up from the force. "I want you to think of how I make you feel when you're away from me." Liam slams into me again, and I claw my nails into his shoulder. "When you move, I want you to feel me right here." He rears back and the slapping of skin rings loudly through the air. "You belong to me. Not him. Not anyone else."

I can't speak as Liam sets a punishing rhythm. He growls as he pushes harder and harder. Each time he hits a little deeper, and I bite my lip to fight from crying out. This is rough, but it's exactly what I need. We had our sweet lovemaking . . . now we're fucking. There's no finesse, no love. Just primal and urgent. The need to sink our bodies so deep that we don't know where I end and he begins.

"Do you understand?" he asks and pushes so hard I can't control the cry. I welcome the pain from his body. I'd rather feel him hurt me than all the other forms of agony I'm in.

"Hurt me! Make it stop!" I scream out.

Liam stills and looks down at me as tears build in my eyes. "I'll never hurt you." His voice is calm and unlabored, as if all of that minutes ago was nothing. He flips me on top and grips my hips. "I love you," he says tenderly.

Tears fall from my eyes and splash against his chest. "I love you," I reply.

He moves me slowly and I rock, allowing his cock to fill me. "Stay tonight," he requests.

I don't reply because I can't. He knows it, but it hurts. Liam forces me to pick up the pace but still stays affectionate. "I'm gonna come, Lee," he tells me as he begins to pump from below.

I lean down against his ear. "I love you. Fill me."

He grunts and releases. Liam's arms wrap around my body, holding me close. I close my eyes and wish I could stay here.

But I can't.

No matter how much I don't want to . . . I have to go home.

CHAPTER

SIX

LIAM

UGH. MY FUCKING head is throbbing. I feel like shit. I roll over and fight the spinning.

That was one hell of a dream. I scratch my head and look at the bed in disarray. I must have really gotten into that one. I haven't had a wet dream since I was twelve.

I get up and head to the bathroom, reliving each moment. She felt so real. I could touch her, taste her, and feel her body beneath me, but there's no way it was her. Natalie's with her fucking husband.

Once I'd gotten myself out of the rope the bastard tied me in, I passed out in bed. I let the alcohol-induced coma take me over. Quinn was right, I need to pull myself together and man the fuck up. So she's gone . . . I have a deployment coming and a team of men who need me to be present. Not some lovesick puppy licking my wounds.

I rub my neck and notice the nail marks on my shoulder. What the fuck?

I turn in the mirror and see them extending down my back. No way. It couldn't have been real. But I can smell her. The smell of lavender filters through the air. I remember the taste of her lips and the way she kept telling me it wasn't a dream.

Well, then where the fuck is she?

The room is cleaned more than I could've done last night. I rush out to the living room to find it picked up as well. Son of a bitch. She really was here. The night comes flooding back, and I slap myself for thinking it was a dream. She kissed me before she left and told me she loved me. I was already half dead between the intense sex and extreme hangover I was nursing. Within seconds, I was passed out again thinking I dreamt it all.

I grab my phone and text her.

Me: When can I see you again?

Natalie: Soon. I promise.

I hope it's sooner than later. I miss her already, but I can't say that. She's got a whole host of bullshit on her plate.

Me: We should talk about what happened.

Natalie: I'll call you tonight.

Me: Okay, sweetheart. I'm glad you came over last night.

And I am. Even though I wasn't sure if it actually happened, it means a lot to me. She was thinking of me enough to sneak out and come over. Of course, I feel like a monumental shitbag for sleeping with her when her husband is home, but he lost her. At least that's what I'm telling myself.

Natalie: Me too. No more drinking like that. I'm on my way to work. I need to get a break from my mind.

I decide not to respond. I need to figure out what the hell to do. I'm on leave, so I don't have to be anywhere. I grab my keys knowing exactly what I need to do today. Aaron and I need to talk, and since he's home alone—looks like it's my perfect opportunity.

Of course my luck runs out when the lights flash behind me. Motherfucker.

The cop strolls over to the driver's side door with his aviators and I'm-bad-ass walk. I would like to dropkick this guy and he hasn't even spoken. I must remain calm since the last thing I want is a ticket.

"Good morning, do you know why I pulled you over?" Officer Brock asks.

Yeah, because you saw a bright red hot rod.

"Sorry, Officer. I must've been speeding?" I say more as a question. I seriously have no fucking clue what I did.

"You were speeding. This is a thirty-five. I need your license, registration, and insurance."

I pop open the glove box and grab the papers, handing them over along with my military ID. The officer looks them over and nods. "You're active?"

"Yes, sir."

"I don't think you meant to hand me this," he says and hands me over an envelope with my name on it. I look at it and realize it's the letter from Aaron. "I'll let you go with a warning. Just slow it down. Thank you for your service." He hands the rest back and walks back to his cruiser.

I sit here stunned and I feel like I got hit by a bus. Well, fuck. Do I read it or shred it? I pull into the parking lot right across the street from his house and stare at it. What he had to say is irrelevant now, but curiosity gets the best of me.

Liam,

Hey, man. I'm sitting here before heading out on this deployment and I have this weird feeling. I can't explain it, but I don't think I'll make it back. I know we're not supposed to think like that, but, well . . . it is what it is. I have a few things I want to ask of you and you're the only person I trust.

Take care of Lee. I haven't talked to anyone about this, but things have been hard for her. We've lost another baby and it's killing her. I'm watching my wife dwindle to nothing, and I can't stop it. She used to be full of love and light, but now she's miserable. Make her smile and help her find happiness. I can't give her the life she's desperate for. So please, watch her, help her, dry her tears, and be there, because I don't know how she'll handle it. If you realize the gift she is and you fall in love with her, treat her right or I'll fucking haunt you. There's no woman in the world like her, and if she has to love anyone else other than me, I hope it's you. I want her to find someone worthy, so if it's not you, make sure he's not a prick.

If by some stretch of a miracle she's pregnant now, I want you to be like a father to him or her. You're like a brother to me, and I need to know they won't grow up not knowing anything about me. Tell them about all the trouble we caused and protect them from doing the same stupid shit.

I've thought a lot about some of the things we've talked about. How this life will eventually destroy you and a family, and I think you're right. I'm not the same guy I was. I've seen too much, and while I'm proud of the things I've done, I carry guilt about Natalie. I'm a piece of shit. I don't deserve her, but for some reason she loves me, and I keep hoping she never sees the bad in me.

Anyway, be good to her. And even in death, I'll have your six.
—Aaron

Once I pull into the drive, I grab on to my anger. He fucked around on her, got another girl pregnant, and then has the balls to be pissed at me. I respected her, loved her and his daughter. He even asked me to do all this and then he wants to act like I broke some damn man code. He can fuck off.

Aaron steps off the deck as I close the door.

"Didn't think you'd be back so soon."

I step closer. "I thought we could use some time to discuss the last year."

He nods and turns toward the back deck. "Seems I've missed a lot."

We sit in the chairs and we both stare off. I'm not sure if I should start or let him ask the questions. My training kicks in and I decide to let him go first. Typically, it's the best way to get answers you want.

I wait, but he doesn't say anything or move, just stares.

Then I remember the fucker is trained to do the same thing. It could be hours before either of us budge. The thing is, he's not a terrorist, he's a friend and deserves to be treated like one.

"I'll go first," I say and he turns. "What do you want to know?" I give an inch but still try to maintain control of the discussion.

"How long have you been playing house with my family?"

So this is going to be how it is.

"First of all, I wasn't playing house." I make sure I keep my eyes clear so he knows that's not what the fuck this was. "Second of all, how long were you making a new family while you had yours here?"

His eyes shift the slightest amount, but it's enough for me to notice. "You don't know everything."

"Neither do you." I give it right back. He didn't see Natalie at her worst or when we were both trying to figure out how we felt. He wasn't here, so he better not fucking judge me.

"Brittany was a mistake," Aaron says and then stands. "A big fucking mistake."

"Yeah, well, your mistake doesn't think she is." This is the part that pisses me off.

"You think I care what she thinks?"

"I don't know what you think. You fucked around on your pregnant wife! Brittany told her everything, and now you come back spewing your shit about me and Lee? Fuck you, man. It wasn't behind your back. It wasn't to shame you. You even told me to love her. You said you wanted me to raise your kid as my own and now you're acting like this?" Once I start talking, it all comes out and I can't stop. "I love her. I helped pick her up when you died. I was at the hospital when Aarabelle was sick, I held Natalie's hair when she was puking, and I fucking defended you!" I push his chest and he winces.

Aaron takes a few steps back rubbing his chest, and I feel like a dick.

"Aaron, I'm sorry, man," I try to apologize, but he turns before I can say anything else.

"I deserve it. I know I was wrong, but I fought to live for them. I don't want to fight you, but she's *my* wife. That's my daughter, and I won't let them go just because for the last year you decided you love her." He steps closer puffing his chest. I clench my fists and release them. "I've loved her almost my whole life, and if you're the man I think you are, you'll walk away."

I step closer and weigh my words. I could be a prick and let him know I fucked her last night. I want to, but I won't. The depth of pain I could cause my closest friend right now is all in my hands. But in the end, Lee will be who is hurt. And I'll fucking slice my veins open before that happens.

"Just know how much you hurt her. She may not want you. And if she walks away, I'm not going to push her back to you."

Aaron nods and pauses. "I'm going to ask you this once, for the sake of my child." He waits and I already know where he's going. "If you love Natalie and Aarabelle, then don't do this shit. Don't be the man who ends a marriage and a family."

"You're unbelievable. Don't you think you ended your own

marriage when you fucked around? The guy who I knew would've manned the fuck up and fixed it before it got that bad. You and I aren't going to battle over this. It's her choice."

Aaron steps closer, and I swear I've been nice, but he pushes me and I'll knock him on his ass.

"What about your word, Liam? Huh? What about the fact that you swore to have my back no matter what?"

I look at him wondering if he sustained some kind of traumatic brain injury, because he seems to have forgotten one key issue—he's the one in the wrong.

"Have your back?" I'm going to punch him. "I had your back. I had your back every fucking day. I didn't do this to you!" I draw a deep breath and try to stop the pulsing in my neck. I can feel my rage boiling over.

"I told you to love her, but . . ."

"But what? You didn't mean it? You know, I read that fucking letter today. I didn't even know what was in it. I fought day after day with feeling anything for Lee. I would tell myself it was wrong and ridiculous. The first time either of us acknowledged anything, we struggled. Being with her was never easy. I always had you in the back of my mind, but I prayed you'd know that I would never let her forget you or let Aarabelle not know the man I knew."

"So you just went forward with her anyway?"

"None of us knew you weren't dead!" I throw my hands up and fight the urge to shake him. "You're missing the entire point. I'm not wrong here, and neither is Lee. You are. You made your choices, and now you have to handle the fallout."

He looks at me with fury burning in his eyes.

"I didn't expect to come home to this shit! You didn't say a word on the plane."

My mind spins as I try to find a way to not go to blows. "What did you want me to say? I couldn't believe it was you. When we were told about the mission, I thought it couldn't be you—you were dead. We had a part of your body as proof. So when we get to Afghanistan and I realize it *is* you . . . I'm not sure what the fuck you expected from me, man." I walk around in circles because there's still a part of me that's processing the fact he's standing here. My brother in arms, my friend who I would've traded places with to die instead, is here.

I hope he takes a swing at me. I'll get a good one in for the dumb move he made screwing around on Natalie. But then I look at him. He's been home a few days and looks a little better, but the bruises still cover the one side of his body. He's been broken.

"I love her. I thought about her day in and day out."

There's two sides to me, and both are so screwed up I don't know where to turn. One, he's alive and he thought he'd come home to the life he left. Two, he doesn't deserve her. I do. I'm the man he couldn't be and she loves me. She came to me last night, and I made love to her while he slept. I'm not perfect, but God, if I wouldn't do anything to make this situation different.

"Look, man, you've been through more than I'm sure you'll ever admit. I get that. But let me be clear: if you'd come home from that mission and Natalie would've found out you'd been screwing some froghopper behind her back looking for the next SEAL to hop to, she'd have thrown your ass out."

"If Natalie chooses because of whatever I did, then I'll let her go. No matter how much it'll kill me. But don't pursue her. I'm asking you as my friend. Give her and I a chance to see if we can mend our family for Aarabelle's sake."

The responses roll around in my head. So many things I want to say, but out of respect for Lee and the fact that this man saved my life on more than one occasion, I simply nod. "You really don't get it?"

"Get what?"

"This isn't up to you. You don't get to make demands or requests. I'm not walking away for you. But understand this: I love her. I love Aarabelle. And I'm going to be the man in the end that has them. I don't think you realize how bad you screwed yourself. So, I'll give her the time she needs, because I don't think she knows what end is up. I love her enough not to push her . . . do you?"

"I know her."

"Not anymore. She's changed, Aaron. She went through hell and then got kicked when she was already at her lowest. I was there. I saw it, and I won't let her go down that path again."

This is the best I can do.

He steps forward. "Fair enough." Aaron extends his hand. "Thank you for being there for them. I'm grateful."

No, he's not. He's hateful that I got his girl. I grip his hand and we shake. I don't respond because I'm not sure I can be civil at this point. The urge to tell him to take his request and shove it so far up his ass he sneezes it out is on the tip of my tongue—but I don't. We have history, and ultimately, I can't force Lee.

She's who matters here. And Aarabelle.

I have to sacrifice a part of myself for her and pray in the end she'll come to me. Even if it means my closest friend will be fucked in the end.

chapter

seven

NATALIE

"HEY SPARKLES, CAN I come in?" Mark asks apprehensively.

"I figured they'd send you in first." I grin as I wave my hand to usher him in. "You'd be the one I'd be more likely to forgive."

"It's because we both like to glitter." Mark flops in the chair and slaps his hands on the side.

"Must be that."

You can sense the tension in the air, but Mark is probably the best at masking his discomfort. Coming in here today was difficult, but I needed a sense of normalcy. Aaron didn't notice I'd been gone all night, or if he did, he never said a word.

After I left Liam's house, I grabbed Aarabelle and cried myself to sleep. I didn't mean to sleep with him. I honestly just wanted to see him. But once he touched me, it became impossible to stop and there wasn't even a part of me that wanted to. The lines in the sand are becoming blurred.

Walking in the office was far more difficult than I could've expected. Knowing prying eyes and Aaron's friends surround me makes me want to cower, but I've done enough of that. I work here now, and I needed a reprieve.

People's lives are in my hands—at least that's my excuse.

"What can I do for you?" I ask after a few moments of awkward silence.

Mark grows serious as he shifts forward with his elbows on his knees. "I'm worried about you. I know you may think you can't talk to me, but you can."

I believe that he cares for me. I trust that he has good intentions, but I also know if push came to shove, their whole "bros before ho's" bullshit would be in full effect.

"I'm doing fine." The last word trips me a little. I immediately think of Liam.

"How's Aaron?"

I glance out the window and mull over my words. "Adjusting, I guess—we both are."

Mark waits for me to look back at him before speaking. "I know this is hard on you more than anyone. You moved on, you found out about the affair, you were happy, and now he's back. It can't be easy. Hell, I can't even pretend to know what you're feeling. But he's been through fucking hell. If you're in pain, imagine what he must've gone through in the year he was being held. I'm not asking you to forgive him," Mark pauses. "I'm just asking you to let us help."

My eyes widen at his last request. "Help? How do you plan to help?"

Mark tilts forward. "Jackson and I are your friends, Lee. Aaron can stay with me for a while, you can take some time off, or whatever you need. But all he could talk about on the plane back was seeing you. He never mentioned the other girl."

I huff, "Like you'd tell me anyway." I wait for him to refute me, but he won't.

The stories of infidelity run rampant in the teams, but we all ignore it. We look the other way, because no matter what, they'd never tell the wife who's blissfully ignorant. So many of my friends found out, after their husbands returned, that while they were holding down their homes, their husbands were fucking everything that walked. Some even after they'd made love to them again. It's the worst slap in the face, and I thought I'd been immune to it.

"No, I wouldn't have told you . . . but I would've made sure you knew."

"What the hell does that mean?" My hands come down on the desk with a smack, and Mark looks a little startled. Good. "I'm so tired of these riddles and rhymes. You all talk of honor, valor, and code, but you're all hypocrites!" I stand and the chair flies out from under me.

"Lee," he says hushed.

"No!" I yell and walk over to him. "You don't 'Lee' me . . . I'm tired. You can all tell me that in all the time you spent with Aaron for that year, you never suspected it? You can honestly sit there and tell me you had no clue? I'm sure more times than you know he said he was with you. How does that make you feel?"

Mark stands towering over me, his hands gripping my shoulders gently. "I didn't know. I would've told him to knock it the fuck off or tell you. He made mistakes and he's paid his penance."

"And that's supposed to comfort me?"

"What do you expect?"

What do I expect? I don't know. That's the part that gets me. I can't tell him what I want, because if it were Reanell, I wouldn't run and tell Mason. But there was a baby involved. And it wasn't a one-time thing.

I flop in the chair and hang my head. "I expected it to never happen. But none of that matters because I'm over it. I'm over the affair and all the other bullshit. I was genuinely happy with Liam."

Mark sits beside me. Wrapping his arm around my shoulder, he pulls me close. "Were you happy with Aaron? If you hadn't believed he was dead all this time, would you be with him?"

I rest my head on his shoulder. "I can't answer that. We weren't happy, but we were happy about the baby. Who knows if after Aara was born if we'd have gone backward?"

"Yeah, that's the thing . . . you don't know. But what I do know is you have great friends who love you. And you have Aarabelle. As for the rest, it's up to you."

I lift my head and look at him. "Is it? My choices affect everyone in this."

Mark kisses my cheek, "I think you need to give yourself a chance to breathe before you choose anything." He heads out of the office and then pops his head back in. "Lee?"

"Yeah?"

"Do you think we could give Aarabelle the call sign Moonlight?"

My smile is automatic, and I throw the box of tissues from the table next to me at his head.

He ducks and it misses him, but he smiles. "I'll take that as a no."

Only Mark.

I head back to my desk and get back to work. The people overseas matter, and I need to focus on their lives instead of my own. At least for a few hours.

My phone rings and I answer without looking.

"Hello?"

"Natalie," Aaron's scratchy voice sounds nervous.

"What's wrong?" I ask quickly.

"It's late. I'm just wondering if you're coming home."

I look out the window and then at the clock. Shit. It's almost seven.

"I'm sorry. I got caught up in these projects," I explain.

"Right. Work," Aaron replies disbelievingly. "I figured you might be somewhere else. I don't have a car or anyway to get anywhere. I just wanted to know what to do."

"Aaron," I say softly. "I'm really sorry. I'm leaving the office now and I'll be there soon. Let me call Paige and see if she can keep Aarabelle overnight. Then we can have dinner and talk?"

We need to figure out the logistics of all of this, and I need answers. I need to know from him what exactly happened and how we move forward for Aarabelle's sake. I don't want to move out of my house, but I don't want to throw him out either.

"I'd like that."

"Okay," I smile. "I'll see you soon."

"I love you, Natalie."

"I—" I choke on the words. "I gotta go," I mutter quickly and disconnect the phone.

There's no traffic on the road and Paige was happy to keep Aarabelle. I'm not sure how to handle things with Aaron, but I need to know a lot of things. Where he was for the last year, for one. I'm assuming if Aaron went on that rescue mission, it hadn't been by choice, but I'd also assumed he wasn't sleeping around.

I park in the drive and a text bings.

Liam: We have to talk.

Me: I know. I need to handle things tonight with Aaron.

Liam: Okay. I'll wait to hear from you.

Me: I love you.

The text was easy to say. I didn't stumble over my words because my heart is where Liam is. No matter what my past holds with Aaron, my future belongs to Liam. I need to figure out how to make my present match up with all of this now.

I wait for a text from Liam but it doesn't come. My finger hovers over the call button. How can he not say it back? I'm trying to prove to him that he's my choice. I'm being honest and faithful to him. Hell, I snuck out of my house just to see him.

"Lee?" I drop the phone and cover my mouth to avoid screaming. I look at the window and Aaron is standing there. "You okay?"

Gasping for breath, I look over. "I'm fine. You scared me."

He opens the door and extends his hand. "Sorry, I was worried." Hesitantly, I place my hand in his. I wait for a spark, a zing, anything, however, there's nothing but familiarity there. "I ordered food. I figured it would be easier than either of us cooking."

"Yeah," I laugh. "You and cooking don't really mix."

Aaron places his hand on the small of my back, and I move faster.

"Some things never change," he muses.

"And some things do."

Aaron lets out a breath. "I guess they do." He pauses as we make our way to the deck. I look at the table with candles, roses, and pizza by the side. "I thought, maybe . . ."

I turn and look at him with so much anger and hurt. "You thought what? You would make this a date? This isn't a date, Aaron. This is figuring out how the hell to make this less painful than it already is. I can't just forget that you cheated on me . . ."

"So you're going to take her word as bond? You're not going to give me the chance to explain anything?" he explodes and softens his stance. Aaron lowers himself to the ground at my feet. "You loved me once. We had a love that others prayed for. You and I made vows." His voice is feeble, and it's as if the ground is swallowing him.

I drop my purse and perch myself on my knees in front of

him. "Vows that were broken. And yes, we loved each other once, and we lost ourselves somewhere on that path." Aaron's eyes meet mine, and I want to cry. "Let's not do this to each other. Please," I plead.

"Let's just enjoy dinner and talk."

I nod and we both shift. "There are things I need to know. Like, what happened in Afghanistan?" I decide we have to start there. I need to know about the affair, but at the same time I don't know if it will make a difference. I need to put each of our issues into their appropriate box. *Again with the damn boxes.* But I think it'll help me keep each of the mounds of bullshit contained so I can handle them better.

"I know you have questions, and I'll answer the best I can. I'm still fuzzy on some parts." Aaron says and stands extending his hand.

I stand on my own, knowing I need to keep my composure and appear in control. We sit in the chairs illuminated by a soft candle glow. I fight the urge to blow them all out. This isn't a date. But I need him to be honest, not set him off.

"Tell me about the explosion." My voice is low and calming.

Aaron puts a slice of pizza on both our plates and then he grabs my hand. "Is this okay?" he asks looking down.

It seems like he needs this from me. Like my hand is the lifeline that will ground him. "Yeah, you can hold my hand." I speak the words and squeeze his hand.

"Thanks, baby."

"You can't call me 'baby,'" I reply more harshly than I meant to. Aaron's eyes drop to our joined hands.

"But I can hold your hand?"

"I think you need a friend. I think you need support to talk about what's going on and what happened. I've been your friend since we were kids. I'll always be your friend."

Aaron nods and lets out a deep breath. "I don't know how much will make sense. But I remember getting in the caravan to head out to the site where we were having issues. There were four of us in the truck just talking and laughing." His eyes glaze over as he retreats into his story. "There were a bunch of kids throwing their arms up screaming. They were trying to stop us—I guess. I don't know what they wanted. I was sitting in the passenger side and urged the driver to keep going. I know better than to slow down, but instead of listening, he let up on the gas. As soon as we slowed a little, the explosion happened. It hit my side of the vehicle, and I remember feeling like I was flying. Everything was weightless but chaotic at the same time."

He takes a deep breath and his hand tightens. "What happened then?"

"There was screaming and blood everywhere. I remember being dragged by the neck, and I assumed it was one of the guys in our car. I was going in and out so much, I honestly don't know much more than that."

As a tear falls down my face, Aaron releases my hand. "Who was pulling you?"

"They did."

"Who's 'they'?" I encourage him to tell me more.

"Who do you think, Lee?" Aaron says as his jaw tightens. "I was losing a lot of blood. I thought I was dead. They made sure I wouldn't die, but I wouldn't tell them anything. Not my name, not anything. They knew I was American, even though I only spoke French so they'd be confused. I would go unconscious for long periods of time. I honestly don't remember much. When Charlie came to the site, she apparently was following around some high ranking terrorist pretending to be his new toy."

"Is that the agent that found you?" I ask.

"Yes, she literally stumbled on the camp where I was being

held. When she realized I was American, I started to get the care I needed and got some information. But I wasn't sure any of it was real. I'm still not sure what was reality versus not."

I sit quiet and try to absorb all he's telling me. It was a year and we never looked. None of us searched for him. "They told us there was no way you could've survived the blast. It was so bad that no one would. There weren't many remains of the others. Did they survive?" I look at him and he shakes his head.

"I shouldn't have. The blast was bad, but apparently, I got pulled out before the secondary explosion of the vehicle. I was mangled and in bad condition when I woke up the first time. I would wake for a few hours and then go back out for who knows how long. There wasn't exactly good medical attention. Charlie was the only thing keeping me alive. It took her months to gain my trust. I wasn't sure if she really was CIA or if she was full of shit. I couldn't rely on my training because nothing made sense."

"I hate this for you," I admit.

He tangles his fingers with mine. "All I knew was that if there was any chance, I needed to stay strong. I would let her help me so that I could come home to you," he says, hushed.

"Aaron," my voice shakes. I hate that he's been hurt. I know he won't tell me, but I care. "Did they . . . ?"

"I've been through worse. I'm alive, so all of that shit doesn't matter."

"I can't tell you how much your death affected me. I was a mess. Each night I would pray it was a lie. I refused to get rid of your things for almost the full year. I can't tell you what it was like when Mark came to the house to tell me," I let out a shaky breath. "I latched on to every good memory we had. I held them like lifelines, praying they would keep me afloat. When I went into labor, Reanell practically had to carry me to the car. I knew once Aara was born, things would be different for me." I stop and take a gulp of wine. "I did it though, I gave birth to that beautiful little girl, alone. Each time I'd push I would think of you. How you went through so much and always stayed strong. When I held her for the first time, it was agony. I hated being alone."

"You think I didn't want to be there?" he asks incredulously.

"No, of course I don't think that. Let me finish." I wait for the vein in his neck to stop pulsing. "There was this baby we fought so hard for. She was everything I wanted, but you weren't there. It was the end of me feeling sorry for myself. I found strength and determination. I was still sad, lonely, and missing you terribly, but you were gone. When I had the memorial, it was horrific, but again, I did it. I had to get up each day because she needed me, but that was about all I could do. Then Liam came to Virginia."

"No," Aaron cuts me off. My eyes snap up, and he rips his hand back. "You're not going to sit here and tell me about how Liam put you back together. Natalie, you're my wife." He leans forward with determination in his eyes. "We have a child. We have a life people only dream of. You and I are meant to be together."

"You slept with another woman. You keep forgetting that. And I don't think we had a life people dream of. I think we were comfortable and content. You were seeking what I wasn't giving you! You said it yourself."

"It was a one-time thing, a fucked up night," he says, and my retort dies on my tongue.

"One night? You can look me in the eyes and tell me that?" I ask hesitantly.

Aaron stands and comes around the table. My heart falters as I look at my husband, my best friend since I was sixteen. He stands over me and pulls me to my feet. "One horrible night after we'd lost the baby. After I had to watch you lie on the bathroom floor begging for God to kill you. You held your stomach and prayed that someone would just end it all because you weren't good enough.

I was broken after that. I didn't know what to do, so I left."

"I remember. I came out and you were gone. You left when I was in the middle of pure torture." I look at him recalling that night.

It was the last failed procedure, and I was distraught. I thought that baby was the one. I was ten weeks, we were so close to the safe zone. I started cramping and then I saw blood. I sat there trying to convince myself that it wasn't really blood. That it wasn't a sign that we were going to lose the baby, because I was so close. The pain was unlike anything I'd ever felt. I would cry and clutch my stomach as the life I'd been desperate for left me.

I told myself that if the pregnancy didn't stick, I would stop trying. I needed to move forward and stop hoping for something I wasn't meant to have. We'd spent so much money and energy. I was consumed by everything regarding fertility.

Aaron's hands hold my face. "I couldn't watch. I felt like I failed you as a husband. I couldn't watch you like that. I went to the bar, got drunk, and I fucked up."

Turmoil boils in my body as I try to figure out if he's lying. None of this makes sense. "Brittany said it was months. She said . . ."

"She lied," Aaron says, so sure.

"Why would she lie? What does she have to gain? We all thought you were dead. So it makes no sense for her to be vicious and mean to me. But you lying right now would make sense," I say, feeling angry that I don't know what the damn truth is.

There's so much between us, so much history, and throwing it all away isn't something I take lightly, but I think about Liam. How far we came. How much we loved. And how hard it would be to lose him. I've already lost Aaron once, I know I can endure it. Besides, this man in front of me isn't the same man I loved. I look at him now and see betrayal and deceit.

"Why would I lie to you, Lee? I always told you the truth!" he exclaims and turns his back.

"You didn't lie? You think for one second even if it was only one night with her, that's okay? Do you not see how disgusting that makes you? On the night we lose a child, you sleep with someone else. The night I had to crawl into bed on my hands and knees because the cramping was so bad, you were fucking someone. While I was in horrific pain, you were enjoying the night of your life?" I spit the words, hoping he feels the knives embedded in them. I hope they tear into his heart and shred him to pieces. "Some man you are. Some love and honesty we have."

Aaron stands behind me unmoving. I feel the heat radiating from his body. But he doesn't touch me, and if he'd like to keep his hands, he won't try to.

"I never told you because it meant nothing. She means nothing and neither does the affair."

I spin on my heels and slap him in the chest. "Fuck you. It meant everything to me! *You* meant everything to me! I hate you right now. You stand here smug as if *I'm* doing *you* wrong. You were a coward."

"I deserve that." He steps closer, but whatever emotion is showing on my face causes him to retreat.

"You don't deserve me." I step closer. "No matter what your relationship was with *her*—which I don't believe for one second it was a one-time deal." Another step.

"What does it matter? I'm here right now trying to fix things."

"You then came home that day saying you slept at work. Two months later, we found out I was pregnant with Aarabelle." Aaron takes two steps back as I vibrate with anger. "So you did whatever the hell you did and came home and then made a baby with me."

He looks away. "You're not going to listen to me at this point. Apparently, what I've been through doesn't matter. You're no better than me, Lee."

"Unreal," I huff. "You went through hell over there. I hate that you were hurt. I hate that you ever had to endure one ounce of pain," tears stream down my face. He's been through so much. We both have. Now we have to hurt even more. "But it doesn't erase our past. There are no free passes because you're holding up the argument that what I did is the same. Me moving on and finding love again doesn't equate to cheating. I can tell you don't want to tell me everything. I see it in your eyes that there's more."

Aaron steps closer and grips my shoulders. "Damn right there's more. But it's in the past. She's in the past. I went through more hell than you can fathom. I didn't think I'd ever see you again. You. Not her. *You!*"

Confusion sweeps over me as I soak in what he says, conflicting emotions rioting within me. I have no doubt he went through a lot. I also don't doubt him when he says that it is me he loves. That's the part that kills me. But it's not enough.

"I know you love me. And if I'm being honest, I love you. I will always love you. You were the first man I ever loved. But you're not the only one anymore," I reply somberly. "I let Liam into my heart, and he and I share something special. I never meant for this to happen. I had no reason to expect you were alive. But things failed way before then, Aaron. Were you happy? Because I wasn't." I let out a deep breath. "We have to let each other go."

"So because of what I suffered, I get to pay even more? How is that fair? You even said yourself you love me."

I shrug out of his hold and walk toward the end of the deck. "I don't want to make you suffer. No matter what you think, this isn't easy for me. And there's no 'fair' here. I would never intentionally hurt you."

"But I am hurt."

"Well, so am I."

The silence lingers between us. Years of love and trust are gone. They've washed their way out into the sea, leaving behind shells of who we were.

Aaron blows out the candles, and I can't help but feel like the light inside of him just went out too. He walks over, grabs the dishes, and starts to head inside. I turn toward the ocean and wait for the calmness it usually brings, but instead, I feel cold and alone. Both of us have had to deal with so much in one year.

The plates crash to the ground, and when I turn around, Aaron is already in front of me. He grips my face, and before I can say anything, his lips press against mine. My mouth stays still and he pushes hard. It's painful, like this entire situation. He holds me against him as my hands shove against his chest, but Aaron just holds me closer. His tongue sweeps against the seam of my lips, and I turn my head. As our lips break apart as he stares down at me.

"Why can't you love me again? I would do anything for you."

"Then tell me the truth."

"You want to know everything?"

I stare at him, waiting. "I don't think we can ever move forward if I don't know everything."

"I told you everything that matters."

"That's just it. Everything matters."

"I choose you, Natalie. I'd choose you every day until the day I die. I want you. I need you. And I don't know how else to make you see that. Everyone and everything else is in the past."

"And so are you. You're living in the past where I'm your doting wife. I lived the last year of my life knowing what it's like without you. I found out the truth about who we were—hell, who I am. I'm not the same woman you fell in love with. I've changed." I touch his arm and he flinches. "I'm not that girl anymore, Aaron."

"Fine."

"Fine?" I ask skeptically.

"It's done, Lee. You want me to go back to her?"

"I thought it wasn't about her?"

"That's right," he sneers. "It's about Liam."

I don't say anything as he turns and heads into the house.

W E DON'T MENTION the kiss. We barely acknowledge each other's presence. It's awkward and it's as if we're walking on eggshells. I cleaned the stuff from outside while Aaron looked through photo books of Aarabelle.

"Do you want to sleep in the bedroom? I can take the couch," I offer.

"No, I think I'm going to head to Mark's. Maybe spend the night there. Jackson offered the condo he owns as well."

"Oh," I reply. I can't fully explain why this bothers me at all. I should be happy, but it saddens me it's come to this. He just got home, and I've already displaced him. "You can stay here, Aaron. I mean, if you want to spend time with Aarabelle. I know things are . . . strained . . . between us, but this is your home."

"My home is where you are. You're not here with me," he says and then goes back to the picture book.

The reactions play out in my mind, but my mouth stays closed. I could tell him he's wrong, but he's not. I could give him false hope, but I won't. "I don't know what to say." Which is the only honest thing I can reply.

He closes the book and I sit next to him. "You can say you'll try. Maybe you can forgive me, see how much I love you. Are all the years of marriage worth so little to you?"

I look over as tears begin to fall, painting my face with the pain in my heart. "It was never easy for me to let you go. I struggled so much with it. Even at my angriest, I never wished you dead." Aaron brushes the tears from my face. "But you hurt me so badly. Even *if* you had only slept with her once, you did it on one of the worst nights of my life. She loved you, Aaron. I could see it in her eyes. She came to your memorial."

"She's irrelevant to me. It's you who has my heart. It's you who has my world."

I don't acknowledge his statement, because right now, I don't believe him. I know what it's like to be someone's world.

The bruise on the side of his face is starting to fade, and my hand reaches up to feel it. I try to remember what his skin felt like beneath my fingers. How his clean shaved face would allow the pads of my fingers to slide down with no resistance. The way our bodies would come alive at each other's touch. His head leans into my hand as if I'm comforting him. How long did he endure pain? How much was he awake for, and how did he suffer?

"Did they torture you?" I don't respond to his statement because all I can think about is his marred skin. The way the Aaron I knew is gone in every sense of the word. His body, which was once strong enough to lift me even when I was pregnant, doesn't look like it could lift much more than Aarabelle.

His eyes close. "I can't talk about that. I was badly injured and barely holding on. It wasn't until the end that anything really happened, and then Charlie got word out."

"But they hurt you. Why did she wait so long?"

Aaron grips my hands. "I think it looks worse. Remember I was in an explosion. Some of these are injuries that didn't heal right. There was a medic on site of the extraction and he said I'm really lucky. She had a job to do, exposing me would've sacrificed everything she'd worked for. Her helping me was a huge risk. I respect her mission. I feel like I need to tell you something."

I brace myself for whatever it might be. "I don't know how much more I can take."

"I'm going to fight for you. I didn't live for nothing. I'll be damned if you think I'm going to fade away. You and I are for life, Lee. You, me, and our daughter. We have a lot of adjusting and a lot to work through, but we make sense."

"I need you to stop and listen to what I'm saying," I plead hoping he won't make me say it. I'm battling everything inside of me to not tell him I went to Liam's last night. I'm fighting to not tell him I want to be there right now. But I know it'll break him, and no matter how badly he hurt me with Brittany, I know that this will wound him deeper.

Brittany was a nobody in my life. Liam is his friend. The man who went and rescued him and then brought him to me. They share a bond that I never had with her. I try to imagine what it would feel like if I still loved him the way he claims he loves me and it were Reanell. I would be devastated.

"I told Liam the same thing."

"What?" That stops the words that were forming on my tongue.

When the hell did he talk to Liam? Did Liam tell him we spent the night together? Oh my God, maybe he knows.

"Liam and I talked today. I told him the same thing—I'm not giving up. I asked him to step aside and let us have a chance to fix this."

The color drains from my face and my throat goes dry. "W-what did you . . . ? Why?"

"Because you're my wife. Because you've been my girl since we were kids. He understands that this isn't just some relationship.

You and I, baby, are the real deal. We don't quit because someone died."

My eyes snap open. "I didn't fall in love with him because you died. That might have been what forced us together, but I love him in a way you can't understand," I say and see the way his jaw ticks.

"You can't convince me you love him more. I know you. I know your heart and your soul. I can see everything you're feeling before you say it. So I told him to step aside before he destroys us all."

"How dare you?" I rip my hands from his and stand, needing to dispel some energy. "You don't get to make that decision for me."

"We made vows."

"You broke them."

"Is this your whole argument? That I broke promises? You did too, babe. You promised to love, honor, obey. You fucking fell in love with someone in under a year. What does it say?"

Anger rips through me as I clench my fists. If I were a violent person, I would've punched him by now. "What does it say, Aaron? It says we weren't happy. It says we had problems. It says that I met someone, fell in love, and moved on. It says that you met someone while we were married and did the same."

"Well, we'll see, because Liam and I have an agreement," he says smugly.

Fuck him.

"I hope he told you to go to hell."

Aaron stands and walks away. He stops and turns toward me. "He said he would give us time."

My heart plummets. "Of course he did." I nearly choke on the words.

"I'm not a fool to see that he loves you. But he knows we have a life, a child, a home."

Liam and I are going to have words. His text message now

makes sense. He's giving up on us. After all we've shared and how far we've come. All the promises are lies, just like those of the man who stands in front of me.

"Had," I say and stare into his eyes. "We had. You keep forgetting what we had is now past tense. Right now, we have a mess to clean up. Do you even want to acknowledge the fact that you were going to leave me for your whore?" I bite back the nasty retort floating around in my mouth.

"I'm not with her now, am I?"

"And if we don't work out, will you go back to her?"

"Is that what you want?" he asks, watching my reactions.

I huff, "I can't even believe you. You sit here telling me you love me, spouting off how we have a love no one can ever understand, but you can't even answer me honestly once. Are you going to admit what your relationship was with her?"

His story has too many holes. There are too many nights I remember being alone or wondering. The times I pushed down my woman's intuition and smothered it. Ignorance is a beautiful place sometimes, but I don't plan to live there anymore. The hardest part in all of this is that I'm going to be the one to hurt Aaron. I was supposed to be his lifeline. Just as Liam has become mine.

Then I think about what Aaron said about him stepping aside. Fuck them both.

I get a say in who I'm with, and they're both going to learn that quickly.

"Who knows?" Aaron says and then shakes his head. "What is the truth anymore?"

"Then I'll be sure to talk to Brittany tomorrow. She doesn't have any issues saying what happened between you two."

"You love my fucking best friend! She's nothing compared to that," Aaron's voice trembles.

"How can you say she's nothing? You were with her for a long time. You went to her many nights, didn't you? What about the time you stayed with Mark for two nights? What about all the times I would call your phone and it would go to voicemail? The late nights you'd come home so tired you'd fall asleep on the couch. I remember them all, Aaron. Clarity isn't something I'm lacking."

He can play dumb as much as he wants, but he's a master at deceit. I always believed he kept his work away from home, but as the truth unravels, it reminds me it's a part of who he is. He worked to get information from others, concealed himself and the truth from those he had to. Aaron can withstand torture, injuries, and this to him is probably a walk in the park. I was a lovestruck idiot, hoping my husband was the man I wanted.

"Jesus Christ," he groans and throws his hands up. "She means *nothing* to me! Nothing."

"I don't believe you. She sobbed and cried saying how in love you were, but you still can't be honest."

Aaron looks to the left and shakes his head. "You have no idea what you're talking about."

"Then tell me! Tell me the truth. You want your chance . . . this is it!"

His face becomes stone. "I told you what matters. I was with her more than I ever should've been. I hated myself. I thought I could stop, but I was too weak. I didn't deserve you then and apparently I don't now. But we've had a year that we've been apart. I can be better. I don't want her anymore."

Even though we're not together it hurts. The word 'anymore' hangs heavy in the air. I'm the runner up. When he wanted her, he had her. Now, for whatever reason, I'm his choice but what happens when things get tough? When our lives aren't filled with laughter, but we're swimming in tears . . . does he go back? Too much has happened.

His hand extends, but I move before he can touch me. "This

is why I didn't want to tell you. I knew you wouldn't understand."

"Understand? I can't even look at you. I don't know how you can say this is what love is. I need to leave," I start to move back. "I'll be home later. Or maybe not," I say grabbing my purse. There's no way I'm staying in this house with him. I'm hurt, livid, desolate, and more than anything, I'm devastated that Liam would cast me aside so easily.

"Don't leave," Aaron begs.

"Don't lie anymore." I grab my keys and head out the door.

Once in the confines of my car, the need to scream overwhelms me, so I let it go. I punch the steering wheel and scream at the top of my lungs. Nothing coherent comes out, just yelling, trying to cleanse my body of all the confusion. I look at the window and see him standing there. He watches me lose it in my car and the contrast between him and Liam is glaring in this moment. Aaron chooses to let me go while Liam would've been at the car already.

Speaking of Liam, I turn the key and back out of the driveway while my husband watches me leave to go to my boyfriend's house.

The drive isn't long, but it allows me the time to form a plan. I'm so hurt that he would just toss me away. We need to talk and figure things out. I'm not either of their doll and they can't pass me off to the other. Aaron and I may be married legally, but he's been dead for a year. He and I aren't married in any other way.

I knock on the door and hear a woman's laughter.

Please, God, don't let him have another woman in here. I can't handle it.

Liam opens the door smiling and it falters when he sees me. "Hey," he says, closing the door behind him, pushing us out into the hall.

"Wow," I say in disbelief.

"Wow?"

"You're kidding me, right? You have someone else here? Not

only do you tell Aaron you'll step aside, but you move on so quickly." I'm so beside myself I can't think. I push his chest and slap him. "I hate you all!"

Liam's arms wrap around me and stop my physical assault. "What the hell are you talking about? Calm down," he commands as I struggle to get out of his hold. "Natalie, stop."

"How could you? I trusted you!" I begin to cry.

"What the hell are you talking about?"

"I heard a girl laughing, and you pushed me into the damn hall." Tears fall like rain as he refuses to let me go.

"It's Quinn and the girl he's talking to." He releases me a little so I can look at him. "Did you think I had another girl in there?"

My eyes meet his with drops streaming down my face. "I don't know what to think anymore."

"Only you. I wouldn't be able to be with anyone else." Liam holds me close, and I try to melt into him. His words soothe me, and being in his arms allows me a sense of comfort.

"Don't give me up so easily," I cry against his chest and he lets out a deep breath.

"Let's go inside?" he offers.

I nod and he pulls me to his side.

As we enter, I see no broken bottles and everything is cleaned up better than when I left. It's been not even a day since I was here. So much has happened in the last few days, but my mind and body feel as if it's been a lot longer.

"Hey, Lee," Quinn says and looks at Liam then sits. "We'll get out of here and let you guys talk," he offers and grabs his date's hand. She stands and smiles at me.

"I'm sorry to run you off."

"You didn't. Ready, Ash?" I look at her and she looks familiar.

Liam juts his head toward the kitchen, and Quinn nods and heads there. "I just need to talk to Quinn a second," Liam quietly tells me in my ear before kissing the side of my head.

She walks over and waves awkwardly. "Hi, I'm Ashton Caputo. We kinda met, but didn't really, because well, it wasn't the time for introductions. However, I think that may be our thing," Ashton rambles. "Anyway, I'm Catherine's best friend from New Jersey." It takes a second, but I remember she was with Catherine. She's absolutely stunning. Her long, red hair flows down her back and her eyes shimmer.

"I sort of remember."

"I'm visiting Mark, but he pawned me off on Quinn while they left for a few days to go . . . well, anyway, so we came here to meet Liam," she explains.

"Are you and Mark . . . ?" I ask with wide eyes.

"No!" she waves her hands animatedly. "We tried that and it was like putting the same person in the other and one trying to claw its way out. We're just friends."

"Ahh, so you're both smartasses?"

"Well, he's an ass and I'm smart." She pauses and I smile.

Ashton seems uncomfortable, and I instantly hate that I've ruined their night. "What brings you down here?"

Her eyes close and she shakes her head. "I needed a break from my life, so Mark suggested I come to Virginia for the week. Just so happened to be a busy week here as well."

"You could say that," I half laugh.

"I know you don't know me, but I feel like I know you. Cat talks about you a lot and she's worried about you. I don't know much other than what I've overheard, but are you okay?"

I sit on the couch and Ashton sits beside me. "Short answer . . . no. I'm so far from okay I don't even know what it looks like. I'm sorry, I shouldn't burden you on your vacation."

"Please," she scoffs. "This is an escape from my self-inflicted hell. Plus, with Cat gone, I don't have much girl talk, so please don't feel bad. I miss this. She's practically married to Jackson, and they're in a good place, so I get nothing." She grins, and I feel at ease with her. "You have a lot going on, and believe me, I only know what I'm overhearing from G.I. Joe over there. Mark told me that he had to go do something and then dropped me off at Quinn's. So I've pieced a few things together."

I smile and even if she knows everything, I'm grateful she's allowing me the sense of privacy. "Quick version . . . my dead husband isn't dead. Liam is his best friend and has told him he'll back off. I'm in love with him, and Liam deploys soon. Basically, I'm losing my friggin' mind."

"Well, who do you want?"

"Liam," I say without any hesitation.

"I'm not trying to talk you out of it. But do you think you should give yourself some time to really be sure? Again, you can tell me to eff off and I'd understand. I tend to give unsolicited advice." Ashton gives me an out, but I feel oddly comfortable. She reminds me of Reanell, and I almost wish I would've gone to her instead of coming to see Liam. I'm too conflicted and emotional to be rational.

"Aaron and I weren't in the best place when he died—well, went missing—I don't know if we could've survived it. He cheated, lied, and I'm not sure we can move forward. Liam has been my rock this last year. I know it sounds crazy, but our love is different than I had with Aaron," I explain.

It's true though. My love with Aaron was almost infantile. The way you adore something so much that you only see the good. We loved each other because that was what you do. It's all I knew and so I thought it was all there was. It doesn't diminish the time we were together, but when I fell in love with Liam, it was like a part of me clicked. I could've never told Aaron things that I can tell Liam. If I told Aaron why I was mad, he'd make me feel stupid. Put me down and tell me I was being ridiculous. Liam draws me out.

"Different is good. Trust me, I'm the last person you should be getting love advice from, but I'll be here for a little while, and if you want to grab a drink or whatever, let me know." Ashton stands as the guys walk into the room. "It was sincerely nice to meet you, and I hope I'll see you soon?" she asks.

Quinn walks over. "I was going to bring Ashton to Aarabelle's birthday party, if that's okay?"

Her party. I completely forgot. "Yes," I say snapping out of my head. "Of course."

"Great! I know Catherine and Jackson are coming too, so thank you."

"All right, man, see you at work tomorrow." Quinn slaps Liam on the shoulder and leaves with Ashton. I give a short wave and she smiles.

I turn to Liam and remember why I'm here. He stands there uncomfortable but I don't care. He's not going to play the martyr.

"You don't think I should get to decide?" I ask with venom dripping from each syllable.

CHAPTER

NINE

LIAM

"**I** DON'T THINK you should have to," I state while glaring back at her. She comes here pissed off, hits me again, and then breaks down. "You're a mess, and you can't tell me it's me you want when he's waiting at home for you."

"He's only there because you won't come get me." She drops to the couch.

"Do you hear yourself? You need to give yourself some damn time. I need time too," I explain.

She doesn't see how this alters everything. Aaron being alive makes me the other man. I'm not Aarabelle's father; I'd be the guy that stole her mom from her dad. Besides the fact that it makes every family gathering the most awkward thing there could possibly be.

"This is impossible for all of us." Her body almost goes limp. "He's dealing with coming home after God knows what happened. You're not wanting to break some code with him, and I'm torn in the middle." She wraps her arms around her stomach and drops her head.

"Lee," I say and tilt her head with my fingers. "If we truly love each other, not time, another man, or distance will keep us apart. Do you trust that enough?"

There's so much at stake, and while I want to be a selfish asshole, I can't. My loyalty has nothing to do with what I said to Aaron. Truth be told, I couldn't give a fuck less what he wants me to do. He lost her, but on my way home, I realized she lost herself too. I don't doubt she loves me. I don't think she doubts it either, but we need a minute. We both have to figure out the best way to handle it, and I can't be the one to tell her what to do. I leave for deployment in two weeks, and there's talk about leaving a week earlier. The deployment gives us the time and space to work through it all and really see if what we have is strong.

"I know I love you. I trust that right now all I have in my heart is you."

"I think we need to take my deployment as a break," I utter the words and instantly wish I could take them back.

The last thing I want is a break from her, but it's the only choice we have. I won't put her through trying to sort things out with him while I'm deployed. I don't want to worry about what she's doing while I'm gone. I need to focus on my men and keeping myself safe. This type of shit is what gets guys killed.

Her face falls and I see the pain spark in her eyes. I hate hurting her. "I seriously can't believe this."

I take her hand in mine and savor the feel of her skin beneath my fingers. "I love you, Natalie. More than I should, but I can't have this shit hanging between us when I go. We won't be able to talk a lot when I'm gone, and I already knew I would go batshit crazy when I leave, but now . . ." I trail off.

Her blue eyes pierce through me, and I see how hard this is for her. "Can I write you? Can I see you before you go?"

Every part of me disintegrates with her questions.

I hope to God there's a way we can find a way back through this, because if I lose her for good, I don't know that I'll ever go through this shit again. There's a part of me that always wondered if he was actually alive who she'd choose and if we can stand the test. This is the time to prove it.

"You don't get it. I don't want to be away from you. I don't want to do this, but I think we have to. I need to focus when I'm away, and imagining Aaron moving in on you will get me killed. Do you understand?"

"Please don't say stuff like that. He's not moving in on me and nothing will happen to you."

I bring her against me and close my eyes. If only it were so simple. If I were Aaron, I would fight to the death. Which is exactly what he'll do. Brittany isn't who he wants to be with. It's Lee, who happens to be who I want as well. I won't ruin myself in the process though. If she wants to be with him, I won't stand in her way, because he had her first. Even if it kills me.

"Nothing is guaranteed, sweetheart. Know that each moment I'm away from you, you'll be in my mind. There won't be a moment that you won't be what I'm thinking of."

We recline back in the couch then she wraps her arm around my torso. "I don't want you to go."

I sigh, "I know, but maybe this is what we need."

"No, it's not what we need, but it's what we have. I'm going to ache for you every day you're gone. I'm going to wish you were here so I could snuggle into your side and remind you why you should love me."

I pull her closer and rub the side of her arm. "Loving you was never the issue. It's keeping you when you're not mine to have."

She looks at me as a tear falls. "I think I was always yours to have. I'm just hoping you'll see that soon."

chapter

ten

NATALIE

"L EE?" REANELL CALLS out from the back deck. It's Aarabelle's birthday party and she came early to help set up.

"In the kitchen!" I call out and wipe my forehead. The house is a mess. There's flour all over the floor, eggs on the floor thanks to my clumsy hands, and Aarabelle laughs at me from her highchair.

She opens the sliding door and stops. "Wow . . . I mean . . . wow."

"Yeah, can you help me?"

"Where's your devoted husband? Visiting his girlfriend?" she asks with hostility.

"Reanell!"

"Too soon? Yeah, probably too soon. Sorry." She bends down and starts to clean up the eggs. "So, where is he?"

"Mark picked him up and took him out for a few hours since the tension was enough to suck the air from the house." I point over to the newspaper that featured his rescue. "Read the last paragraph."

Considering I used to work for the local press, you'd think they would've given me a heads up. Nope. They did a huge piece on him and how he's a hero. But the worst was how Aaron told them how determined he was to make his family whole again. How he loves his wife and child more than his own life and we're what kept him alive.

"He really laid it on thick." Reanell puts the paper on the table. "Mason seriously feels bad, but he couldn't say anything—not even to me."

I put the mixer down and huff. "I know. I'm not mad anymore. It could've risked Liam and the other guys' lives."

Still sucks, but I get it.

"What time will your mom be here?" Rea asks, tiptoeing around the mess. "Did you get anything in the damn bowl?"

"Shut up. I'm not a great baker, but I wanted to make her a cake."

Reanell laughs, "Maybe I should head to the store and get her an edible one. Jesus, you're like Betty Crapper—this doesn't even look like cake mix."

I drop the mixer and start to laugh hysterically. Tears drop from my fit, and I slide against the counter to the floor. "Oh, God, Betty Crapper . . ." I continue giggling, unable to stop. I laugh on the flour-covered floor as Reanell stares at me as if I'm losing my mind. Hell, I am. "I can't . . ." The laughter rages on.

"What the hell is wrong with you?" Her voice is full of concern.

"I mean . . . it's funny," I say, trying to calm myself.

"I'm not sure I follow. You're scaring me, Lee." Reanell hunches down and puts her hands on my knees. "I'm really worried about you. The last few days you haven't been yourself."

Her fear is valid. Since I left Liam's house and he basically told me we need to take a break, I've been a mess. The only thing that kept me going was knowing I had him. Aaron hasn't said a word about our last fight. He's here trying to help and be a part of our lives.

We've met with doctors, psychologists, and he met with some liaison from the government. But I'm robotic. I drive him there and listen to everyone tell me how blessed I am to have him home. They tell me it's a miracle and how happy they are for us, but I feel no joy. I've placed myself back in my bubble of void. It's easier than feeling, and I'm emotionally drained. The only thing that gives me any light is Aarabelle. I try to keep her around me at all times.

"I'm broken."

I haven't told her about what Liam said, but I'm sure she notices.

She grabs my face. "Oh, honey. You're not broken. No one is. You have Aara, me, Mason, and so many other people who love you. This isn't easy. This is real life and it fucking sucks."

"Yeah," I reply dejectedly.

"Seriously, this isn't some movie where it'll all work out in the end. This is ugly and raw. No one has the answers, babe. The thing is . . . there's not really a choice. I feel like six months ago you made your choice. You let Aaron go when you allowed yourself to love again."

She's right. That's the issue. I can't go back not just because of the affair and the lies between us. But because I let go of that love. I forgave him. I found a place where I learned how to truly love and not have to see what I wanted. Will my love for Liam always be that want? No. We'll struggle and we'll fight but there's no one else I want by my side. He thinks he's giving me time to make the right choice. But he's a fool.

Reanell places her hand on mine. "I know something happened with Liam, but you won't let me in again."

"He doesn't want me," I mutter. "He said he wants to take the deployment as a break. I need to focus on here, and he has to worry about the mission."

"First of all," Reanell's voice morphs into her serious tone, "He does want you. You're an idiot if you believe that he doesn't, and since I'm not friends with idiots, I'm going to say you don't. He wants you so much, but can't you see how hard this is for him?"

"Of course I do!" I push up off the floor. "I see it all, and I'm the one who has to deal with all of it! I have to deal with Aaron, Liam, Aarabelle, and last of all, how I'm coping." I throw my hands in the air and wipe my face. *I will not cry. I will not cry.*

She doesn't get it. No one does. This whole damn situation is ridiculous. Aaron and I agreed he could stay here until Aarabelle's birthday party. Then he's going to stay at Jackson's until we can make a decision. It was his idea to go there since the psychologist recommended we get a little space. His night terrors wake us with his screaming, he zones out in the middle of a conversation . . . he's definitely getting better, but it's a long road for him. But the worst is that Aarabelle hasn't been the same, and he wants to allow us both some sense of normalcy.

"Is Liam coming today?"

"I don't know. I can't imagine he would, but he loves Aara, so who knows?"

"He loves you too."

I scoff, "I don't know at this point. He hasn't called or shown any sign this is affecting him."

"Sit," she commands and points at the chair. "Natalie Gilcher, you are so much fucking stronger than you know. Liam is not the only man alive. If he gives you up so quickly, then fuck him. But I think there's more there. I think he's in pain and guys are idiots. They do dumb shit because they don't know how to handle these situations." She smoothes her hair. "Think about it. If he calls you, then he's breaking his own rules. He's giving in, and then he has to break you and him all over again. So . . ." I see the gleam in her eyes as a plan forms in her mind, "You make him break them."

Her smirk forms, and she raises one brow.

"How the hell do I do that?"

"You go upstairs and make yourself irresistible. He seems to have a weakness for red, doesn't he? After all, you're the host . . . shouldn't you look presentable?"

I sit there with my jaw slack at her plan. But she's right. If he comes in and sees me a crazy mess, it won't help my cause. So I muster the strength I have left and stand. "Watch her please . . . I have some freshening up to do."

Reanell smiles as I head up the stairs and decide he's going to miss me no matter what.

I GIVE MYSELF a once over in the mirror before heading back downstairs. Thank God Rea came early. I made sure to wear my red dress from our first date. I have my hair in soft curls down my back, and I went very natural on my makeup, except for my cherry red lipstick. I'm not sure how to handle this. I don't want Aaron to think there's a chance in hell we're getting back together, but at the same rate, I need to wake Liam up. Make him see that giving up isn't what he wants.

I slip on my heels and head to see what Rea thinks.

"Holy shit!" Reanell says as she holds Aarabelle. "Sorry, I mean . . . hi there. Are you trying to give him a stroke?"

"If that's what it takes. My mom said they're on their way. I figure the mommy should look good, right?" I no longer feel sexy and in charge . . . I feel stupid. Maybe this isn't the best idea.

"Do not even think about changing," Reanell chastises as she walks over. "You own this man. Now remind him just how much."

"Gimme the baby," I say with arms outstretched. "I'm going to get her in her party dress before anyone gets here." I bounce her and she smiles, turning to Reanell, I give her something to do. "Everything should be set up, other than the cake, which my mother called and said she's bringing one since she figured I botched this one. If you can make sure my mother never sees the kitchen, I'll love you forever." I laugh and shake my head. It's the running joke that baking and I do not mix.

She nods and waves her hand. "Go make that baby shine for her first birthday!"

Aarabelle is in her pastel pink dress complete with little jewels on the bodice. I went a little crazy on this party, but I wanted to celebrate her birth. The reminder that something so perfect came at a dark time.

"Lee," I hear Aaron's voice as he knocks. "Wow. You look incredible, ba—" He catches himself.

"Thanks."

"Hi, my beautiful girl," he smiles and makes his way over to Aarabelle. He extends his hands, but she clings to me. "Mama's girl through and through." Aaron laughs it off, but I see that it hurts him. I'll give it to him that he's been trying. He spends as much time as he can with her and offers to help. "Who all is coming?"

I hear the undertone to his question. He wants to know if Liam is going to be here.

"A few of our friends, and you know my parents are here. Is your mom coming back down?"

Aaron shrugs and winces. I hate that he has some residual pain, but his right arm took the worst from the IED. The scars are more prominent. He explained the weather has a lot to do with his pain as well.

"She said she couldn't stay this long. I'm going to visit her in a few weeks."

"Okay, what about Brittany?"

He huffs then looks away. "I haven't seen her since I've been here."

"I'm only asking." I try for nonchalant, but I'm sure I fail. There's a part of me that wishes he would choose her so that I didn't have to be the bad guy here. Yes, he cheated, but according to him it meant nothing. He says he wants a life with us, and even if I want to dismiss him, there's a part of my life that belongs to him. "I'm sorry. That was out of line. I'm just nervous about the party."

Aaron steps forward and brushes the hair off my face. "Can we ever get back to us?" His voice trembles with hope.

I look at him and let out a breath. "I don't think so. I can't explain what learning about your relationship was like, but it opened the door to seeing what our marriage truly was, and I can't forget that. And I may not have been with Liam for very long, but I don't know that I could go back. I know that hurts you, and I hate it. I don't hate you, Aaron. I'll always love you in some way."

"I'm not giving up. I won't let you walk away so easily," he warns as he heads toward the other room.

He knows me better than anyone. Aaron can twist my heart so that it's unrecognizable, and it scares me, but it wouldn't be out of love. Loving someone is being unselfish and sometimes relinquishing your own wants for that person. It's being noble in the face of knowing it would obliterate your world—like walking away. Like the man I love is doing now because he loves me.

I head down the stairs, and my mother and father rush over.

"Hi, sweet pea!" she yells and holds her arms out. She beelines straight for Aara and ignores me.

"Hello, Mother," I chide, laughing.

"Hi, baby girl," my dad says and pulls me into his arms. "You look like you're going on a date." He appraises me in a fatherly way.

"Nope." I decide not to elaborate. My dad was always very protective. Hell, Aaron wasn't even allowed in the house until I was eighteen. My father was the one sitting around talking about a black belt he never had and cleaned guns that I swear he only bought once I turned fifteen. He's all bark and no bite.

"Wouldn't you be more comfortable in jeans?" he asks and I laugh.

"Give it up . . . how's the hotel?"

"Fine. Your mother wanted to stay another night sightseeing in Williamsburg. I couldn't get out of there fast enough. That woman can spend money like no one else." He shakes his head and my mother slaps him in the chest.

"Where's Aaron?" she asks.

"He was upstairs last I saw."

She looks at my father and sighs. It's got to be killing her to keep her mouth shut. There's no way she doesn't have an opinion on what I should be doing.

"Well, I think for Aarabelle's sake, you should be trying to find a resolution."

"Mom—" I cut her off.

I didn't want to tarnish Aaron's memory for my family or his, so I kept his infidelity a secret. To them, Aaron is still husband of the year. But now that he's back, I'm glad I chose to keep it hushed. It's between us regardless, and our mistakes don't need to be broadcasted.

"No. I'm saying that he's your husband and her father." She raises her hand as if it's just her friendly advice.

I reach out for Aarabelle and decide I've had enough pleasantries. "We're going to make our rounds." I smile and walk toward Reanell, who's laughing at my discomfort. Some help she is.

The party is in full swing, and I can't help but look over at the door for him. How can he not show up for her birthday? He's been a father to Aarabelle since she was a baby. He was the man in the hospital with her. Liam cared for her when I was sick and held her in his arms. For him to not be here breaks me in two.

"Hey, there's my goddaughter!" Jackson calls out and Aarabelle smiles. He pulls me and Aara into a hug. "You both look stunning."

"I think she's a little young for you, babe." Catherine chuckles from beside him. He rolls his eyes as he takes Aarabelle into his arms. "Hey!"

"Catherine, you look amazing!" I say and we hug each other. "California agrees with you." She's cut her hair to her shoulders and it's pin straight. She looks so much more a classic beauty now. Her skin is bronze and she has this natural aura around her.

"Please, you would never know you had a baby. You look insane, and that dress . . ." We both smile knowingly. "Anyway, I'm glad we could be here. Muffin told me all about everything, and if you need anything please call me. Is he here?"

"I'm going to take this one and make the rounds. Women love a man with a kid," Jackson says and heads into the kitchen with Aara.

"Such an idiot," Catherine scoffs. "So . . . is he?"

"Which one?" I ask.

"Either, I guess."

"Aaron's here somewhere. Probably with Mark."

She nods and we walk over toward a quieter corner. Jackson has Aarabelle and is probably feeding her God knows what, but right now, I don't care.

"I'm sure he'll be here." She pats my arm.

I wish I could be sure. I've fought the urge to text him all day, but I need to keep my strength. He needs to come to me, because I keep running to him but he's shut me out. I miss him.

A few more guests arrive, and my hope dwindles. Reanell and Catherine keep me busy and try to stop me from spinning into a downward spiral. This isn't the Liam I know. There would be nothing he wouldn't do for us.

"I'll be right back," I say to Reanell and she nods.

As I head into the hallway, I run into someone. "I'm so sor—" The words die on my tongue as I look up and see him. My heart rate accelerates as he holds my arms.

"Hi," he says, still not releasing me.

I focus on breathing and try to ignore that he's touching me. I want to kiss him so bad it hurts. "I wasn't sure you were going to make it."

"I had to help a friend first. I wouldn't miss her birthday." His warm, rich voice washes over me and I shiver. "Cold?" he asks, not missing anything.

Liam releases me, and his eyes travel my body. He gazes over my skin then to my dress. His breath catches as he makes his way back up to my lips. Deciding to make this a little more difficult for him, I slowly lick my lips. He watches my tongue and presses his body against mine.

I'm flush against the wall, and his warmth is blanketing me. "Are you trying to fucking destroy me?" His voice is low against my ear. "Do you want me to lose my mind, sweetheart?"

I whimper softly at the term of endearment he uses. "No."

"Really? Because that's exactly what you're doing."

I straighten and stare at him. "You're doing that on your own."

"You're making me hate the one person who I shouldn't. You have no idea how torn up I am. How I fight the urge to come here at night and rip you out of his house. How I had to smash my phone to stop from calling you. I'm begging you . . . go change." Liam's plea is full of bitterness, and as much as it makes me want to ease his pain—I won't.

I push against him and he backs up. "I've got guests waiting. You could've been here." I step toward him and he retreats. "You could've been in my house every night, but you need space. With space comes this." I turn on my heel and head toward the party, hoping he's watching my ass the entire time.

Liam stands to the side of the party by Quinn and Ashton. They talk, but his eyes never waver from me. I can sense the way he watches me and almost feel his hostility when Aaron is around us.

Aaron does his best to give me space, but I try to include him. He's different though. It's almost like he's not really here with us. Everything feels forced and uncomfortable. While he may not have always been overly social, he would've been at least engaging in conversations, but now he only responds to questions he's directly asked.

I can't help but be concerned that this is all too much for him. "Do you need a break?" I ask him quietly.

"I need to lie down," he admits.

"Go ahead upstairs. We won't do cake until you come back." I place my hand on his arm, but he flinches.

Immediately he tries to soothe me. "Sorry, I just . . ."

"You don't have to explain."

Aaron turns, but then looks back. "I'm sorry, Lee. For everything."

"I'm sorry too." And I am. I'm sorry our lives have come to this. I'm sorry that we can't go back in time to a place where there was no affair, no other people, just us. Maybe if I hadn't been desperate for a family, things would've been different, but the bottom line is, sometimes sorry can't fix the hurt. Sometimes the pain is so deep that no words can heal the damage, and knowing the man you spent months grieving slept with another woman . . . is one of those hurts.

chapter

eleven

JACKSON WALKS OVER looking nervous. He keeps wringing his hands and wiping them on his pants. I can't remember a time I've seen him looking frayed. "Hi," he says glancing around.

"Hi?" I reply skeptically as I smile a little.

"So, I'm going to propose to Catherine. I wanted to do it after the party, but I have something set up on the beach for ten minutes from now. I wasn't sure how long these kid party things last . . ."

My eyes alight and I'm so happy for him I could scream. "So go. Don't be stupid. Where are you taking her?"

"The lighthouse," he smiles and checks to make sure no one is near us. "I would love for everyone to come in about a half hour, but I don't know now since I apparently have shitty timing."

The joy in my heart is overwhelming. He deserves this so much. After he lost Madelyn, none of us were sure he'd recover, but when you see him with Catherine, you can't help but be happy. They've been through a lot of troubles, but in the end they endured. There's nothing more I'd like than to be a part of their special moment.

"I'll have my parents watch Aarabelle and round everyone up." I place my hand on his forearm. "I'm genuinely happy for you."

He smiles down at me. "Thanks, Lee." Jackson kisses my cheek and then nudges my arm. "I'm gonna grab Cat and head there."

I nod and watch him walk off. My eyes drift to Liam who's looking at me. Our gazes stay connected, and I suddenly wish we were that happy. He's the man I want to come home to, wake up next to, and fall asleep with, but for some reason he's trying to be noble.

Jackson and Catherine walk off to the beach while I head over to our friends. Mark, Ashton, Quinn, and Liam all look over as I approach. "Did Jackson fill you all in?" I ask, and they nod. Liam looks away for the first time, and my anger builds at his dismissal. "Okay, I'm going to change my shoes."

"Are you sure you want to walk on the beach in that dress?" Liam asks seemingly annoyed.

I smile at the fact that my plan is working. "Yup. I'm *very* comfortable."

"Glad someone is," he mutters under his breath.

Mark and Quinn give each other a look and slap each other on the chest. Apparently, they notice his crappy attitude.

I climb the stairs and check on Aaron. He's sound asleep and for once not thrashing around. I decide not to wake him and grab my shoes. Liam is waiting at the bottom of the stairs. I stop on the bottom step and have to restrain myself from either leaping into his arms or slapping him again.

"You can't be mad at me because you don't like your decision."

Liam steps closer and we're eye to eye. "I don't like the situation. This is fucking impossible."

"What is?"

"Not touching you," his hand lifts and he holds my cheek. "Not talking to you," he keeps me captivated with his voice. "Not kissing you," Liam leans in and our lips are almost touching. "Is it killing you, Lee?"

I don't answer. I hold my ground for a second before I can't hold back any longer. My lips press against his and I melt. His arms drop, he grips my hips, holding me tight as my arms wrap around his neck. I won't let go . . . I can't let go. I need him to fill my lungs and awaken me again. There's a house full of people, but right now there's no one else but us. His lips mold to mine and our tongues meet. Liam pushes me back against the wall, hiding us from anyone's view. He kisses me languidly, and I find myself in his touch.

Someone clears their throat, and we break apart. I look over at Reanell who has her hands on her hips. "At least find a spare room." She shakes her head and walks away.

"We should go," I say, feeling conflicted. He tilts back against the railing, wipes his mouth, which smears the lipstick even worse. "You have lipstick on your face," I say moving closer. I wipe his mouth, relishing the way his lip feels against my finger. The smell of his cologne filters around us.

He grips my wrist before it drops, "I won't lose you."

"You're damn right you won't."

Liam releases my arm, takes my hand in his, as we head toward the lighthouse. Everyone is ahead of us, and I savor the fact that we're alone. Neither of us fills the silence, we just walk hand in hand. Liam's thumb rubs the back of my hand, giving me comfort in his touch. Once we're out of view of my home, he drags me close, and wraps his arm around my waist. He pulls me tight against him, and dips me back. I watch his blue eyes shimmer as his mouth slowly moves toward mine.

Our lips touch and there's no rush. He kisses me like I'm a treasure in his arms. He cradles my head as he holds his mouth to mine. I could stay like this forever.

Liam pulls me back but keeps his arms wrapped around me. "I'm sorry."

"For kissing me?"

We start to walk again and I wait for my answer. "No, sweetheart. For how this is for all of us. I hate that you're hurting and that I'm hurting you. The deployment got pushed up."

I stop moving. "You're leaving sooner?" I thought we had another week or two. Time to mend a little, or at least find a better resolution than him stepping aside so my husband can have a go at this.

"Yeah, I got the call earlier today. We leave in three days." Liam's voice is resolute. You can tell he's going into what we call deployment mode. They close off the world around them and start to focus on the mission.

The lighthouse is within view, and I still can't respond. My mind is going a mile a minute with how to handle this. Liam stops me before we reach everyone else. "I want to see you before I go."

I nod with tears in my eyes. "I'm going to miss you."

Liam gives a sad smile, but before he can respond, Quinn whistles us over.

We head toward our friends right as Jackson and Catherine exit the lighthouse. Catherine is smiling, and then she sees us and her face falls in confusion.

She looks back to Jackson as he drops to his knee. I watch with tear-filled eyes as she clutches her chest.

"Catherine Pope, you've given me more love in the last two years than I've ever known. You taught me how to love again, how to be a better man, and how to forgive myself. I want to spend every day of my life making you happy. I will cherish you, protect you, annoy you." She laughs as tears fall down her cheek. "I'll give you everything you could ever want. Will you marry me?" Jackson's voice is full of promise, and we all stand with smiles and love for them.

He's gone through a lot of hell to get here, and I have faith

I'll survive just like he has.

Catherine falls to her knees and grips his face. "I will marry you today if you want."

He holds her close and kisses her passionately. Jackson leans back and places the diamond on her finger and wipes her tears. "Tomorrow we leave for Hawaii."

She laughs and he pulls her close. "Always so damn sure of yourself."

"You can't resist me, baby." Jackson smirks and kisses her again.

We all join in their joy and hug the happy couple. Ashton squeals over the ring and the guys joke with him about losing his touch. I stand off to the side sharing stolen glances with Liam.

Fear that he won't make it home consumes me, but more than ever, I'm terrified we won't make it back to each other. There's so much at stake for both of us, and six months is a long time. Part of me understands his need for a break, but I worry it will be too much.

Liam walks over after the group disperses. "Do you want to walk with me?"

"Sure," I reply.

"I don't know how this works, Lee. If Aaron weren't here, I would be with you on my last night. I would make love to you and—"

"Don't," I lift my hand to stop him. "Don't tell me how you would be doing things if he wasn't alive. Because you could be doing them now, but you don't believe me. I chose you. I came to you and told you."

"And he's living in the house. What do you want—family dinners? I'm doing the right thing by staying away. I'm giving you *both* a chance to figure out what the fuck you want."

"He's moving out soon, but I can't just throw him out. He's Aarabelle's father. Jesus, he's been tortured and God only knows what. It's our home," I try to explain to him. This isn't easy on me or him, but Aaron has it the worst. Sure, he screwed up and there's no going back, and at the same time I can't be cruel. I know Liam isn't asking for that, but I'm at a loss here.

"Your home with him. Do you get it now? It's not our home. It's the home you made with him. Where you share a child. Where I would come crash for the night on the couch when I would visit while you two did whatever upstairs. I'm always the outsider."

I turn and fire burns through my veins. "I think you want to believe that. It's easier for you to walk away this way. Make me the bad guy so you can deploy and carry out your life without having to worry about me. I'm not the bad guy here. None of us are. Aaron is moving out soon. He wanted to give me and Aara some space so we can adjust and figure out a life."

"Did he tell you he'd let you go?" Liam fires off.

"No."

"I'll never know for sure, Natalie. I'll always wonder if you really loved me or if I was just the consolation prize. So take the six months and figure it out. Know that no matter what, when I get back I'll be hoping you're there. If you are, I'll marry you. I'll do anything you want to prove how much I want you."

My heart rate quickens, and I wait for him to say more.

"This isn't about me fighting for you. I know you keep saying I'm giving you up, but I'm not. I'll never stop hoping you'll still choose me when this is all over. I just can't watch you decide. I see the way he looks at you. He's made it clear he wants you back. I never wanted to lose you in the first place."

I grip his shirt and pull myself to him. "You never will."

"I hope that's true. You have no idea how much I want that to be the case."

"Have faith in us, Liam."

He presses his lips to the top of my head. "I do, sweetheart.

I just need a minute."

Liam walks me back to the party with his hands in his pockets. Both of us keep our heads down. I don't know how I'll endure six months of not knowing. But I do have faith in us, and I won't let that falter. I have to make him believe me. As we approach the deck, Aaron is standing there watching us.

"Hey." He looks at both of us and guilt eats at me. "I woke up and your mom said you all headed to the lighthouse."

"Yeah, I came upstairs but you were asleep. Jackson proposed to Catherine and he asked us all to come," I explain, hoping he'll drop it.

He looks toward the ocean. "Where's everyone else?"

"They're coming. Do you feel better?"

Aaron looks at Liam with hate in his eyes. "I did until now."

"Stop it," I chastise him. "I've been honest with you. I'm not sneaking behind your back and doing God knows what while we were still married. I'm not keeping half truths or secrets."

"I thought you would give us time before you moved in on her again?"

Liam steps forward, pushing me behind him protectively. "I wish you'd seen the wife you love so much when she found out about your girlfriend. The pain in her eyes, the way she cried and then drank herself stupid. Or maybe you could've seen the way she wanted to kill Brittany after she found out about her pregnancy. My word means something to her . . . does yours?"

chapter twelve

I NEVER TOLD Aaron about the baby. I wanted to see if he was really lying about his relationship with Brittany. So much for that plan.

Liam stares Aaron down, and I push him back, but he doesn't budge.

"What?" Aaron asks.

"You didn't tell him?" Liam turns to me with his jaw slack.

The blood drains from my face leaving me colorless. As much as I wanted to not mention the baby because I wanted him to tell me, I also didn't want to acknowledge it. Aaron and I had a host of fertility issues, but the main one was me. I have PCOS, therefore I was the biggest contributing factor. Polycystic Ovary Syndrome causes my hormones to constantly be unbalanced and renders me practically infertile. My doctor explained even if I could get pregnant, I needed to be aware I was very high risk.

"I didn't know how," I mutter.

"Lee, look at me." Aaron steps forward, and my heart begins to sputter. It hurts all over again.

Liam's eyes implore me to tell Aaron. "Acknowledging the baby to him is a reminder that it's me who couldn't have a baby. I didn't want to face that so soon."

He nods and then I turn to Aaron. "I know it all. I know about your relationship you keep telling me is nothing. And I know about the baby you and your girlfriend were having." I look at the now practically empty home except for my parents and Reanell. "Now's the time to be brutally honest because there's nothing that can hurt me more at this point." Aaron sits on the step and now I wait.

"I think this is something you and I should discuss privately."

I half laugh. "I didn't get that luxury finding out. I had to be in a crowded bar with all of our friends when I found out that you, the man I would've never imagined, cheated. I had to stand there and have her tell me about how much she loved you. And while you may not have loved her the way she did, I saw her pain." My voice is low, but he cringes.

"All I could think about was you," he says, not fully admitting what he did. "So you're going to throw it all away? Our whole life?"

And there it is. For the first time, he's not denying or circumventing how deep their relationship was. "Did you know she was pregnant?"

"Yes," Aaron says, barely audible.

No matter how much I love Liam, this still hurts. Aaron wasn't just some guy. He was my partner and the one person who promised to love me and honor me. I was guilt-ridden after he was gone about having any kind of feelings for another man.

"So was all of what you said a lie? Were you in love with her?" I ask him unsure if it matters at this point.

Aaron stands, and Liam's arms hold my shoulders from behind. Here I am between them both. "No, I loved her. It wasn't even an inch of the love I have for you. Being held over there reminded me of that. I made vows and promises to God and anyone who would listen about the man I'd be when I came home," he says looking straight into my eyes. "I love you, Natalie. I always have and I always will."

"You broke the very core of our marriage."

"I can fix it," he pleads with me. "I fought for you. I lived for you. Please, give us a chance."

We stare at each other, and I see the man I promised to love in sickness and in health, for better or for worse. I'm torn in half and burnt to ash. Everything inside of me is dead. How do I do this? How do I break him when he's already broken? I know that my answer right now will kill him in some form, and if I spare him it'll be in false hope. Then, the added pressure of knowing Liam will hear whatever I say.

"I can't do this with you both," I finally reply exasperated and overwhelmed. "You're literally killing me. Inside I'm a mess. I cry all the time, I can't remember the last time I slept without waking in a pool of sweat. You broke me when I found out. I literally tore everything you touched apart. I don't know who you are anymore," I say and clutch my stomach.

I turn to Liam and prepare to unload on him. "And you. I love you so much it is physically hurting me to be away from you. But you keep pushing me into someone else's arms. You leave in three days and I'm dying inside. How can you push me away and then know you could get hurt or worse? All I want to do is curl into your arms and you tell me it's all going to be okay, but you won't give me that. Instead you tell me we need to spend time apart?" I ask as the tears fall. "I hate what you're all doing to me. Am I the only one here that sees how fucked up this is?"

I look to them both and they stand there. I want to throw something, scream, cry, and lose it for once. I'm always the one holding it together. Trying to make our lives easy. I'm a mother, friend, daughter, and lastly I get to be a woman. Well, this time . . . I'm a woman first. I have to give myself a chance to come through this.

"Sweetheart," Liam steps forward.

I put my hand up. "I need a minute," I say the words that I've been biting back. I see the flash of pain across his eyes, but right now I'm going to save myself.

"No, there are no more minutes." Liam's entire body is tight and ready to fight. "I'm done with us taking time. I love you. I would never betray you. You and I make sense. So I'm done shoving you away."

These two men have the ability to destroy me, and I won't let that happen. I push past them and head inside. My mother stands with Aarabelle in her arms. Tears fall from her face, and I know she heard it all. I walk over and wrap my arms around them both. Her arm holds me close and Aarabelle puts her head on my shoulder.

"Dada!" she yells, and I turn to see Liam walking in the house.

Aaron's face falls, he turns, and then walks out the door. "Aaron!" I call out and rush onto the beach after him. "Aaron, stop!"

He turns and pain lances across his face. "You let her call him Daddy?" There's no judgment in his tone, only hurt and disappointment.

"No," I shake my head quickly. "And he never encouraged her. It's just what she called him."

"I can't . . ." he begins and then stops talking. He walks closer to the water and stops and screams.

I wait in silence, unsure of what to say or do. You can feel the turmoil rolling off him.

"Everything I hoped for and lived for is gone," his voice breaks at the end. Aaron turns and his brown eyes cement me to the ground. "I wanted to die so many times. I could've begged at the end for them to kill me, but I lived because I kept seeing your face. Each night I closed my eyes and saw you and imagined what she looked like. Now, I come home and you're in love with another man. No, not just another man. Liam. My best fucking friend and my daughter is calling him Daddy!" he yells, and it's my turn to break.

I step closer to him, the urge to comfort him overwhelming me. "It wasn't like that. You died in my world, Aaron. There was a paper that said you were gone. No hope of a return. We said our goodbyes, and I grieved." My hand touches his. "I was dead inside. Then he came to Virginia and made me live again. He brought joy, laughter, and love back to us. Liam didn't steal anything." Aaron's eyes close and I go on. "In your letter, you told me to move on. I wasn't sure I could at first, and then when things shifted further into more with Liam, I found out about Brittany."

"You'll never know how much I hate myself for sleeping with her." I touch his face softly and he squeezes my hand. "It was my worst mistake. I felt so incapable of making you happy. Everything was about the baby and I couldn't cope. Then, I convinced myself while I was gone it never really happened. If I could deny it over and over then maybe, just maybe, we could find a way again. But once again . . . can you see how fucked up I am? Can you see how I don't even know who I am anymore?"

"You're in there, Aaron. You're not a bad guy, but you can't keep doing this. You have to deal with everything."

"Please, Lee. Save me," his voice is desperate.

There are two options right now—I can hold on to the hate and anger toward him or forgive and try to move forward. He made a horrible mistake, but it's not within me to make him suffer. "I can't save you. But I forgive you."

His eyes snap up and I see a small piece of relief. "Does that mean we have a chance?"

"Please don't ask me that. I may have forgiven you, but I don't want to hurt you. So please, don't ask unless you're really ready for the answer," I implore.

Aaron reaches his arm out tentatively and we embrace. He needs this, and in a way, so do I. The life we shared together was filled with happy times. There was love and passion, but the end was where we failed. It's both of our faults the marriage was where it was. I know he wants a chance, but my heart is with Liam.

"I know what your answer is." Aaron looks away. "I'm going to stay here for a bit."

"Okay," I reply. "I'm going to make some arrangements for Aarabelle. Liam deploys in three days, and I want to see him off. I want us to do what's best for her, so I can ask my parents to stay here so you can spend some time with her or they can take her?" I give him a little, hoping he'll see that while I'm not asking for permission, I'm taking into account his feelings. He is Aara's father, and I won't begrudge him the time with her.

"I'd like to spend some time with her, so if they agree to stay here . . ."

"I'll ask," I smile.

Aaron nods and looks off toward the water as I head to the house.

Liam stands on the deck as I advance. "He okay?"

"I think he's getting there. That hurt him a lot," I explain.

He looks at the sky and then back at me. "I never wanted that to happen. I should get going."

"Don't leave yet," I request. "I'm going to have my parents stay here with Aaron and Aarabelle. You and I are going to spend your last days here together."

Liam's lips lift as his eyes brighten. He steps closer hesitantly before his fingers graze my cheek. "Are we?"

"We are, and if you're a good boy, maybe you can break out that eggroll," I raise my brow and for the first time it feels normal.

"I'm not sure you deserve my eggroll," he jokes.

I lean close to his ear and use the tip of my fingernail to scrape down his chest. "I think you and I both know you can't resist me. So, you can go home, and then I'll be over with a bag soon."

Liam's lips just barely touch my ear. I shiver involuntarily as his breath wisps across my skin. "Don't bring any clothes, you won't need them."

I close my eyes and try to get myself under control as I now need to get the rest of my plan set. "I'll see you soon."

"I'll be waiting." He kisses the side of my cheek and walks off. God, I love that man.

MY PARENTS WERE all too happy to stay at the house with Aarabelle. I explained the situation briefly, and they seemed to understand. Aaron was surly but didn't say much when I left. Once I arrive at Liam's, I grab my bag and head to his apartment. He opens the door before I have a chance to knock.

"I was beginning to think you weren't coming," he grins and leans against the door. His dark hair shines in the sunlight, and his white shirt accentuates his muscles. My mouth waters at the sight of him as my body burns to see it all.

I lick my lips and drag my bottom lip between my teeth. "Well," I say pushing my hand on his chest. He doesn't move, but I shove him a little harder and back him into the apartment. "What are you going to do with me now that you have me?"

Liam grips my hips and then kicks the door closed. He lifts me into his arms while pressing me against the door. "Do you know how much that dress made me fucking crazy?"

I nod and tangle my fingers in his hair. "I hoped it would. Nothing else seemed to get you to stop being so stupid."

His head rests on mine as we both breathe in each other. "You came to me. You're here instead of there."

My hand pulls his head back so he can look at me. I watch the turmoil flicker through his eyes. "I choose you. I just wish you'd believe me."

"Let's skip the heavy shit. I have an idea."

"Now I'm intrigued."

"As much as I'd love to strip you down and make love to you for hours," he pauses.

"I'm good with that."

He laughs and kisses me, but before we can get hot and heavy he shifts back. Liam glances at his watch and puts me down. "We gotta go now."

"Go where?" I ask confused.

Liam smiles and holds me against him. "Trust me?"

"Always."

He takes my hand and grabs a bag by the door. I reach for mine but Liam grabs it before I can reach. I smile at him and he winks. "We gotta hurry."

We sit in Robin, and Liam starts her up. My mind starts to wonder if we're going to Corolla. I would love to spend time with him completely alone and enjoy having that house again. Instead of bugging him, I let him surprise me. We only have a few days before he has to leave, so it's not like we can be going very far.

I notice we're not heading south, and now I'm really curious. We continue to head in the opposite direction, until we pull into the airport parking lot. He's got to be kidding me. How the hell can we go anywhere requiring a plane ride? It's not feasible.

"Why are we at the airport?" I can't hold back any longer.

"Because we're going on a plane."

He parks the car in the garage and exits. I sit here wondering what in the world he has up his sleeve.

"Lee?" he opens my door and looks at me. "Are you going to get out?"

"Where are we going?"

"Jesus, you're killing me. Just get out of the car." Liam grabs my hand and lifts me out. He kisses me quickly and then hoists the bags.

"Did you plan all this from the time I told you I was coming over?"

"I did . . . are you impressed?"

More than impressed, I'm in awe. He trusted that I would come to him. So as much as he says he doesn't know if he can believe me, this gives me the assurance he does.

We step up to the ticket counter, and we hand over our identification.

"Welcome, Mr. Dempsey. I see you have two in your party traveling to Charleston."

I look over at Liam with a smile. He knows how much I've always wanted to go there. The cobblestone streets and little romantic restaurants are all Reanell talks about. She and Mason go there every year, and in passing, I mentioned how much I'd love to have a getaway there.

"I love you," I say, feeling overcome with emotion.

Liam wraps his arm around my back and holds me close. "I love you."

"Your flight will be boarding in about thirty minutes so you should head to your gate immediately," the woman smiles and hands us our boarding passes.

We head through security, and it dawns on me that I didn't pack for this. I didn't grab cute clothes and shoes. I don't even have enough toiletries. I figured we'd be in his apartment. "I'm not prepared for this."

"What?"

"The trip. I didn't bring anything I need."

Liam smiles and we make it to the gate as they begin the boarding call. "Relax, they have stores in South Carolina. I doubt I have everything either, but all I need is you, and I've got that."

He leans in and our lips touch. Everything I was worried about fades away.

"Yeah," my hand rests on his chest. "You do."

chapter

thirteen

W E CHECK INTO the Harbour View Inn. It's magnificent with its old, historical, brick exterior and plush interior. Everything is upscale and pristine. Liam opens the door to our room, and I can't find my lungs. A four-post, wooden bed takes up the middle with white linens. The opulence is in every detail. The suite features a balcony that opens to a view of the water. It's stunning.

Liam stands behind me as I take it all in. His hands brush my shoulders and he sweeps my hair to the side. I close my eyes as his lips touch the edge of my neck.

"Are you happy, sweetheart?"

"More than you can imagine." I turn into his arms and kiss him.

Our mouths connect and Liam deepens the kiss. His tongue swirls with mine and my hands wrap around his torso. In all of this mess, he's the only person I want, and right now, he's all mine.

Without breaking, he walks me backward, and I feel the bed hit my knees. He lowers me slowly and tenderly. I devour every moan and sound he makes as our lips stay fused. His hands graze my body, and I squirm beneath him. I'm desperate to make love to him. I want to show him how much he owns me. Give him every part of me and let him take whatever I have to give.

His teeth tug my bottom lip and he pulls back. My eyes roll back as his hand finds its way under my dress. "We're going to go very slowly," he rasps. "Do you understand?"

I nod, unable to find my voice. He lifts my back up and glides the zipper down. My hands move of their own accord and trace his body. I lift his shirt and tear it off. He watches me, and my fingers touch his face. The scruff is longer than usual and almost a beard. I inhale the sea air mixed with the sandalwood scent of Liam and commit it to memory. I allow my fingertips to trail to his neck then to the hard lines of his chest. I trace the muscles and feel each dip and mountain. Lower I go until I reach his abs. I stare into his eyes as the pads feel his satin skin tense as I slide down the middle of his stomach.

"We can go slow, but I want this to be equally torturous for you," I whisper. I want to drive him as crazy as I'm sure he plans to drive me.

I reach his belt and slowly undo it.

"Seems you're a little overdressed," he grins while he pulls the straps of my dress off, exposing my frilly, white lace bra. It's one that I can only wear with certain fabrics. Everything is visible and Liam appears to be fine with that. "God, you're magnificent."

His mouth descends on my breasts, and he licks me through the fabric. The heat from his tongue against the friction from the lace is too much. I moan and quiver as he moves to the other. The cool air breezing through is blissful agony as it hits the wetness on my skin.

"Liam, please." I beg for what, I don't know . . . more of him, more of us, more of this.

He doesn't let up as he drags the strap of my bra down and alternates between each breast. Bringing me higher and higher. His teeth scrape across my nipples, and I claw at his back. I'm going out of my mind. Finally, he removes my bra and sucks hard, pulling my taut nipple into his mouth.

I'm so lost to his touch that when his finger presses against my clit, I cry out. He pushes and swirls, applying pressure at the right times.

"I'm gonna come," I say, breathless.

"Not yet," he replies and lifts up.

I nearly weep with need. He sits on his knees and removes my dress, leaving me in my underwear. My eyes travel his body until I meet his eyes. Liam looks down and tears my underwear off then removes his pants. He stands there at the edge of the bed with his erection begging to be touched. I shift onto my knees and press his lips to mine. My hand travels down and grips him. I pump him slowly while we devour each other's mouths.

Liam's hands travel my body as he fondles my breasts, paying extra attention to my already sensitive nipples. I moan and his mouth moves to my neck as he nips at the skin by my ear. My hand releases him, and I press against his chest as I climb off the bed. He looks at me before I drop to my knees.

He groans before I even touch him. I smile and keep watching him watching me. My mouth opens, and I take him between my lips. Liam's head falls back with a deep sigh. His fingers thread in my hair as my hands grip his ass.

"Fucking hell. Your mouth . . ." he mumbles as I glide his cock to the back of my throat. Every muscle in his body tenses, and I repeat the motion. "Natalie, I can't. You're going to make me. I-I . . ."

I take joy in the fact that he can't form a coherent sentence. My fingers snake around and grasp him while using my mouth to perform the same motion. His hand grips my hair harder, and he pulls my mouth off him.

"The only place I'm going to finish is inside of you. Get off your knees."

I stand, and he lifts me into his arms. Even though we're only a foot away from the bed, he carries me there. Liam places me down and crawls on top of me. My love for him swells and overwhelms me. "I love you, Liam Dempsey."

Liam stares at me and closes his eyes. When they open he looks at peace as if the world just righted itself. "I love you, Natalie. More than my own life."

"Make love to me," I request.

As if abandoning his plan, Liam settles between my legs and then enters me. The emotions engulf me. I never want this to end. He's going to leave soon, and I'll have to hold on to this in the days where it's hard. I try to take myself back years when this was the life I lived. When the last kiss could be my last kiss. The times where loneliness could annihilate me if I let it—and I can't let it. I have to hold on to this feeling when he's gone.

"I'll never be able to leave you again," he tells me. "Now that I've had you again, I can't walk away."

Liam thrusts harder as I cling to his shoulders. "Good."

"You fucking own me and you're mine."

He pushes deeper inside of me and my orgasm builds. "Liam," I whimper.

It astounds me how attuned we are in every way. He knows my heart, soul, and body. He can elicit pleasure from every fiber in my body. He flips us so I'm on top.

"Ride me, sweetheart."

I rock back and forth, my hands resting on his chest. I climb higher with each bit of friction. My eyes close as I lose myself in the moment. My orgasm takes me over the cliff and I fall. Liam holds my hips as he follows me over, and we ride out the moment together.

My chest falls to his and I smile against him. Being in his arms is everything I want.

But he leaves soon.

I stop myself from going there. If I start preparing for goodbye, I won't enjoy the time we have.

Liam's hands glide up and down my back as we remain connected. I lift my chin and rest it on my hand. "Hi," I beam.

"Hi yourself," his smile mirrors mine.

"This was quite a way to welcome me to South Carolina."

He chuckles and pushes my hair from my face. "I'm happy to welcome you any time."

I start to get up, but he pulls me back against him. "I need to clean myself."

"No point. I'm going to enjoy making you dirty again," he says as his hands drift to my ass. He lifts a tiny amount and rolls me onto my back. "I told you this was going to be a long day."

His lips press against mine and we get lost in each other once more.

"WHAT TIME IS our flight tomorrow?" I ask Liam as we walk along the harbor with his arm slung around my shoulder.

He sighs and kisses my temple. "Too early. I'd like you to stay with me and see me off. I know that's asking a lot, but if it's possible, I want your face to be the last thing I see before I get on that plane."

We stop and I turn into his arms. "I don't know if I can."

Aaron used to ask me the same thing, but I never could. There was something about having to say goodbye in front of everyone that was too much. I tried once and driving home was a nightmare. I ended up sitting in my car for almost an hour sobbing as the plane took off. You feel so helpless watching the one thing you want more than anything possibly leaving you forever. It's heartbreak and fear on overload.

"I don't understand."

"I can't watch you leave and then have to keep it together. I don't know if I can handle it," I admit. I hold back the rest of my concerns because I know he can't worry about it. He needs to be focused, and my fears will only weigh him down.

Liam rubs my arms and stays quiet. "Then we'll say goodbye at my apartment. I don't want you to drive if you're going to be upset."

"Of course I'm going to be upset. You're leaving for six months. We're barely at a secure place in our relationship," letting more out than I planned.

Liam grabs my hand as we sit on the bench with the water behind us. "There's a lot I worry about with leaving. Aaron is living in the house and I won't be around. I worry it'll be easy for you both to fall back into your old life. I wonder if when I'm gone you'll think it's too much." He looks at our hands, and I follow his gaze.

His fears are valid. We have a lot of obstacles in our way, but small holes of doubt will only leave gaping issues. There are no guarantees. Neither of us can assure the other that the fears we are struggling with aren't real.

"I worry you won't make it home. That I'll be dealing with this all over again," I huff. "We're quite a pair."

"I'll do everything I can to be sure I come home to you."

"I promise to handle things with Aaron so we can move forward."

We both stay silent as we make the only promises we can to each other. They aren't concrete and I can only assume mine doesn't give him great comfort. I refuse to make things worse for him, but I can't lie.

"How do we do this, Lee? I may sound like a fucking idiot, but

I don't know how to do a deployment with someone at home."

I sometimes forget that in a way we're both learning all over again. Liam hasn't ever had to think about the consequences of his actions at home. I've heard from Aaron and Quinn how he's the risk taker. While he never gambles with anyone else's life, he's more than willing to put himself in danger for the success of the mission.

My head rests on his chest while I try to form the right words. "Well, you focus on coming home, I guess. We email, Skype, write letters, and you call when you can."

"Do we get to naughty Skype?" he asks and raises his brow.

I start to giggle and slap his leg. "You're so stupid."

"Imagine how fun it would be . . ." he trails off with a glimmer in his eye.

"We'll have to see how well you behave," I toy with him.

I nestle back into his chest and try not to let my worries get too far ahead of me. *He'll be safe and he'll come home.* That's going to be my new mantra, because otherwise I'll lose my mind.

"I'll do my best to keep in touch with you. You know once we go to wherever we're needed, I won't be able to, but I'll do everything I can to let you know it's coming. It just depends on how long we'll be in Germany before heading to whatever hellhole we're needed in," he says before kissing the top of my head.

"Yeah, last time Aaron went to Germany he was only on a mission for two weeks. It's so hard for most wives to understand these new deployments. I mean, just send you guys from here. I hated when he'd be gone for what felt like no reason." Liam stays quiet and I wonder if I've upset him. I lean up and see him looking off. "Liam?"

He looks back and gives a small smile. "I know you were married to him. I get it, but right now, it feels different when you talk about your life with him. Maybe I'm a prick, but before when we thought he was dead, it didn't feel like I was competing as much as I am now."

"You weren't then, and you aren't now." My voice rings strong with honesty.

"I'm having to adjust to the fact that when you think of him, he's sleeping in your house."

"I can't just kick him out. Regardless of what he did and who I choose, he's Aarabelle's father. He's been through hell and back, and he was my husband," I speak the words measuredly. I know he's not asking me to kick him out, and I can't imagine how hard this is for Liam.

"This is why I thought we should take a break during the deployment," Liam says and lets out a heavy sigh.

I sit up and wait for him to turn his gaze back to me. "Is that what you need?"

He waits and closes his eyes. "I don't know. I don't want that. I honestly don't know how the fuck I'm going to be thousands of miles away and not wonder."

"Do you trust me?" I ask.

Liam grips my hand and tangles his fingers with mine. "I trust you, Lee. But I'm a guy and you being in a house with another guy—one that wants you back—is a lot to carry. Imagine knowing I was going to be with someone I loved once."

I glance at our intertwined fingers and decide that I have to make this easier for him. We both have a lot of fears we're dealing with and the only thing worse than not being with him is having something happen to him. I would never be able to handle that again. If he were to not make it back home, it would be the end of my heart.

"Maybe we can have tomorrow's goodbye be easier on both of us?"

"How?"

"Know that I love you and every moment you're away you have half my heart with you. And when you come home, you'll make me whole again. I don't want you to worry about Aaron, and we'll handle everything so when you come home we can move forward," I say with conviction. I need him to believe me, because it's the truth.

Liam links his fingers with mine. "I'm a lucky son of a bitch."

"Yeah, you are," I joke with him. "There's a part of me I never knew was missing until you came along. I thought I had it all. I really believed my life was perfect because it was easier than seeing the cracks. If things hadn't happened the way they did, I wouldn't know a love like this exists. I wish we could be . . ." I pause as I remember how hard this is for him. "I just want you home already."

"And when I come back, if you still want me, then I'll do everything in the world to make you mine."

I press my fingers against his cheek. "I look forward to that."

"Me too."

CHAPTER

FOURTEEN

LIAM

"READY, ASSHOLE?" QUINN slaps my back as Natalie and I stand here looking at each other. "Wheels up in ten."

I nod and grip her hands. Even though she didn't want to come to the airport, she said she couldn't leave me at the apartment. This is the first time I'll leave someone behind. Even though we are in a good place, it feels like I'm leaving my life behind. She's everything I need. I love her more than I can ever explain. All I can do is pray when I get home, she'll be fully ready to move forward. And if she chooses *him,* then I'll know what six months apart feels like. Maybe that'll make it more bearable.

I'm fooling myself, but I know we'll be called up and I need to be ready. It's not just my ass on the line, it's the men in my team.

"Hey," she says drawing my attention back. "I'm going to miss you." A tear forms, but she wipes it before it can fall.

"No tears. You'll make me have to kiss you." I try to joke and lighten the moment.

Her laugh is short and then she looks down. "Maybe I should cry then."

"Lee," I pull her chin toward me. Her blue eyes look gray

and hollow. "You have no idea how much I'm going to wish I was here with you. Usually, I love deployments, but I can already tell I'm going to hate this one."

Her perfect lips attempt to smile. "I need to say this," she hesitates. "If you . . . I mean . . . if you get lonely . . ." She gnaws on her bottom lip and looks away, but I turn her face back.

"If I get lonely?" I know what she wants to say, but I'm going to make her say the words. First, it's keeping my mind off the fact that I'm going to touch her lips for the last time in a few minutes. Second, it's kind of cute.

"Just tell me. Please don't let me find out the other way. If you meet someone and you fall in love or whatever . . ."

"If I get lonely, how about I call or email you?"

Her eyes snap up. "That would work."

"Good," I say and lean down so she hears me clearly. "No one is going to fill the void of you. There's no woman in the world that will be able to make me forget you." I hope she hears the conviction in my words, because there's no one else. Selfishly, I want to add on, "Unlike your husband."

The announcement comes over, "Three minutes. Say your goodbyes."

Natalie's chin quivers, and her hands grip my shirt. "I hate this."

"I do too, but remember our trip. Remember what I said. I love you."

She pulls me close against her and my arms are locked around her. I want to hold on to how it feels right now. When the nights get long and I need to feel peace, I want to have this moment. And if God forbid she decides she can't do this again . . .

"Be safe, be smart, and please come home to me," Natalie says quickly. "I love you, Liam. You can't even begin to know how much you own my heart. I wish this were different right now. I wish you had no doubt that you're who I want, but I'll prove it. I'll show you that in six months when you come home, I'll be standing here waiting for you." Tears fall and once again my heart breaks.

"And then I'm going to marry you."

"I'm going to hold you to it."

"I'll call you as soon as I can," I promise.

She nods and presses her lips to me. "Okay."

"And then we can naked Skype," I smile.

She shakes her head and kisses me again. "You can keep your eggroll in your pants."

"And I'll be home as soon as I can," I assure her.

Natalie's eyes lock with me as I bend to kiss her. "Not soon enough." Another tear falls and my throat dries.

Fuck. How the hell am I supposed to get on that damn plane? This was a bad idea and I should've listened to her. Walking away is going to break me. It's my job, and usually I'm the first on that plane, but I can't get my arms to release her.

I look over and see my men grabbing their bags and a few guys starting to head toward the plane. It's time. I have to let her go.

"I gotta go, sweetheart," I say gently.

I expect a scene. Her crying or unwilling to let me go, but I watch a shift happen in her face. She straightens a little straighter. Natalie's entire demeanor morphs into strength and determination. It's the same as when we're ready to head out. We shut down the emotional side and are ready to battle. There's no place for pussies during missions.

"I know," she smiles and releases my uniform then pats it down. "Okay, we got this."

I pull her hips closer one more time and kiss her with everything. I press against her lips as she opens her mouth and I dive in. I need to taste her, feel her, and make her remember how much I belong to her. Her arms wrap around my back and she moans. I'm kissing her like she's the only thing here. I hate myself for making her think we should be apart. I wish everything were different, but it's not, so I give her all I can right now.

"Let's go!" I hear Commander call out.

We break apart, and I rest my forehead on hers. I can't look at her eyes again or I'm not going to be able to get on that fucking plane.

"Come home to me, Liam. Please, just come home," she pleads and I nod.

I bow down and grab my sea bag. This is it.

"I'll see you soon."

I keep my eyes on the ground, and I hear her breath catch.

Don't look. Just get on the plane.

"I'll count the days." Her voice is soft and quiet, but I hear her. I think I could hear her voice even if there were a crowd of people yelling. She calls to me on every level.

With my arms full, I turn and head toward the plane. Two other guys are beside me with the same faces. We're ready, but this blows. There's no happiness getting here, but this is our jobs. We signed up for this, and we serve with pleasure. But no one ever told me this is the other side of this shit.

I'm leaving the woman I love in the arms of her husband. This is so fucked up. But she's not mine fully. I have to use this time to figure out if we have a chance. The life we're both entering into if we stay together is complicated, and there are a lot of people's lives at stake. Aarabelle being number one. I know she's Natalie's primary concern.

As I round the corner, I can't stop myself from looking back. She stands with her long, blonde hair pulled over her shoulder, her arms are clutched in front of her as she watches me walk away. I lift my chin and her hand lifts a little. Then she presses her fingers against her lips and blows me a kiss.

Right there . . . she just broke me.

chapter

fifteen

NATALIE

I STAND HERE as he turns the corner before allowing myself to truly feel what just happened. My body is stiff, and my chest heaves. His desert camouflage uniform is taut and he adjusts his cover. How I wish I could trade it for his jeans and beanie. It would mean he wasn't putting his life in danger. But that's not who he is, and I knew this. Doesn't make it any easier because my heart is sitting on a plane.

This is pure hell.

Reanell walks over and places her hand on my shoulder. "Each time I promise myself I'll stay home, yet I can't stay away." I turn with tears in my eyes as we both grab each other and hold on.

"I hate this. I forgot how much I hate this." I cry against her shoulder, and she stains my shirt with her tears.

She sniffs, "I never really forget, I just block it out." Rea pulls back.

"How can I miss him so much already?"

"Because you love him. As soon as Mason walks away, I start to yearn for him," she says longingly.

I know what she means. "It's like we know we *can't* have them, so we want them even more."

She nods, "I always want him home, but it feels like even when he's home we're gearing up for our next deployment."

"Sometimes even when they're not active it feels like that," I muse. I think my life was worse once Aaron chose to separate from the military. While he wasn't deploying anymore, a part of him was missing.

Rea turns to me and points to the plane. "Those men, they're built differently. They love differently, and they need different things. We're the same way. This is the life we know, and while some may not understand it . . . we do. Our love is stronger than most couples, and you and Liam are no different."

I see Liam enter the plane and the door shut behind him. I want to run and kiss him one more time, but I know it won't ever be enough. There will always be times of missed moments we could've had. She's right though, we love differently, and we accept that our lives aren't up to us.

"How do I do this as the girlfriend?" I ask Reanell. I've always been the wife. I was privy to the information and the support. As a girlfriend or whatever I am, I have no rights.

She snorts, "I'm the Commander's wife, Lee. Any information, you know I'm not going to keep it from you."

"I need to go," I murmur. She looks at me perplexed. "I can't watch the plane leave. There's no way I can."

Reanell nods in understanding. It's one thing for me to be here to see him off, but watching his plane take off, that goes beyond my limit. I've tried in the last hour to put myself back to what I used to be. The military wife in me is rusty, and I know I need to dig deeper. I need to be the strong, silent partner and keep his mind as free as I can. It's one of the parts I loathed. Being angry or upset, but needing to be happy and cheery when they call.

I learned very quickly how to mask my feelings and all the

things that went wrong when Aaron was gone. I had to be a somewhat less creepy version of a Stepford wife.

I smile as I unlock the door to Robin. I sit in the driver's seat and find myself grinning. He drove her here, so I get to drive her home. My eyes close as I inhale deeply. It smells of Liam, and if I try hard enough, I can almost feel him here.

"Okay, Robin . . . let's see why he's so protective of you," I say to the car and decide I need therapy.

I look over at the passenger seat and there's a note with a rose. I smile and try not to break down in tears.

Sweetheart,
You have my heart and now you have my car. Take care of both until I get home.
Love,
Liam

A small laugh escapes me as I start the car. The drive back to my house is a blur. I try to focus on the joy that awaits me. I haven't seen Aarabelle in seventy-two hours, and I missed her desperately.

I open the door and she looks up. "Mamama!" she calls out and my heart swells with love.

"Hi, baby girl!" I call out and rush toward her. I scoop her in to my arms and nestle her close. "I missed you so much."

"Hey," Aaron's voice is low and gruff. "You okay?"

I turn, wondering if he's being serious or sarcastic. I decide serious. "I'm okay, thanks." The small act of kindness means a lot to me. This is the Aaron I always tried to remember.

"The team get off okay?"

"Yeah," I smile.

Aaron shifts his weight as Aarabelle pushes against me to get down. "Good. I'm glad." He looks away awkwardly, and my chest hurts. This is hard for him, and I wish it didn't have to be. It's hard for me too if I'm being honest.

None of these issues are easy for anyone. It really sucks being an adult.

"How was she?" I ask, looking at her as she runs over to her toys.

He smiles and gazes at her. "She was great. Your parents left about an hour ago. They said they needed to get on the road. She's amazing, Lee. You did such a good job with her."

I try to fight the tears, but they come flooding forward. Between Liam's farewell and then this . . . it's too much. "I'm sorry," I say trying to gain control.

Aaron's arms are around me in a heartbeat. "It'll be okay," he comforts me, and I push back gently.

"Aaron," I pause, "You don't have to comfort me. This isn't fair to you. I'm so sorry."

I shouldn't be crying in his arms. I won't be that girl. This is no place for the weak. My emotions need to be better managed.

"I did a lot of thinking this weekend," Aaron says as we move toward the couch. Aarabelle lifts her block and then shows me the other ones.

"Yeah?" I ask, watching my daughter in admiration.

"I realized how bad I fucked up. Lying to you, cheating on you, it isn't the way it was supposed to be."

This isn't exactly the conversation I feel like we've been having lately. "What are you saying?"

"I'm saying I get it. I sat here this weekend knowing you were with him, and it fucked with my head. But if I didn't know and thought you were on some girls' weekend or something and found out, I'd kill someone."

I sigh and wish this could've waited a little, but it's the first time I feel he's being sincerely honest. "The issue was the lies.

You lied about Brittany. You lied about the baby, and then you went so far as to tell me it was a one-time thing. That's not the man I loved. You and I had issues, big issues . . . but they weren't something we couldn't have tackled. We didn't talk though, and it cost us everything."

Aaron looks at Aara. "She's the best thing we ever did."

My lips turn up as I look at the reason for my existence. "Yeah, she is." My eyes prick in sorrow. "It's hard for me to know you were willing to throw it all away." I look over at him and see him nod.

"You and I fought so much. It wasn't a good time for either of us. Do you remember how much you hated me?"

Both of our guards are down, and we owe each other the honesty. "I didn't hate you, I just didn't like you. You were so angry all the time. Everything I did or said turned into an argument. Right now, you love Aarabelle and for that I'm so happy, but when I found out I was pregnant with her . . . you walked out."

He stares at her and then turns to me. "I wanted her for you. But there was a huge part of me that worried how you'd ever survive the loss of another baby. So the pregnancy was another way I thought I'd lose my wife. And in a small way I didn't think we deserved her."

It's heartbreaking how two people who genuinely loved each other can go so far off track. I had my fault in this. I pushed him away and made everything in our world revolve around getting pregnant. It was the only thing I could focus on most of the time. But I did try to be there with him. I never stopped loving him, and I couldn't imagine seeking out another person. Aaron isn't a bad guy, he made bad choices.

"Instead of talking to me though, you sought out another woman?"

"You know how you're torn apart right now? You probably feel like you're split in two. I know you love me, Natalie. I see how you want to hate me, but you can't. We have a child, a life, and memories." He takes my hand in his.

I look over at Aaron with watery eyes. "I'm begging you, please don't do this to me today."

My emotions are everywhere and today . . . I just can't. It's a conversation we could have tomorrow or the next day, because today my heart hurts. I miss Liam. I had to see him off, and it's too much to process this heavy of a discussion.

"I've spent a year away, baby. I know who I want, and maybe with Liam away, we can find our way back. He's not able to interfere and you'll see I'm where your heart really is."

"You couldn't give me today? You had to say it . . ." I'm not even angry just hurt.

It was selfish to come at me about this today. He knows my defenses are down, and he's fighting dirty. I don't need selfish . . . I need strong. I deserve someone who's going to take my feelings into account. With Aaron it's all about him. He saw the opportunity before him and tried to break me. Liam may not be here, but that doesn't mean my heart and soul aren't filled with him.

"Lee," he squeezes my hand and I pull it back. "I just figured . . ."

"You figured he's gone and you have an opening. Knowing what it feels like to leave behind people you love and what he must be feeling. You've spoken to me the day after you left. You know how sad I was. This," I point between us, "isn't what we're discussing today. I can't even possibly think about us. So please, don't be a self-centered asshole for today and let me put myself together."

I stand, grab Aarabelle, and head into the kitchen. Too bad it's not even noon or I'd contemplate a damn drink.

THE ROUTINE OVER the next few weeks after Liam left is exhausting. I email every morning, usually I can catch him online and then we Skype. Seeing his face makes those days a lot easier. I don't have to imagine the angles of his face or the way his jaw curves at just the right place. His blue eyes are the perfect color of crystal blue and the full- blown beard he sports makes me melt.

He's there on my screen, alive and smiling.

"Hi," I smile coyly.

"How are you, sweetheart?" Liam asks rolling onto his side. His shirt is off and he's been doing that a lot lately. Not that I mind.

"Better now." I sound like a lovesick twit. Which I guess I am.

Liam smiles and stretches, giving me a full view of his chest and abs. "Me too. Seeing you is the highlight of my day."

"Put a shirt on."

"Take yours off."

I deadpan and wait for him to laugh, but he just raises a brow. "Fine," I reply playfully and take off my top. I have my cute bra on and he leans in close as if that'll help him see better.

"Bra . . ."

"Not happening, buddy."

He huffs, "You get to see my chest, it's only fair."

I reach behind my back and then Aarabelle screams on the monitor. I laugh and sit up. "Looks like Aara has other plans. No dirty Skype session for you."

"Ugh," he groans and flops back. "Go get her, I want to see her too."

I smile and get my shirt back on, "I'll be right back."

Liam nods and I rush into Aarabelle's room. Aaron usually sleeps in the spare bedroom off to the right, but the last two nights he hasn't come back. He's been sleeping at Mark's, or so he says.

"Wanna see Liam?" I ask her as she bounces holding onto her crib. She smiles and gives me my morning kisses.

"Aarabelle!" he exclaims and now is suddenly in a shirt.

She smiles and presses her hand by the screen. "Dadada," she calls him and looks at me still beaming.

"Hi, beautiful! She's getting bigger."

"Yeah, she and I are both apparently gaining weight," I laugh. I swear I've always been an emotional eater, but this is ridiculous.

"You're both beautiful," Liam says as Aarabelle tries to touch him through the computer.

"Dada, up?" she says with her arms raised.

"Awww, she wants you to pick her up." I smile at how much Aarabelle connects with Liam. She calls Aaron the same name but she still won't lie with him.

He tries and he's a good father. Aaron is always here to put her to bed with me. He's genuinely trying to be a part of her daily routine.

"I wish I could, pumpkin." Liam's face drops a little like the air was let out. It's hard for all of us, but I can't imagine knowing your family is home and living their lives while you're gone. I hear some commotion behind him. "I gotta go, Quinn and Barnes just got here. I'm going to be down-range soon." He looks at me, and I get what he's trying to say.

He's going on a mission and won't be able to talk.

"Okay, stay safe."

"Always, sweetheart. I'll be in touch soon. Bye, Aarabelle."

She waves goodbye and he blows her a kiss.

"I love you," I say with my hand hesitant over the disconnect button.

"I love you, we'll talk soon," Liam says and ends the call.

I look over at Aarabelle who stares at the screen with her head tilted. "Dada," she says looking back at me.

"Liam had to go bye-bye. Let's go baby girl. Mommy's gotta work."

I take her into my arms and get ready to start our day. On the days I do get to see him, it's harder to pretend I don't miss him so much. When he's on the screen, I don't feel like he's so far away. He's in our house, in my room, but I wish he knew that he's always in my heart.

chapter

sixteen

"COME ON, LEE. I need a reliable gym partner."
Reanell tries to pry me off the couch. The last thing I want to do is work out.

"Not this again. We barely lasted a week the last time."

"When Mason gets back, I want him to see I have a nicely toned ass."

She's ridiculous. Reanell has one of the best bodies out of anyone I know. She eats like crap and yet somehow manages to stay looking like a swimsuit model.

"Go away." I lie back down on the couch so she can't get me up so easily. I'm not sleeping well again. I have horrible dreams of Liam being hurt where I wake screaming. Last night was so bad that Aaron came in to check on me. I was crying and flailing around.

Reanell lifts my legs and sits under me. "Still not sleeping?"

"Nope. Last night was the worst."

"You know if I knew anything, I'd tell you. OpSec be damned. Mason told me all the cocks would soon be in the henhouse. So that's good."

We all speak in code. Operational Security is top priority when they're gone. It's one thing for the enemy to catch them because of whatever, but if it was because they heard somehow from our end, it would be unforgivable. Previously, Aaron and I had words that would alert one of us to where or what was happening.

It gave me a sense of solace through the dark times. It's hard not knowing where or how long, and many of us have our ways of giving just enough information to keep each other calm. When they are deployed to Germany, you know they'll be called out. But when you talk daily and then nothing . . . you can't help but be scared.

"Mason needs a better phrase than 'cocks in the henhouse,'" I giggle.

"He knows I like when he talks dirty to me."

Aaron heads down the stairs slowly. "Hey."

"Good morning." I look at the clock. His schedule is completely off course. He can only sleep in small intervals, so he naps throughout the day. The doctors told him to rest and take it easy. He has counseling three times a week and physical therapy the same days.

"Mark is on his way over and we're heading out for a while."

Reanell slaps my leg and hops up. "I'm going to run. I'll swing by and grab you tomorrow for the gym since you're obviously not going today. But tomorrow—no bullshit."

"Fine. Whatever." I watch Aaron as he stares out the window. Sometimes he looks so lost and it shreds me apart inside. I wish I wasn't responsible for some of it.

Reanell opens the door and gasps. "You're fucking kidding me, right?"

I turn to look and see Brittany standing in our doorway.

I don't move or speak. I wait to see what he does. I've made it abundantly clear that we're not together, so Aaron has a right to do what he pleases. But I can't deny this hurts. For the first time, I can truly empathize with what he must've felt seeing me with Liam.

They're both standing there looking at each other. Brittany

has tears in her eyes and she waits.

"I'm sorry. I heard and I just needed to see if they were lying," Brittany tries to explain as she looks at me, then Aaron again.

"You shouldn't be here," he says from behind me.

"You're alive and . . ." The hurt rings loudly in her soft voice.

I grab my cup sitting on the table and start to head into the kitchen. I don't want to watch this, and I don't want to hear their conversation. It's too much. I may love Liam and want to be with him, but I can't sit here and look at Aaron with another woman.

Aaron grips my arm as I pass by stopping me. "Stay," he demands. I look at him and he doesn't take his eyes off me. We stand here as she waits at the door of our home.

"I can't."

"Because you still love me."

"Because I don't want to watch you with her. Because she represents the tear in our lives."

His hand releases my arm but travels to my wrist. "I didn't call or get a hold of you because I'm trying to win my wife back." Aaron's voice doesn't shake. He's strong and in control for the first time.

Brittany whimpers slightly, "I heard and I waited for you."

I close my eyes and try to fight back the urge to scream.

"I'm sorry I hurt you."

"Sorry?" she screams. "Sorry you loved me?"

Aaron releases my wrist. "No," his voice softens a little. "We shouldn't have been together. I fucked everything up for both of you."

"So you're going to choose her? What about the fact that she was with someone else?"

I keep my back turned because I'm barely holding on. All of the pain resurfaces. The lies and mistrust that hang heavy between Aaron and me. The nights I spent sobbing on the floor and waiting for him to come home. Times his aloofness left me wondering, but now I know—he was with her.

"She always would've been my choice."

"You two need to talk," I say and Aaron grabs my arm again.

"You're a liar! You told me we were going to build a life together! You promised you'd leave her, and what? Now you want to play the doting husband?" I turn and see her face. Her hands are in tight fists hanging at her side. She looks at me and then back to him. "Was it her name you were screaming when you made our baby? No. So, fuck you and your bullshit apology," Brittany cries and my pain streams down my face.

"Am I at your house?" Aaron yells at her.

"God, you selfish prick. You told me we would get married. You told me she was cold and barren. You said I was the warmth you needed and that I gave you something you never knew you were missing. I loved you. I gave you what you said you couldn't live without." Brittany's voice is loud and full of hurt.

I hate her. I hate her for making me hear this. I hate Aaron for holding me here against my will.

"You two are the most selfish people I know. You deserve each other!" I cry out and Aaron's arm drops. "How dare you come to my house? How dare you hold me here and make me hear this? This isn't love. This is destruction. You don't hurt people you love over and over," I spit the words at him. "And you," I turn my attention to Brittany. "You just can't stop, can you? It's not enough to ruin me twice, you needed to come back for the knockout punch? Is there a place you won't hurt me? You slept with my husband, you got pregnant, and then when he doesn't choose you . . . you come here. You want him? Have him!" I say and run up the stairs.

"Natalie, wait!" Aaron calls after me, but I keep going.

In the confines of my room, I pray I don't have to hear anymore. The baby is what gets me every time. It's the one part of everything, no matter what, I couldn't forgive him for. I know it's not for lack of trying that we didn't conceive naturally, but they did.

A few minutes later Aaron opens the door. "Get out," I say dejectedly.

"Lee, please."

"No, I didn't need to see that."

He steps further into the room that was once ours. "I needed you to see. She isn't my choice."

"Aaron, you don't get it." I look out the window and let out a deep sigh. "She isn't the issue, it's us. Yes, we were going through so much with trying to get pregnant that I think somewhere in there we both broke apart. I wasn't the woman you remembered, and you weren't the man I needed. We failed each other. But instead of either of us talking about it, you went off and slept with her."

He sits quietly at the edge of the bed. I'm not angry. I'm just over it.

"Not only did you have sex with someone else, you had an affair. A full blown I'm leaving my wife and having a baby affair." It reminds me of the second part of my argument. "Then you lied—again. You got back and told me it was *one* time."

Aaron turns slightly and grabs my hand, but I snatch it back. "I knew I'd lost you."

"Don't you think we both deserve to be happy?"

"That's all I want. I want us to be the way we used to be," Aaron admits.

I wish he would understand me.

"We can't ever be those people again. I'm not the same woman you married. I've gone through a lot. Learned a lot about who I am and what I want in life. I want a man to stand beside me and walk through the fire holding my hand. I want a man who, even though we're not even dating, will leave a woman to come to my side at the hospital. Who will sit with me when I need it. Hold me when I cry and give me love even when it hurts us." I stand and walk to the nightstand. I see the scrap of paper that came out of his clothing during my rampage. "I found this," I say as I hand it over.

Aaron takes the paper and his eyes darken. "I was leaving you."

"And you did that day." I hold on to the back of the dresser feeling a little dizzy. Today has been crazy and I still haven't eaten.

"I never gave it to you. I couldn't."

The words hang in the air between us, but they have to be said. The guilt of being the person to say them weighs heavily on me. "We need to separate. I need to move forward with my life."

Aaron stands and takes my hand. "I never did this to hurt you."

"How did you think it wouldn't? Being pregnant while you had your mistress pregnant? Or sleeping with her and then coming home and telling me about how our child would finally be here? If you didn't want to hurt me, you shouldn't have kept going back. But here's the thing—I love Liam. I know that's so incredibly hurtful to you, but he's who I want to be with."

I could go further to tell him all the reasons why Liam and I are meant to be, but it wouldn't help heal us. And for Aarabelle's sake, we need to be civil, and truth be told, he's been my best friend since I was a kid. Aaron knows about the first time I snuck out of the house and drank. He was the one who taught me how to drive a car. He carried me down the street when I fell and broke my leg. In his arms I remember thinking how we'd always be together.

I was young and naïve. It doesn't diminish my memories, but it was an immature way of thinking.

"And if you and Liam weren't together?"

I take his other hand in mine. "I would still be saying good-bye. I can't get past the images of you two. I can't forget the pain I endured alone during all of that. Wondering if you left after I told you about Aarabelle to go to her. These are the thoughts I play over and over. I can't live like that. Then there's the fact that even when you had all the time in the world to come back, be a different man . . . you didn't. You lied to me—repeatedly."

Aaron releases my hands and holds my face. "I'll never know how I was able to do that to you."

I hold his wrists and pull his hands down. "I'm not angry. I will always be your friend."

My head starts to spin and I wobble a little.

"Whoa, are you okay?" Aaron asks, but everything sounds far away.

"I don't feel good." I sit on the bed and the room spins a little. "I think my blood sugar is low."

"I'll get you some juice." Aaron leaves the room and I lie here thinking about all that's happened the last few weeks. Him being alive, Liam and I dealing with the aftermath, Liam deploying, and now Brittany.

He returns and I sip the juice. I need to do better at taking care of myself. All of this stress is going to wear me down.

"Aaron?" I pull his attention back to me. "I want you to know I don't hate you. Maybe if things had unfolded differently we wouldn't be able to talk like this. But in a way, you being gone might have saved a lifelong friendship."

He sits beside me. "I lost myself before the explosion. I loved you, but it was almost hard to come home. I would look at you and it was like we weren't Aaron and Natalie. Does that make sense?"

I nod, "I get it. When you died, I blocked it all out. I literally couldn't remember how bad things were. I needed to only remember how much I loved you and how wonderful you were. Then, it all came undone."

"I think I'll move out this weekend. I've been putting it off, but I can't keep doing this. I'll always love you, Natalie." Aaron lifts his hand and then drops it.

I smile sadly. This is harder than I expected. I know where

my heart lies, but having this conversation is immensely sad. The strings that tied us together will be snipped by our own choices. This isn't death where you feel robbed of your decisions. "You'll always have a place in my heart. And you'll always be a part of Aarabelle's life."

He leans in and kisses the top of my head. The pain in his eyes breaks me a little more. Aaron doesn't speak as he exits the room, and when the door shuts, I grab my pillow and cry for the marriage I just lost again.

"**I**'VE GOT A few things on the calendar I need to make sure we're ready for," Mark says in his command voice. We had a small issue on the mission in Kuwait. Some of the guys had rounds missing that I know for a fact I ordered. It reminds us all of the problems that led to Aaron's explosion and Jackson's shooting. All of us are on edge and double-checking everything. There've been two more things that seemed fishy, but we caught them before anything could happen.

"I don't know what the fuck is going on, but until we do, everyone is on their 'A' game. I want nothing overlooked, and if you have to check it ten times, then do it. I won't have another life lost on our watch."

Everyone nods and starts to filter out.

"Lee, can you hold up a minute?" Mark asks.

"What's up?"

"I want to run a few things by you and make sure we're all on the same page."

I tilt my head wondering where he could be going with this. "Okay?"

"We want to bring Aaron back to work. His doctors think he needs to establish some kind of consistency, and I know it could be uncomfortable for you both, but . . ."

"I get it." I glance away and try to think about Aaron. These are his friends and this was his job. I shouldn't feel disappointed, but I love it here.

"No, Sparkles . . ." Mark smiles and I roll my eyes. "I'm not asking you to step down."

"He deserves to be here," I say and place my hand on his arm. "I can find a job somewhere else."

"Fucking hell, woman." He grabs my shoulders and shakes me gently. "Are all of you this damn dense?"

"I know you're not talking to me like that." I widen my eyes and he smirks.

Mark has been strange the last few weeks. I haven't taken too much notice because I've been so out of it myself, but he's been irritable and very unlike him. He even mentioned going to spend time in Washington D.C. for a meeting with some top officials.

He speaks but everything suddenly goes tunnel vision. I feel lightheaded again and I try to grab the table. I'm going down.

"Lee?" I hear Mark call out.

But my hand is weak, and I fall to the floor. Then, everything goes black.

"We're on our way to the hospital." I hear Mark talking as I start to wake. "She's fine, she passed out."

I open my eyes and I'm being loaded into an ambulance. What the hell? "Mark," I grumble. I'm so tired.

He puts his phone in his pocket and grabs my hand. "You know if you wanted some attention, you just had to tell me."

I think I smile but I'm not sure. "What happened?"

"You went down. It wasn't long, but we want you to get checked out. And since the ambulance happened to be a block away, they got here really quick."

The EMT pushes Mark back a little then starts to take my

vitals. "I need some information." He asks me all the basic questions and continues to ask about the frequency of the dizzy spells. He checks my sugar levels and asks if I'm diabetic.

Once we arrive at the emergency room, I answer some questions before they start running some blood tests. I've been poked and prodded more than I care to know.

"So," Mark puts his feet on the edge of the bed and reclines back. "We can avoid burning vacation time if we talk work, and I'm all about making Jackson pay, so let's chat."

I shake my head and try to rest.

He nudges me with his foot. "I'm not kidding. I'm planning a giant vacation and I need all the time I can get. You're not dying, so it's billable hours."

"I'll call Jackson now if you want," I say as the room spins slightly.

The doctor walks in and smiles. "Hello, Mr. and Mrs. Gilcher. I wanted to go over the results of all your tests."

"Oh, he's not—" I start to say but Mark cuts me off.

"Comfortable in hospitals. My wifey here is concerned I will end up in a bed with her."

He's lost his damn mind. I stare at him, waiting for him to correct himself, but he grabs my hand and smiles. "For the love of God."

"She's just tired . . . please, Doctor." He pauses and kisses my hand.

I yank my hand back and slap the top of his. Idiot.

"Well, your blood tests came back and showed your blood sugar is low, but it also showed that you're pregnant."

My mouth falls slack and my heart rate accelerates. "No, that's not possible."

"Congratulations," she smiles.

Mark laughs loudly, snapping me out of my trance. "It was

all my super sperm. Glitter and Sparkle, baby."

"Doctor, please can you run it again. It's not possible for me to be pregnant," I say urgently.

She looks at the chart and walks over to the side of my bed. My blood pressure is rising and she checks the wires. "I need you to calm down."

"Lee," Mark's voice morphs into concern. "It's okay."

"I can't be pregnant. You don't understand . . . I can't get pregnant. I had to go through five rounds of IVF to conceive. I lost four babies because of my PCOS. Please, I'm telling you it's not possible." The panic bubbles in my throat, and I start to hyperventilate.

The doctor places her hand on my shoulder. "Focus on breathing, Natalie. I can do a secondary blood test, but your HCG levels are high indicating you are in fact pregnant. I can have the OBGYN on call come in and check you over as well. Just rest, stay nice and calm, and we'll get everything settled."

I nod and try to do as she says. My hands settle on my stomach and tears form. I look over at Mark and he looks unsure. "All joking aside, are you okay?"

"No, I mean, if I'm pregnant . . ." I trail off thinking about what it means. Liam and I would be having a baby. Two men . . . two babies . . . one broken heart.

"I'm happy that we'll have a little Starlight." Mark tries to go for funny.

I look over unimpressed. "You do know we're not married and this is not your baby, right?"

Mark smirks, "I think you need to be happy and laugh. You went through hell trying to get pregnant before, and now you are without even trying. I know it's the worst timing possible, but maybe this is your time. Liam's my friend too, and all of this shit is going to be ugly, but you all need to do what's right so everyone can move forward." He grabs my hand, and the kind and compassionate jokester becomes the strong man. "I know I fuck around a lot, but I'm worried about all of you. You're passing out, Liam's overseas, and Aaron is a mess. He wasn't right before he went to Afghanistan, and Jackson and I failed to handle it."

"What do you mean?" I ask as he sits by my side.

"He wasn't himself. We all chalked it up to the fertility stuff or other stress at home. He didn't talk to us much on a good day," he laughs.

Aaron was always quiet. He lived in his head a lot because of the Navy, but even before that, he wasn't overly social. With me, it was a little different. We both knew what buttons to push and how to make the other lose it.

"After we got back from the mission where we lost Brian, Fernando, and Devon . . . I don't think any of us were right. I'm, you know . . . me," he pauses and I smile. "Jackson had Maddie, and we know he didn't handle it well, but Aaron was just quiet. I figured it was him dealing with it. I feel like we all failed each other."

Mark pours his heart out, and for the first time, I really try to see when it all happened. That mission destroyed and bonded the three of them. Aaron, Mark, and Jackson all left the Navy after that. Aaron was injured, but he finished his enlistment. He went through his therapy and never spoke about it. I just assumed he was dealing with it.

"I think I'm as much to blame for that. After all of that, having a baby became my only goal. If he died, I would have something of him," I sigh and look away.

"Forgive yourself, Lee. We all make choices and some of them aren't the best, but in the end, none of us are perfect. Aaron made some pretty shitty decisions, but you don't have to bear his demons—he has to," he squeezes my hand. "Now, about our beautiful bundle of joy . . ."

My hand rubs my stomach and I get choked up. "I don't even know if I can be pregnant, let alone carry. You have to promise me you'll keep your mouth shut." I look at him as fear begins to swirl. *If* I'm pregnant by some miracle, there's no guarantee I can carry full term.

He raises his hands. "I won't say a word."

"I'm serious. Liam has been out of touch a few days, and again, I don't think this is possible." I start to tremble.

"Hey," he wraps his arm around me. "Relax. We'll see what the doctor says and go from there."

I focus on staying calm and wait for the OBGYN to come for a consult. My mind wanders to Liam and how he'll feel about me being pregnant. We never used protection because I never thought this was a possibility. Mark stays with me, and of course, continues to drive me insane.

We talk about the investigation into Cole Security Forces and how he found something suspicious in the files. He explains how he'll be heading out of town a little more often to check on things.

"Charlie and I are working together on some leads," Mark says absently.

"Mrs. Gilcher, I'm Dr. Wynn." He enters and heads over with my chart. Mark stands and shakes his hand.

"I'm going to step out and call the office . . . let them know you're alive," Mark winks and I nod.

"Do you want to wait for your husband?" the doctor asks, looking perplexed at the fact he left.

I scoot up and shake my head. "No, he's just a friend."

"Okay, I ran your labs again and you are in fact pregnant," he confirms.

My lips turn and my heart races. I'm going to have a baby— Liam's baby. "I have a lot of history." I attempt to rein it in. The bottom line is that I've lost a hell of a lot more babies than I've given birth to. I know the pain that comes along with getting excited or being hopeful. I need to make sure I don't get too far ahead of myself.

I go over my past fertility issues and miscarriages. He listens patiently as I give details and start to get slightly emotional. I explain that the baby's father is overseas and how I need to be certain everything is okay. The big mystery is how pregnant am I. Because I don't have regular cycles, I could be a few weeks, or I could be a few months.

Dr. Wynn steps to the side of the bed. "Well, I'd like to do an ultrasound and see how far along you are. Then we can get you set up with your doctor, but at least we'll get a good idea today. Sound good?"

I brace myself and let out a deep shaky breath. This is it. "Let's do this."

CHAPTER

EIGHTEEN

LIAM

"I'M JUST POINTING out you're whipped," Quinn razzes me as we unload the gear. It's been two weeks since I've heard her voice. Two long weeks where I've wondered and worried. All the damn shit I swore I wouldn't do.

Our simple in and out mission was of course delayed once we got boots on the ground. I'm tired, irritable, and need to see her.

"At least I'm not calling and going to voicemail."

Quinn shouldn't talk shit considering he's called Ashton at least five times and she refuses to answer. But the asshat keeps trying.

"She'll come around."

"Whatever . . . I'd rather be whipped than a pussy who can't get the girl."

He snuffs, "I am what I eat."

We both laugh and finish with the offload. Unfortunately, I still have a ton of shit to do before I can even be close to calling home. There's a stack of paperwork with my name on it.

After about three hours of mindless crap and a debrief with the Commander, I head back to my barracks. Luckily, I have my own room and don't have to deal with anyone. I want to sleep for days, but tomorrow we have another meeting for an upcoming mission and need to prepare.

I grab my phone and pray to God the Wi-Fi isn't going to give me shit today.

"Liam?" her voice is sleepy, and I would give my left nut to be able to touch her.

"Hi, sweetheart."

"Hi, are you okay?" she asks disoriented. I look at the clock for the first time and feel like shit. It's three a.m. her time.

"I'm sorry I woke you. I just got back to my room and missed you."

She groans and I picture her stretching. "I miss you. I'm awake."

"Go back to bed," I give her an out.

"Liam Dempsey, shut your face and talk to me."

"Kinda counterproductive there, isn't it?" I joke and smile, lying back down.

If I close my eyes, I can pretend I'm with her. The silence stretches between us as I imagine myself holding her.

"Everything okay?" Her quiet voice soothes me.

"Now it is."

The mission was one thing after another. And I'll be gone a lot more frequently as there's movement again in Africa. My team is the most ready to handle that region and the other team is already tasked to another area. I don't want to fucking think about it.

"Good." She sounds wary. "How long will we be in touch for?"

"Not long. I swear this deployment is going to destroy me," I admit to her. "I can't fucking handle the bullshit. Every time I get something in place, something goes wrong. My mind is all over the place, and I'm snapping at everyone. I swear one more person adds something to my plate, and I'm going to lose it."

"You seem overwhelmed." Her voice rings of defeat. But why?

"What's wrong, Lee?" Her long pause does nothing to calm

me. I hear her sigh and my adrenaline spikes. "Natalie," I say, sitting up.

"Nothing's wrong. I'm fine."

"That word again." My voice is harsh, but I hate this. "Talk to me, sweetheart." I calm myself because she doesn't need to deal with my shit.

She lets out a deep breath. "I'm just missing you. Aaron moved out this week, and there's some stuff going on at the office."

Just the news of Aaron moving out of the house is enough to make me feel better. I would've never been the one to push it, but knowing he's gone will help me relax a little. The idea of him being there when I couldn't was killing me.

"How's he doing?" I wonder. No matter what, our friendship will never be the same. I could never look at him knowing he got the girl and I can't imagine he'll be calling me for a beer anytime soon. There is no way this can end well enough for either of us to the point where we can go back to what we were. If she picked him, I could never go around there. Looking at her with him would destroy me. Aaron will always be tied to Natalie through Aarabelle, and I respect that. She's his daughter, and though I may love her like she's my own, she's not. The loss of his friendship weighs heavily on me.

"He's good. I hope he is at least. He's in counseling and Mark is helping a lot. Is this weird?" she asks.

"It's not pleasant, but he's a part of our lives."

"Yeah," she sighs.

"I was thinking of Krissy today." I mention my sister for the first time in a long time.

"Oh? You never mention her anymore," Natalie notes with her voice sounding more alert.

I feel like a dirtbag for not talking about her. Krissy was my younger sister, and I doted on her. When we were kids, we were best friends and later I protected her from asshole guys who wanted to fuck her. Which, considering we were Irish twins and only ten months apart, meant I broke a lot of my friends' jaws.

"Just wishing she could see me now . . . changing diapers and shit."

Natalie laughs and I smile. I love the sound she makes and how her eyes brighten. I can see it in my head. "You don't change diapers. You massacre them. But you'll have a lot of time to learn."

"Fuck that. I'll let you handle all of it." My eyes close, and I could pass out.

"I don't know . . ." she trails off.

"I hate to cut you off, but we just got back and I'm exhausted. Can we talk later? I'm beat and I have another shit day tomorrow. Let's hope everyone steers clear because I'm liable to snap."

"Of course. Get some sleep. I love you." Her voice is low and my eyes keep closing.

"Yeah, I need a nap. Love you. I'll call soon." We say our goodbyes and I swear I'm asleep before we disconnect.

chapter

nineteen

NATALIE

"**Y**OU STILL HAVEN'T told him?" Reanell asks as we sit at the Plaza Azteca. She grabs another nacho and pops it in her mouth, waiting for my answer.

"No, I don't want to stress him out, and when I miscarry, I don't want to have to tell him. It's easier this way."

It's been a month since I found out I'm pregnant, and whenever I talk to Liam, he seems stressed beyond his max. Each time I go to the bathroom, I'm terrified. It's like I know it's coming and I just wish it would happen.

"I think he deserves to know," she says, grabbing her giant fishbowl-sized margarita.

"I fully plan to tell him. But if I tell him now and then lose the baby, he'll be devastated and still be deployed. If I tell him and his mind goes elsewhere and he gets hurt—then what?" I ask her and stare. She knows I'm right. He's been stressed, crabby, and he leaves again for another time down-range, as he calls it. So, for now it's better for me to keep this quiet and keep him focused on the task at hand.

She nods and sits back. "I get it. You have a good point. There are so many things I don't tell Mason when he's gone."

"Like?"

"Well, he doesn't know about how the stupid, piece of shit hot water heater went out again. He'll get upset that he didn't fix it, and then I'll have to stroke his ego about how he's so amazing. And really, I'd rather buy myself some Jimmy Choos and say it was my reward."

I laugh and snort, "I don't know how that man deals with you."

Rea smiles and throws back her drink. "I promise that Mason has more cracks than the San Andreas Fault. He spends more money on his stupid sports memorabilia than I do in shoes and purses. We even out and we don't have kids."

Reanell's eyes fall and I know what she's feeling. She and Mason tried for years, and instead of killing themselves over it, they just resolved that if it happened, it happened. I admire that they put their marriage first, but I couldn't possibly imagine a life where Aarabelle didn't exist. My hand drifts to my stomach and I think about the baby inside. If I lose him or her, it will wreck me. I know the pain both emotionally and physically. The agony of not being woman enough gnaws its way up my throat.

"Lee?" Rea's hand touches my arm.

"I can't lose this baby," I admit with tears forming.

"No matter what happens . . . I'm here. I'll hold your hand, rub your back, and then we'll get drunk, but I think this baby is a miracle." She raises her glass, and I raise mine. "To Dreambaby."

"Dreambaby?"

"Well, he's Dreamboat, so he has Dreambabies."

"Oh, Jesus."

We both laugh and talk about my doctor's appointment. According to them, everything is on track and I conceived while we were in South Carolina. I'm only six weeks pregnant and my plan is to let Liam know once I make it through the twelve week period. I've lost two babies during the first trimester and the other was at fourteen weeks. I can't worry him, and I don't want to have him distracted.

Reanell sits back in the booth with a look that I know too well. "What?" I ask.

"How are you handling Aarabelle and Aaron?"

I sigh and look away. "It's hard sharing her like this, but it's the way it is. Aaron is trying really hard and we're getting along surprisingly well. He's going to therapy and he loves her."

Right now he's taking her for short periods of time and nothing overnight. He said he's not ready with his sleep schedule and the nightmares being as bad as they are. I'm proud that he's aware of his PTSD and how it's affecting him. The decision not to keep Aarbelle overnight is his decision instead of something I have to fight him on. Our lives have drifted through rougher seas, but he's trying to calm them.

"How do you think he's going to handle . . . ?"

"Not well. But he knows I'm moving on. I filed for divorce and he signed it."

"Wow, that's surprising."

It was a shock, but I was glad it wasn't drawn out. Aaron and I had tears in our eyes when I gave him the papers, but nonetheless he didn't fight me. It was probably one of the hardest things I've ever had to do. It was truly admitting that the marriage was dissolved on our own choice.

"He said he loves me and he wants us both to be happy." She nods and looks around. "You don't think so?"

Reanell smiles. "I think you both are handling this difficult situation the best you can. I keep trying to imagine how I'd act if this was me. I think the divorce was more than a long time coming. I just want you all to be happy and in a good place. I know he was in a bad way when he got back, but considering he's in counseling, it should help when he finds out about the baby."

Since the fertility problems were basically the beginning of the end for us, I know this will kill him. I've thought about it and how to handle telling him, and I come up empty each time. Mark is the only person other than Reanell who knows. I owe it to Liam to let him know before anyone else. While having more children has always been something I wanted, I never thought it was a possibility. Now here I sit, pregnant with Liam's baby.

"Do you think Liam will be happy?" I ask the burning question.

"Did you guys ever talk about it?"

"No, not really. I mean, he loves Aarabelle so much, I assume he won't be upset, but . . ."

It's the one black cloud that looms over me. I worry that he'll think I tricked him before he was ready, but then knowing Liam, I doubt that at the same time. He loves me and we weren't some one-night fling. He's already made mention of marrying me and moving forward together.

Reanell grabs my hand. "I think Liam and you have a love that's real and true. He's patient, kind, loyal, and most of all, he adores you. He's chosen you over a friendship that lasted far longer and he loves Aara. I mean, not many men would do what he has. Liam is your forever love."

A tear falls as I allow my wall to come down for a minute and think about him. I miss him and can't imagine my life with anyone else. Liam fills the cracks that formed in my heart. He makes me whole again, and gives me something I didn't know I was missing. Just the sound of his voice can calm or excite me. I fall asleep thinking of him and wake up wishing he was next to me. I don't think I could ever get over him. He would forever exist inside of my soul.

"I'm such an emotional mess. Damn hormones," I laugh and wipe under my eyes. "I think Liam allowed me to see the difference between a comfortable love and a love that shatters your world. I loved Aaron, don't get me wrong . . . but it was just something I think we did. We dated, got married, then having children became what we should do next. When we couldn't, I felt like we were broken. Does that make sense?"

It's Reanell's turn to wipe her eyes. "It does."

My heart breaks for her. As much as she puts on the front about her purses and shoes, she wanted children. "I'm so sorry, Rea."

"I didn't want to go through it. I couldn't after watching you. My faith in God broke each time you'd call me and say it didn't work or you lost a baby. You're so much stronger than me, sister."

I come around the other side of the booth and hug her. There's a sisterhood we share. One of understanding, support, and unending friendship. When half our hearts leave, we bind our remaining pieces to get through the days. Not everyone can understand what we do. They say they can, but it's not all sunshine and unicorns. We put our fears aside and wear plastic smiles because that's what you do. Military wives aren't strong because they want to be. They have to be. I know the chance that Liam can be returning in a box is real, but I love him regardless.

Reanell returns my hug and sniffles. It's not often she breaks down, and she never shares this with Mason. "You have no idea how strong you are." I pull her close and we both cry out a little of the pain we share.

ANOTHER TWO WEEKS pass.

Another two weeks of Liam being gone.

I hate deployments.

I look at the beach filled with happy couples, and I want to scream. Aarabelle and I are playing in the sand. Liam hasn't called in a week, and I keep having horrible nightmares. I woke up last night and ran to the front door thinking someone was there to tell me he died. It was so real. I was already crying hysterically when I ripped the door open.

"Hey," Aaron's voice calls out from behind us.

"Hi." I smile as he looks at Aarabelle.

In the last six weeks, Aaron has started to look like the man I fell in love with. We haven't really spoken about anything deep, but he said he understands my need to move on.

"How are you?" he asks as Aara gets up and runs to him.

"Daddy!" Her tiny arms wrap around him and he kisses her.

"She just . . . !" I trail off as he smiles with his whole heart. We've been saying Daddy more and more to her in regards to Aaron. It warms me that he's being such a great father to her. She's lucky that she'll know the love of two men.

"She did! Hi, my beautiful girl." He lifts her into his arms and I hold my heart. Even with everything we've suffered, there's a small measure of healing through Aara. She is the glue that holds us all together.

Aaron carries her over and sits next to me. "That was amazing."

"Yeah," I grin. "I've been working with her on Mommy too. I'm glad she said it with you here."

"Me too. So, how are you?" Aaron asks and starts to play with Aara in the sand.

"I'm hanging in there. You?"

He looks at me and lifts his hand, but drops it before touching me. "I'm doing okay," he admits.

"Good, I'm glad." And I mean that. I don't wish anything bad on him. Aaron has suffered enough in his life, and I know the man he was. He was happy, loving, and fun. I want him to find that again.

"I wanted to ask you if you thought we could have dinner this week? There's some stuff I want to talk about and I owe it to you."

My heart sputters and I'm not sure what to do. Aaron hasn't done anything to make me wary, but I remember the last dinner we had.

"Is something wrong?"

"No, I just want to talk about going forward."

"Okay, I can get a sitter for Aarabelle."

"Great."

We play with Aara for a while and talk about work stuff. Aaron has been working with Mark on a lead outside of the office on what's been going on in Cole Security Forces. This will be the first time he's back in the office for more than a day or two. They both have been steadfast in checking every clue as to who could be behind the issue that caused Aaron to go over there in the first place. Jackson is flying back this week and wants to have a staff meeting. It's hard to believe anyone is intentionally messing with all of these guys, but it seems that way, and Mark is all too happy to work a little closer with Charlie in D.C.

After we discuss work, we transition into how he's handling everything. Aaron's been working hard in therapy and seems to be doing much better at opening up. His therapist has urged him to talk more about what he went through.

"Seeing Charlie this week was good I think," he muses.

"Why is that?"

"She was able to fill in some of the gaps of time and how she was able to get me the hell out of there."

Aaron looks off at the waves and I place my hand on his. "Can you tell me about the rescue?" I ask.

We start to pack Aarabelle's toys and head to the house. It's already getting dark and we've spent the afternoon talking and laughing. It was nice to spend time with him like two old friends. There wasn't anything awkward or uncomfortable. We just enjoyed the day with our daughter.

"What do you want to know?"

"How did it all go down?" I really want to know how they knew where to find him and what happened.

Once we reach the deck, I can tell by the way Aaron stiffens and the way he keeps clenching his hands that this is difficult for him. I reach out and touch his arm. "You don't have to tell me." I offer him the out.

"No, it's fine."

"Do you want to stay for dinner? I have chicken in the crock pot."

"Are you sure that's okay, Lee? I'm not saying I don't want to, but you need to be sure. I don't know if I can really be friends with you like this. You chose him."

My stomach clenches. "Aaron, I wasn't trying . . ."

"I know. You asked me to leave. You asked me for a divorce. I don't know how Liam or Brittany would feel."

"You're back with her? Even after all the shit you said to each other?" I ask.

"Do you hate it?" he asks and steps closer. "Do you wish I wasn't?"

I shake my head. "No. If you were willing to ruin our marriage over her, I would hope you cared about her enough to try. You were planning to leave me."

I thought we were making progress, but it seems not. I don't know if he's playing a game or what.

"I would've never done it."

"You'll never know that."

"I do know." He lifts Aarabelle in his arms. "I don't want to fight with you. I came here to see if we could talk."

My phone rings and it's Liam's number.

"I gotta answer," I explain.

"Liam?"

"Hey, Lee." He sounds exhausted and worn. "I only have a minute, but I needed to hear your voice."

"What's wrong?" Fear starts to course through me. This doesn't sound like the man I know.

He huffs and something crumples behind him. "Everything. I'm ready to be out of this hellhole. It's going to be a long deployment, and I've never been like this. I'm the guy who's counting down the fucking days, Lee. I'm not this guy. I don't do moody bullshit. The whole damn time I was away, all I did was worry about you. This isn't normal. I don't care about being away. It's money and fun, yet here I sit all pissed off and ready to come the fuck home."

"Lee, I need the keys," Aaron says loudly and I know it is on purpose. I hand him the keys and give him the nastiest look. Asshole.

Liam goes silent and then his voice morphs to anger. "Aaron's there?"

"Yes, he came to see Aarabelle."

"But he needs the keys?"

"Don't make this a fight because you're looking for one. It wasn't anything you need to worry about. Our divorce paperwork is submitted, but he's going to be a part of our lives. You're pissed off because you're gone, and I get that, but there's nothing here."

"My mind goes crazy. I think about him being there when I'm not. I wonder if he's telling you how easy it would be with him. I'm going out of my mind, Natalie."

I wish I could take his worry away, but I know if it were me, I'd be the same. I don't blame him for it. He's away and my husband who I loved for more than half my life is here. One who made it abundantly clear he wasn't going to give up.

I look back as Aaron and Aarabelle enter the house.

"Listen to me," I say as I walk down by the beach. "You have my heart. You have my soul and you have my body. No one else. You have to trust me and know that I would never betray you. I love you, and you're not getting rid of me so easily."

"When I get home, I'm going to show you how much you mean to me. I'm going to marry you, Natalie. I'm going to give you everything I have. Just wait for me."

"You already give me everything. Now, come home soon."

Liam disconnects the call. I close my eyes and I rub my stomach. "You've given me more than you know."

chapter

twenty

"YOU'RE NOW SIXTEEN weeks," Dr. Contreras says as she smiles and grips my hand. I've been with her from the beginning of my very first failed pregnancy, and she knows more than anyone how I've been terrified. Each week, I start to gain a tiny flick of hope this might be okay. "You are still high risk, but right now you're on track."

"I keep waiting," I say aloud.

"Don't live like that. Everything looks great right now, and you've made it through the most trying time." She walks over and gives my hand a squeeze. "Have faith, Natalie."

I need to harness my faith that no matter what, I will be okay. I can't be worried because the stress won't be good for the baby either. "Can you give me any insight about how this happened? Years I went through hell, and now when I'm not even trying . . . it happens?"

"Sometimes after you have a baby, your body resets itself in a way. Kind of like 'been there done that.' Your cycle restarted after Aarabelle, and while you might not have been regular because PCOS doesn't go away, you were ovulating when you did happen to get pregnant. It's a good sign." Dr. Contreras smiles and writes some things in her chart. "I want to see you back in four weeks."

"Are we doing this like we did with Aarabelle?"

During my pregnancy, I was considered high risk. My visits were more frequent and they monitored me very closely. I also was on a very light lifting ban. We were very careful, and I felt like I should've covered myself in bubble wrap.

"Most of it, yes. I don't want you doing anything strenuous. If you can keep off your feet then do it. I know that's hard with an eighteen-month-old, but try to take it easy. Do you have help from the father?"

I look away and shake my head, "Aaron has been helping a little with Aarabelle, but he doesn't know. Liam is deployed, and I can't tell him while he's gone."

She laughs, "I'm sure that'll be a fun homecoming."

"It'll be interesting for sure."

She pats my hand. "I'm sure you will get everything worked out. We'll keep you monitored and next appointment will be an ultrasound. It's all good things, Natalie."

"I have so much stress right now, between Aaron and Liam, I'm not sure what the hell to do. I'm concerned all of this is going to affect the baby." This is my worry I battle each day. I've been doing so well with keeping myself calm and in check so far though.

Aaron and I get along, but I'm sure that all could change very quickly. Liam will be home soon enough and then the dynamic shifts again. Plus, there will be an even bigger sense of betrayal. Liam was able to get his wife pregnant when he couldn't.

"I know this is a difficult time for you, but I want you to focus on you for once. Not Aaron and all the issues in the situation, but really give yourself the best care possible. Can you do that?" Dr. Contreras asks.

"Yes, this baby means everything to me. No matter what happens, it's a miracle and I'm happy."

She smiles, "Good. Now, I'll see you in a few weeks and then we can see your baby."

I leave the office feeling buoyant and hopeful. I dreamt of having more children, but I never expected it to happen, and I sure as hell didn't think it wouldn't be without help. Liam and I have a tiny miracle growing inside of me. I don't know how he's going to handle it, but I can't stop the joy that builds.

I'm going to have another baby.

Once I arrive back at the office, I float around in a daze. I was so sure by now I wouldn't still be pregnant that I didn't really allow myself a chance to process what it all means. Aaron will need to be told delicately and not until Liam knows. God, I hope I don't show early.

"Earth to Lee." Jackson smiles waving his hand in front of me.

"Hi! Sorry." My cheeks flush as I realize I've been staring off into space.

Jackson laughs and leans back. "How are you?"

"Good. I'm good."

He smiles knowingly and I wonder if Mark told him. I'll kill him.

"Dempsey doing okay?" he asks.

"Yeah, Liam is out doing . . . well . . . you know," I sigh. "It'll be a few more days until he's back in touch."

Jackson nods and steeples his fingers. I forget sometimes how far he's come. The man who used to play beer pong as a sport is now a company owner. He took all of the bad things that happened to him and used them for good. "How are you handling his deployment?" he asks.

There's no judgment in his voice. He must know how difficult this is for me. I may do a good job of masking my fears, but they're there. They lurk in every shadow, waiting to jump out at me. The fear that someone will come to tell me he's died weighs heavy. It's the reality of loving him, but he's worth battling my demons.

"I have good days and bad days. When he's in Germany, I'm fine. We talk more often and it feels like he's just down the street, but he's been out of touch for a while now."

"It won't be too much longer."

"No, we're half done. It's that last month that's always the most agonizing," I laugh.

"For us too." His warm smile and blue-green eyes light up.

"So, you didn't come all this way to just talk about me . . . what's up?"

Jackson sits forward and explains what's been going on in their investigation. It affects my job because that was the initial issue. When Aaron went out to Afghanistan, it was to see why supplies were going missing. The issue seemed to die out after Jackson got shot, but when they started to delve deeper, they found something was amiss.

"Anything you need and I'll help," I offer.

"I was hoping with your journalism background, you'd be able to look into a few things, but I want you to be comfortable."

"As long as I don't have to travel, I can help. I don't know how great my contacts are and what I can find out, but I still have some friends."

Jackson nods, "Great. Thanks, Lee." He looks around awkwardly and I can tell this isn't the full reason he's here.

"Is there something else?"

"Aaron will be in the office more. I know you guys are talking and both moving on with your lives, but I felt you should get a heads up. I don't condone all the shit he did, but he's been my friend and saved my ass. If you want to cut back here or work from home more, I'll do what I can to make this as comfortable as possible."

Aaron and I have found a way to cope through all of this. We're civil and kind, but I'm not sure working together is the best idea. Especially with me being pregnant. But Aaron isn't responsible for supporting me, and I don't expect anything from him. I need to produce an income.

"Can I think about how to handle this?"

"Of course. I just want you to know I'm your friend too, and I won't let you and Aarabelle suffer either." Jackson gives me a pointed look. "I mean it, Lee."

I grin and nod, "I know. Now, how's wedding plans?"

Jackson and I talk about their upcoming nuptials and how happy he is. It's nice to see him come full circle and with someone like Catherine. They may not have been each other's first loves but they are truly made for each other. Which is how I feel about Liam.

It may not have been the plan I had, but he makes me impossibly happy. Liam sees into the parts of my heart I never knew were there. He's the clarity in the darkness that brings peace to my soul.

MY COMPUTER RINGS and I fluff my hair. I haven't seen Liam in weeks and I want to look stunning.

"Hi!" I squeal as his face comes into view.

"God, I missed your eyes," he says and smiles.

My eyes start to water as I look at him. His dark brown hair is longer than he usually wears it and the scruff I love so much is a full beard. He still takes my breath away.

"I missed every part of you."

"You look beautiful. How are you?" he asks and leans back on his pillow.

"I'm good. I miss you," I say again. I wish I could find better words because missing him doesn't seem strong enough. I yearn for him in a way that's probably not healthy.

He chuckles, "I miss you too, Lee. Where's Aarabelle?"

"With Aaron."

"Ah," he says and his face falls slightly. "I got an email from Mark the other day."

Panic starts to churn, but I try to mask it quickly. "Oh?"

"Yeah, wanted to check in and see how things were. Let me know you were being watched and were doing good."

"Watched?" I say a little pissed.

"You didn't think I wasn't going to make sure you had someone looking out for you?" Liam smirks.

"I think you forget I've done this a time or two there, Dreamboat." I missed our playfulness. It's one of the things I love most. He makes the most serious of situations easier to tackle.

"Yeah, but I haven't. I needed to make sure my girls were okay." The way he includes Aarabelle makes my heart explode with love. He's going to be an amazing father to our baby.

I bite my lower lip and debate if I should tell him now. I decide to test the waters. "How did the last trip go?"

"Let's not even talk about me and here. I swear I'll never be happier to be stateside," Liam huffs and then continues. "There's been stupid fucking mistakes made over and over. I mean, you'd think I'm with a bunch of newbies this time. My frustration level is beyond high, and I'm going to have heads roll if there's one more screw up. I thought someone would be coming home in a body bag this last one."

Nope. Not going to tell him now.

"I'm sorry," I shrug, partially disappointed. I want to tell him about our baby. Of course I wish it was in person versus over Skype or the phone. "The divorce should be final soon, by the way."

"You okay with it?"

"I'm ready to start our lives with no more ghosts," I reply earnestly.

Liam pauses and then his eyes get serious. He leans in and sincerity rings in his voice. "I'm going to make you happy, Natalie.

I'm going to give you all the things you want, and I'll never betray you. As long as we're together, you and Aarabelle will be what I live for. I know she's not mine, but I'll love her like she is. I'm going to make sure you never know what it feels like to be second best."

My heart soars and tears begin to fall. "You have no idea how happy you make me."

"We're just right, Lee. I'm not saying we won't have ups and downs, but I'll be by your side the entire time. Even when I have to be away from you, I'm with you."

I shift forward and blow him a kiss. This man has shown me love when I never thought it would exist again. He gave me faith to open myself to him and that he'd protect me. Even when he pushed me away, it was to protect us. The love we share is once in a lifetime. It may have taken a tragedy to bring us together, but it's true love that binds us.

"I love you, Liam Dempsey."

"I'm thinking you should prove it," he winks.

"Oh, and how do I do that?" I smile as his eyes begin to smolder.

"I want to see you, sweetheart."

I smile and shake my head.

"I want to hear you, watch you come apart with my voice. I need you so bad and this is the best we can get."

If I ever planned to do this with him, there's no other time possible. I'll be unmistakably pregnant soon and then I definitely can't.

I grab my laptop, shut off the light hoping to hide the bump I have now, and head toward the bed. "I've never done this."

"Me either, sweetheart, but I'm dying and I want to do this with you. If I can't touch you, I need to see you and feel you in my mind."

With just the dim light from the setting sun, I glow. I smother my nerves and take my top off. I watch his pupils dilate and hold on to that to keep my confidence up. My heart races as I watch him settle into his bed. "I'm not going to be the only one naked, am I?" I ask.

Liam grins and removes his shirt. My mouth goes dry as I see the sinews of his muscles move. I want to touch him so badly. My hand reaches toward him, but all I can do is close my eyes and imagine the feel of his skin beneath my fingers. "Remove your bra, sweetheart." Liam's voice is hushed but full of heat.

I watch Liam as I move my hands behind my back and stop. Instead, I move my hands to my shoulders and slowly drop the straps down. "Like this?"

"You're so beautiful," he rasps.

Slowly, I remove my arms from the straps and then reach back and undo the clasp. When my bra falls, the moan that escapes him causes heat to flood my core.

"If I was there, I'd touch you. My hands would be everywhere. Do you wish I was there?"

"Yes," I breathe and my eyes flutter. This is the most erotic thing I've ever done. He's thousands of miles away and still makes me feel sexy. Liam's voice drops low as he groans when I push my hair back, giving him a full view.

"Show me how you want me to touch you, Lee. Where do you want my hands on your skin?"

My fingers move from my stomach to my breasts. I close my eyes and listen to his voice as I imagine it's his hands on me.

"I'd latch my mouth on your breasts. Suck each one and let my tongue roam over your gorgeous tits." His husky voice drawing out a moan.

"Liam," I whimper.

"My mouth would be over every inch of you. I'd kiss you, touch you, lick you . . . I'm so fucking hard imagining how you taste."

I open my eyes and need to see him. I don't care that we're through a computer. All I need is him. "Show me," I request.

Liam stands and removes his shorts and boxers. He doesn't move, allowing me to see every bit of his body. I long to touch him, feel his body in my hands. "I wish . . ."

"I'm there with you now, Lee. I'm right in front of you. Tell me," he commands.

"My fingers would be on you." My voice is breathy as desire courses through my veins.

"Where?"

"I would trail up your arms," I close my eyes and mirror the movement on my own skin. "Making sure I feel every muscle. They remind me how strong you are and how safe you make me feel." Liam moans and it emboldens me to go on. "My fingers would glide across your shoulders and to my favorite part of you—your chest."

"You're killing me, sweetheart."

I open my eyes and look at him as his hand grips his cock. He pumps it slowly with his eyes closed and his head back. I want to crawl through the screen. I've never been so turned on in my life. Watching him jerk off to the sound of my voice and the promise of what I'd do is the sexiest thing I've ever seen.

"I would kiss each part of your chest. Slowly trail my tongue down your torso but keep my hands on you. I'd go slow over each ridge and dip in your skin. Feel how your muscles tense when I touch you before taking you in my mouth." Liam stops and his eyes are molten lava.

"Take your clothes off, I need to see you."

I remove my pants and underwear. We're both naked and so far apart, but right now, we're together in every way.

"Are you wet for me? Show me," he prompts. The heat in his

eyes makes me want to give him whatever he wants. I lie back on the bed and hope the camera angle allows him the visual he wants but still trying to hide a little. "Fucking hell, Lee. What I would do to you right now."

My skin is on fire. I slowly touch my breasts as they're weighted and very sensitive.

"That's it. Touch yourself for me," Liam encourages. "Go slow and pull at your nipples. Yeah," he moans and I imagine him touching himself. "Glide your fingers down to your pussy, sweetheart."

I hesitate for a second, but the need to ease the build is too much. My hand moves from my breasts down past my stomach. I pause, thinking of the baby for a moment, thinking I should tell him, but Liam speaks again.

"I love you, Lee. Let me love you with my voice."

It's not the time and this would surely kill the mood. "Tell me, Liam."

"I'd go slow, driving you crazy with need. I'd push your legs further apart so I could see all of you. Watch you pulse as you crave me. Then, I'd lower my mouth to your pussy and take one long lick."

I swear I see stars. His voice is thick and full of promise and I could come apart right now. My finger presses against my clit and I rub small circles.

"It would just be beginning as my tongue would push inside of you and I'd fuck you with my mouth first. There'd be no finesse, just pure passion. You taste like heaven and I'd want to stay there forever."

"Oh my God," I groan as I climb higher and higher.

"When I feel you tighten around my tongue, I'd stick my finger inside and twist until you were gripping me so hard that your body is begging for my dick."

"I'm begging now," I moan.

"I know. Make yourself come. Show me how bad you want me."

My pace quickens as I listen to his grunts and groaning. I lie on my bed imagining it's his hands, his mouth, and his touch.

"Only you, Natalie. Only you can make me this fucking hard. Make it this impossible to do anything but think about being with you," Liam coaxes me as I writhe. "I'm touching you. Wishing it was my hands on your beautiful body. My tongue would be in your mouth as I sink into you, claiming you with each stroke as you come apart on me."

I explode. My body shakes as I have one of the strongest orgasms of my life. I cry out and my breath comes is short gasps. I turn my head and catch Liam last second as he follows me over the edge. He moans my name and cleans up.

"Well, that was the best fucking Skype of my life," he smiles, and I flip onto my stomach hiding myself.

"It was interesting for sure," I blush.

"Hold on, someone's knocking," he says and gets dressed quickly.

I suddenly feel very naked. I grab my robe and throw it over me. I hear him arguing with Quinn for a few minutes before the door slams.

"Hey," he looks irritated. "Sorry about that."

"No worries. Kind of glad he didn't come knock a little earlier," I giggle.

Liam doesn't respond right away. He wipes his hand down his face, "I don't even know how to tell you this, but I have to go back out. I'm going to be gone a few days or more, again."

"I thought you guys were on a short break."

I know he has no control. But these missions are killing me. I worry and wonder when I don't hear from him. So far, I've been able to keep my mind from running rampant, but at the same time, the fear can come out of nowhere.

"We were supposed to be, but Quinn just came here to let me know we needed to start gearing up. This isn't like me." He looks off and lets out a deep sigh.

I'm not sure what the hell he means. "What's not like you?"

"This stressed out, pissed off, ready to go home guy. You broke me," he laughs. "I worry about you and Aarabelle. I wonder if you're okay and if you need anything. It consumes me. You consume my world. I don't know how these married guys do this."

He seems so forlorn I wish I could take it from him. I give him my best shot. "I know the job you have. I have a very small advantage than some new SEAL wife. I've walked in these shoes. You have to remember who you are when you're there. You're not Liam Dempsey. You're Dreamboat. If you don't do your job, you don't come home to me. So do your job and do it well. Then when you come home you can suck up."

"How did I ever get so fucking lucky?"

"You loved me at my lowest. You healed me by being the man you are. I'm the lucky one."

"I'll call you when I'm back and we can start planning another Skype before homecoming," he grins and leans in close. "And I mean a repeat of today, sweetheart."

"You better earn it," I smile and scoot forward. "Or next time I'll point the camera at the ceiling."

"You wouldn't."

"Oh, wouldn't I?"

"I'll be seeing *all* of you very soon," Liam smirks.

"We'll see about that."

"Kiss Aarabelle for me and get her potty trained," he smiles.

"I will. I love you."

"Love you more. We'll talk soon."

I nod as my throat becomes thick with emotion. I miss him

and I don't want to hang up. But I know he has to go and I need to be strong for him. Liam disconnects the call, and I hold my stomach and start counting down until I can talk to him again.

chapter

twenty-one

"**A**ARON, IT'S FINE," I say to him for the tenth time. He's upset that I've decided to work solely from home. But this was the best choice. I don't want to work side by side with him every day, and this gives me a chance to stay home with Aarabelle and the new baby. I'm now nineteen weeks and starting to feel self-conscious around everyone.

"Something's going on with you." He walks over to where I am and looks at me.

Shit. He's going to know. I've been extra careful about dressing in baggy clothes and keeping everything hidden.

This is Aaron, the SEAL interrogator. The one who knows every trick in the book. He and Liam are cut from the same cloth. The last two weeks, Aaron and I have gotten along really well. Our divorce is now final and we're both free to move on. We've promised each other, for Aarabelle's sake, to not be hateful. He knows where my heart lies, and I know he needs to find his.

He's not a bad guy and he never was. He was a confused man who made some bad decisions. Unfortunately, for him, it cost him greatly. Cost all of us. Even with us not being together, he's proven to be a phenomenal father to Aarabelle. Each week he comes and has dinner with us, and every other weekend he takes her.

"Please don't Jedi mind trick me. I just have a lot on my mind."
I try to brush him off.

"No, that's not it."

"I need you to stop, please," I implore him. I don't want him to
know before Liam. I don't want him to know at all, but there's no
avoiding that. I'm starting to show a more defined bump, but today
I have a sweatshirt on. There's no way he can see my stomach.

"I'm just worried." Aaron stops and waits.

My cell phone rings, stopping this awkward and very uncomfortable conversation. I look at the number and I don't recognize it.

"Hello?" I answer.

"Natalie?" A man's voice I don't recognize asks.

"Yes, who is this?"

"This is Aidan Dempsey, Liam's father. I have your number
from Liam's emergency file he sent before he left."

"Oh, hello, Mr. Dempsey." Concern sweeps in. "Is everything
okay?"

Liam's father sighs and takes a long pause. "I'm sorry to call
like this," he stops again and sniffs, "I just—I don't know what to
do," he says and my heart plummets.

I clutch my throat and Aaron is at my side in a moment.
"What's wrong?" I barely get the words out.

"My wife," he stops and catches his breath. "She was in an
accident. And the doctors . . . they aren't saying anything yet. But
the accident was bad." The pain is evident in his voice and I feel
both relief and tension. It's not Liam, but this won't be any easier.

"I'm so sorry."

"I need him to come home." He begins to cry and my heart
splinters into a million shards. My legs start to shake. I need to sit.
"She's not going to make it, and they said to get the family here,
but it's just me and Liam left." His Irish brogue grows thick as his
emotions swell.

"Is he?" Aaron says, and I shake my head.

"I can help. I need some information from you. He's out on a mission, but I'll do everything I can." Tears well in my eyes as I think of how badly this is going to wreck Liam. His sister died and that was horrible, now his mother is barely hanging on.

Liam's father gives me all the information about his mother's condition and where she is. I write everything down, and Aaron rests his hand on my shoulder in silent support.

His father lets out a deep breath, "I can't tell him."

"It's okay, Mr. Dempsey, I'll get Liam home."

We disconnect and Aaron looks at me with empathy. It gives me a tiny amount of hope that we can all find a way to get along. "This is going to break him, Lee. When Krissy died, he almost lost his mind. I was there." Aaron reminds me.

He went with Liam to his sister's funeral. Aaron told me when he got back from Ohio how bad he took it. How the guy who would laugh and joke could barely smile. Even now, it's difficult for him to talk about her. She developed a blood clot that killed her in her sleep.

I look at Aarabelle and my emotions flood like a dam that opened. I imagine being that mother and entering her room. Seeing her asleep and knowing I was right there. It becomes overwhelming and I start to sob.

"It's too much," I cry out.

Aaron crouches down and grabs my hands. "I can't believe I'm saying this . . . but you need to be strong. He's going to need you. I can handle Aarabelle for a bit if you need to go. I would offer to go, but I don't think we're quite there yet." Aaron looks away.

"Are you sure you can handle her for that long?"

He sighs, "I'm sure, and if not, I'll get help."

"I'm not trying to be a bitch, but I don't want *her* around our daughter."

Aaron looks away and then back at me. "I was never with her. I said it to piss you off."

"Great."

"I'm sorry," he says with shame painting his face.

He lied. Again.

"I need to get an AmCross in." I stand and head over to my binder. The American Red Cross has to put the information in and then it goes to his command. Being that it's his mother, I can't see his command denying him the chance to come home.

Once I get the message in, Aaron and I sit quietly. Aarabelle is asleep and I wait for Liam or his father to call. He'd fly into Virginia, and then I don't know where we go from there.

Aaron clears his throat and I look up. "I can stay here if that's okay with you," he offers.

"I appreciate you helping out." Throughout these past few weeks, we've grown as friends. There's no spark or connection, at least for me, but the friendship that was always there is still strong.

"Why don't you get some sleep? I'll stay here and if something happens, at least I'll already be here."

I nod and look at my phone. It's been hours and still no call. I know these things can take some time, but it's not something we have the luxury of. Every minute is precious and I feel like we're waiting for the clock to stop ticking.

Once in my room, I lie down and my mind won't quit. I'm distraught over the fact that Liam will have to endure any pain. I love him and know what it feels like to lose someone you love. I would never wish that on anyone. The hands of time haven't been fair to either of us. We've both endured immense pain, but through it found the beauty in each other.

I close my eyes and clutch my phone waiting for his call. I don't know how much they'll tell him, but I hope Mason knows enough to let him call me after. Hopefully, in less than twenty-four hours, we'll be together, where I can be the rock he needs.

I awake with the sun shining and leap out of bed. Glancing at my phone, I see there are no missed calls. That makes no sense. He should've called home by now. It was an emergency. No matter if he was on a mission or not, he would have communication with the base unit.

Aaron will know. I rush down the stairs where he's drinking coffee while Aarabelle plays with her toys. "Morning," he says and takes a sip.

"Hey, I'm worried. He didn't call." I waste no time explaining my fear.

"If they're out in hostile territory, he won't be able to. He may have to finish out the mission and then come back. He'll get in touch when he can. Sucks he was out and not at base," Aaron tries to reassure me. "I know this sounds fucked up, but we know the risks when we deploy. We know we may never get to say goodbye to someone dying. We miss births of babies and a lot of holidays. It sucks but it's also the way we live."

"Do you miss it?" I always wondered this.

When he got out of the Navy, I always felt it was more for Mark and Jackson. Jackson was the leader and he was the first not to take another commission. Mark was enlisted and he followed suit. But Aaron wavered. He wasn't hurt in the firefight like they were. Aaron came back different though.

"No, I'm not going anywhere again. I have my daughter, and I wouldn't ever put you through something like this again," he says and looks away. The tone in his voice makes the underlying message clear.

"What does that mean?" I can't help but ask anyway.

"It means that I wouldn't choose deploying over you. I'm here, Lee. I'm not going to leave, or get injured, or die. I'm here." Aaron's voice is low and pleading.

"You did leave, get injured, and hell, you died too. You weren't active then. Don't use this against me," I warn.

He stands and looks at the ceiling. "This is our house, Natalie. It's where we made a home. We conceived a child here, had fights here, made love here, and I thought we'd grow old here."

I don't know where all of this is coming from. He hasn't tried to make a move in months. We've been friendly and I've never led him to believe there was a chance at more.

"I did too. I didn't choose for our life to fall apart. I know you made mistakes. I've forgiven you for them, but it doesn't change how I feel. I don't want to fight with you about this," I plead for him to stop.

"I don't want you to have a baby with him," Aaron's voice cracks at the end. He stares at my stomach and tears fall from his eyes. I follow his gaze and realize I'm in my shorts and a tank top with a very clear baby bump. "I thought maybe you were, but I didn't want it. I've really lost you. Haven't I?"

"Have I led you on?" I ask with hesitation. I tried hard not to ever let him think we were going to get back together.

He looks at Aara and back at me. "I hoped, Lee. I'm getting help. I know I fucked up . . . God, I know it . . . but I've always loved you. I would do anything to prove to you how good we could be. I'm doing everything the doctors want. I'm not seeing anyone because they're not you. We can get back and we can be better."

"Aaron, please don't do this now. First, Liam is deployed. His mother is on life support and I'm pregnant. I love you, I always have, but our love changed. It became friendship and comfort. We let it slip through our fingers and then the choices each of us made defined our future. You will always have my past, but Liam holds my future."

"We define our futures."

"So do our pasts," I say hushed.

Once again, he glances at my stomach and rests his head in his hands. I give him a minute because I can't imagine this is easy for him. The pain of finding out about Brittany was horrible for me, and I certainly didn't want him to find out this way.

"Were you trying? Were you going to tell me?" he asks gruffly.

"Not before I told him, and no, we weren't trying," I reply honestly.

"Un-fucking real. I couldn't get you pregnant after *years* of trying and . . ." he trails off.

Aaron stands and walks over to Aarabelle. He places a kiss on the top of her head before turning back to me. "I'll never stop loving you, but right now I can't look at you. I'll be back later, but I need some time."

I don't want to hurt him. It was never my intention. "I'm sorry you found out like this. I'm sorry you're hurting."

"I guess we're even now," he sneers.

I know he's angry and upset, but it stings. Instead of going back at him, I stay silent. This won't end well for either of us, and I won't break him further.

He looks at me once more and the pain rolls across his face. Aaron cups my face with his hand and then drops it.

Without a word, he walks out the door and the loud sound of it closing slams the door in my heart.

IT'S BEEN THREE whole days. Seventy-two hours that I've yet to hear from Liam. I'm growing anxious and frustrated. I called the Red Cross again, ensuring the message was delivered to his command, which it was. His father called me this morning asking if he was going to make it home, and I couldn't answer him.

I don't know what to do, but I need to do *something*. Paige arrives to watch Aarabelle so I can go get some answers. I grab my purse and rush out the door. It makes me sick that I'm going to go this route, but I have no choice.

Aaron called this morning to find out what was going on. Even he seemed concerned that Liam hadn't gotten in touch. He apologized again, but said he needed some time away to get his mind straight. Then he offered to still keep Aarabelle if I needed. If anyone's lost the most, it's him. He lost his wife and his best friend and the life he thought he was coming home to.

My phone rings and my pulse spikes. "Hello?" I answer immediately not even looking at the caller I.D.

"Lee, it's Jackson."

"Hi," I say depressed.

"I'm guessing you still haven't heard from him?"

"No, nothing, and I'm getting worried."

"I'm sorry, I just wanted to see if there was anything you needed. I can call a few people and try to get some damn answers."

I know he'll do whatever he can, but there's really no way he can get answers. He's not active anymore. He's a contractor. Sure, he has connections but they're not going to hand over information on an active mission.

"Thanks, Jackson. I wish there was something you could do, but we both know it won't help."

He lets out a deep breath. "I know. I hate this, Lee. I'm here no matter what you need. I'm here."

"Thanks, Muff. I'm at the only place I can get answers now. I'll keep you posted."

We hang up and I look at my best friend's house. Where hopefully some of the answers lie. I grab my bag, let out a deep breath, ring the doorbell, and my stomach drops.

"Hi," Reanell says and looks away. "I figured it was a matter of time."

"You know?" I ask with my mouth agape.

"Come in," she opens the door then steps back.

I want answers.

"What's going on?"

Reanell sighs while she chips at her nails. "I can't tell you, Lee. You know I can't, but I can't not tell you either."

My chest tightens and my mouth goes dry.

Please, if there's a God anywhere, I'm begging you to not do this to me. I can't handle it.

Something's wrong and I'm going to lose it all again. Only this time there won't be any coming back.

chapter

twenty-two

WE BOTH LOOK at each other as her face falls. She doesn't want to hurt me, it's clear in her eyes, but she's going to. Reanell, who usually has no problem saying anything, shifts her weight back and forth as she waits for me to say something.

"Rea?" I ask with dread. "You have to tell me."

She lets out a long breath and then her eyes flash with resolve. "Fuck OpSec. I talked to Mason today and he figured you'd be here already," she pauses and I bite back the bile threatening to choke me.

My breaths come in short bursts, "I-I . . . please don't." I heave and put my hands on my knees.

Reanell is at my side rubbing my back. "Lee, calm down. Listen to me, please." I stand slowly, and she walks with me over to the couch. "They're out on a mission. It wasn't supposed to be a long one from what I understand. All Mason said is they've gone dark for some reason. They can't establish coms and can't get in touch with him to relay the information. They've missed the last three checkpoints, but they have one more window. If they don't answer by then, Mason is sending a team in."

I close my eyes and try to focus on breathing. He has to be

alive. There's no way he'd leave me like this.

"He'll be fine," I say with defiance. "He knows what he's doing." I stand and grab my bag.

"Lee, talk to me." Reanell stands and clutches my hand.

"I have to go food shopping. I'll see you later." I squeeze her hand and look for my keys.

"Food shopping?" her voice is high. "What the hell are you talking about?"

"We need food in the house. We didn't have food in the house the last time, and I need to make sure we can eat," I explain as if it should be obvious. "When Aaron died, I remember wanting some chips and we didn't have any. I need to get food. And chips. Maybe some chocolate or ice cream. I should probably have a variety of things, because I don't know what I'll crave this time. If I leave now, I can get home in time to do some other errands."

"Natalie," her voice is soft. "Stop."

"No, you stop!" I can't take anymore. "I need to go grocery shopping. I have to *do* something, because if I stop, if I take a minute to pause, I'm going to go insane. Do you not see the irony?" I pause. "I'm pregnant—again. I'm having a miracle, and I'm going to lose my other one. I need food in the house. I need to clean so that the next time I see you, I'm prepared."

As much as I want to cry, I can't. The tears sit on the cusp, but they won't come. I need to keep moving and get ready for what seems to be inevitable in my life. Hope that was springing to life dies before it blooms. I should've known better than this. Liam warned me that his life would always be like this. He told me before we started this that he could die.

"Okay. You just don't know anything yet. I'm here though. I trust in Mason and Liam. Don't let fear lead you down a road you don't need to be on."

"I'm not scared. I'm just ready for the inevitable."

I lied to myself over and over that I could handle that possibility. I can't lose him. I can't stand by his casket and relive that again. Respecting death is his deal, because if this plays out poorly, it'll be my heart that never beats again.

"Lee . . ."

"No, I should go. I shouldn't have asked you to tell me."

Rea steps closer, "I would've been at your house in about five minutes. I promise I'll call if I know anything. I have hope, Lee."

She pulls me into her arms as I block out the fear. I can't let myself go down this road. There's too many variables and too much at stake. Hope doesn't grant you wishes. It doesn't paint you pretty pictures or give you a place of relief. It's something we hold on to when we need something to believe in. I believe in truth and facts. Right now, the only thing I know is he's missing and could be dead.

Once in the car, I head to the grocery store. I'm in a fog. People move around me, but I don't notice. I just know that I need to keep going. My cart squeaks against the floor as I head through the aisles. I place things in the cart all the while desperately trying to feel a connection to him.

"Ma'am?" A woman in her early forties places her hand on my shoulder.

"Yes?" I ask.

"Are you okay?" The concern in her voice is soothing.

I look around and nod. "Yes, why?"

"You've been standing here for a few minutes and I don't . . ." she trails off, and I look in the cart.

I've been just loading jars of peanut butter into the cart. There must be about fifteen of them. "I didn't . . ." Embarrassment is laced in my tone.

"I wanted to make sure you were okay," she explains.

I'm definitely not okay. I'm back almost two years ago to when my world crumbled around me. Sure, I made it through and I can do it again, but I'll never recover. I won't ever love again. There will be no healing, just being a mother to my two children. I'll give them everything of me because they will be all that matters.

My hand presses against my small bump, and I pray this baby will know their father.

"He doesn't even know," I say aloud.

"The father?" The woman is still standing here concerned.

Tears flood my vision, and I nod. "He doesn't even know I'm pregnant," I say as they fall.

Her Navy Wife t-shirt lets me know she probably understands in some way. She doesn't say a word as she pulls me into her arms. This stranger I've never met before comforts me in aisle three. I couldn't cry before, and I don't want to now, but I lose it. She rubs my back and lets my tears stain her shirt.

"Is he over there?" she asks and I tilt back.

I nod and look at her shoulder. "I'm so sorry," I say and wipe under my eyes.

"Don't be." The kind woman smiles and waits a second before I nod. "Do you want me to stay for a minute?"

"No," I smile. "I'll be fine."

She pats my hand, "I think I'll just check this shelf out, I'm Lisa by the way."

"Natalie," I try to smile but it won't come.

Lisa stands with me for a few minutes and helps me unload my cart of the jars. If something happens to him, I need to be prepared.

"Thank you," I say hoping she knows it's for more than helping restock the shelf.

"Sometimes we all need a little help," she smiles and heads down the aisle. I watch, wishing I could say more. But she helped me more than she can imagine.

I arrive home with bags of God knows what, and Aaron is in

the kitchen. "What are you doing here?"

He takes one look at me and his face falls. His brown eyes shimmer with fear, as he knows I went to get answers.

"What happened?" he asks worriedly. "I got a call from Reanell asking if I'd seen or heard from you. She told me I should talk to you."

"They've lost coms," I say with no emotion in my voice. I can't muster anything. I'm a blank canvas on the easel. One call will define the color that gets painted and whether it's filled with joy or sorrow. "I don't want to think about it. I need to put this away and clean the house."

Aaron begins to pace and it does nothing for my nerves. "Lee, I know you don't want to hear this, but I can't tell you how many times SEALs go dark for one reason or another. Sometimes it's for safety and other times it's because the equipment goes bad. It could be nothing."

Something in Aaron's eyes tells me he doesn't think it's nothing. "But you don't think so, do you?"

"What did Rea tell you?"

"Just that Mason knew I'd be there and that was all she would say. You should go. I should probably make some meals, maybe get his car detailed, and start to get his stuff together." I make a mental list.

There's a lot to be done as I learned the first time.

"Don't get ahead of yourself. Just wait it out. This is the choice you made, and you have to be ready to deal with it. If something didn't happen to his mom, you'd never have known this." He looks away.

"I did. I chose him. It doesn't mean that if I lose him, I'll regret anything. It means I'll hurt and grieve all over again. Now, I need to make some meals and be ready."

I start to walk away, but Aaron grabs my arm. "Goddammit,

Lee, don't you see? Don't you see the life that you have to endure again? I can give you and Aarabelle the life that you deserve. I won't leave again. You'll never have to worry about any of this." Aaron's voice softens. "I won't leave you. I'll never hurt you again."

"You're doing it right now." I rip my arm from his grasp and walk away.

Aarabelle runs into the kitchen to me, and I hoist her up. I hold on to my lifeline and anchor myself. I have to be strong. I need to believe that Liam is okay and that it's only a problem with the equipment. Aara grips my face and gives me a kiss.

"It'll be okay," I say to her. "Mommy will be fine. Liam will call soon and then we'll be okay."

She lays her head on my shoulder, and I rub her back. I rock her back and forth, almost as if we're dancing. "I love you, Aarabelle."

"Yuv you," she says in her tiny voice.

I inhale and memorize the baby smell that's starting to leave her. This moment, in all my turmoil, Aarabelle is the light. I press my lips to her head and she sighs.

We stay like that for a few moments. I close my eyes, and enjoy this fragment in time. Suddenly, a cramp hits me hard. White blurs my vision as the pain radiates across my stomach. Every muscle tightens and then releases. I start to fall but catch myself right as another flash of pain hits.

"Aaron!" I let out a mangled scream and he rushes in.

Another one hits, and he barely grabs Aarabelle before I fold over. "Lee, what's wrong?" The fear in his voice is clear.

"Oh my God, the baby!" I cry out as I hold on to the counter while my abdomen clenches. I lose my grip and fall to the floor holding my stomach protectively.

Aaron puts Aarabelle down and then I'm in his arms. He carries me tenderly with his eyes locked on mine. All the while, I watch the color drain from his face. Very gently he lays me on the couch as I pray another cramp doesn't hit. The terror is splayed across his face because we both know what this could mean.

I look into his brown eyes, and he sweeps the hair off my face. "Just stay still. I'll call the doctor."

I grab his arm as tears spill down my face. "I can't lose this baby today. I can't."

His eyes close and he nods.

I fight the urge to go to the bathroom. I pray I won't feel anything more. No pain, no blood, because it'll put me over the edge. I'm barely hanging on to the ledge now. I have to muster any amount of courage I have, because this . . . this will kill me. If I lose Liam's baby while he's missing . . . I can't let myself go there.

"No, she just crumpled over," I hear Aaron explain over the phone. "I'm not sure if she's bleeding." A pause. "No, she's not, but I'm with her now." Aaron comes back into view and then heads back into the kitchen. "Okay, I'll call again. Thanks."

My voice isn't there when I open my mouth. We both know what they said and now it's up to my body to decide. Even if I am miscarrying, there's no way to stop it. I'm too early and all I can do is stay off my feet.

He crouches down and rests on his knees. "Lee, you tell me what to do."

"Stay and be my friend. Call Reanell and someone should call Liam's father."

"I'm sorry about before," he says and shame is reflected in his eyes.

"You can't keep doing this to me. I love him, and I'm going to be with him."

"I wish you didn't, but I won't hurt you anymore."

I grip his hand and try to get him to hear me. Right now, I only have enough strength to worry about one thing. "If you love me, you have to let me be happy. You signed the divorce papers and said you understood. And right now, I can't talk about all of this. It's too much."

"I know. I thought if I let you go willingly, you'd find your way back." Aaron's hand falls as do his shoulders. "I want you to be happy. I love you enough for that and for Aarabelle. As much as this sucks, Liam is a good man and he'll be a good father."

My hand rests on my belly and I pray he'll get to be a father to our baby as well. I already know the kind of man he is and how he treats Aarabelle when she's not even his. He loves her with his whole heart. "I'm scared," I admit.

"He'll be okay. I know him better than anyone. If they went silent, it's for a reason. I know it seems like you knew a lot of what happened on our missions, but you didn't. There were plenty of times we had close calls. He's one of the smartest guys I served with and I'd let him lead me any day." Aaron stands and looks at Aarabelle. "And if something happens with the baby . . ." He looks at my stomach. "You'll tell him, and if he's less of a man than I think he is, I'll beat the shit out of him. Just rest for now. Rea is on her way."

I close my eyes, try to relax, and pray this doesn't end the way so many have before. I love this child. I love that man. And I want them both.

"LEE." SOMEONE SHAKES me. "Natalie, wake up."

I open my eyes and Rea is sitting on a cushion pushing my hair back. "Hi," I croak. "Have you heard anything? Did Mason or Liam call?"

She looks away and I fight the urge to scream. "Mason said they're still not responding. He won't tell me anything else, just that he's in control of the situation."

"Right," I sigh. To be honest, I'm lucky I'm getting this much. "I need to get up," I start to rise and my stomach clenches.

"You okay?"

"No, I'm not, but I need to go to the bathroom. I can't hold it in anymore."

Reanell helps me stand and walks with me to the bathroom. "I'll be here if you need me."

"Where are Aaron and Aara?" I ask holding on to the wall.

"They went to the park so you could sleep. You were thrashing in your sleep, so I woke you," she pauses. "I know you don't want to go in there, but you can't stay standing here either. I'll be right outside the door." Rea puts her hand on my shoulder, and I fight back the tears.

She's right.

I don't want to look. I don't want to see blood again. The fear floods through me, leaving me paralyzed in a sea of unyielding pain. I'm drowning in my unshed tears, but I have no choice. There's no one that can change the outcome either way. If it wasn't meant to be, then I'll grieve the loss of another child and what could've been. Or if I make it through this with a baby, we'll celebrate the life that was born.

Entering the bathroom takes every ounce of willpower I have. I close the door and say a silent prayer while I muster up my courage.

I know I pray a lot asking for things. I'm not asking for anything any mother in my place wouldn't ask for. I know you're busy, but please don't take them both from me. Don't let me lose him and the baby. I won't be able to function for Aarabelle. Any ounce of hope I've ever had will be gone. So, I'm begging you to please bring him home and don't take another baby from me.

chapter

twenty-three

I OPEN THE door and start to head to the couch.

"Seriously?" she asks incredulously. "You're not going to say anything?" Reanell helps me lie down.

"No blood, but I'm still crampy." It's relief and then terror all at the same time. No clear signs that I'm miscarrying, but then a cramp hits. I hold my stomach as a tear rolls down my face. "I can't do this."

"You can and you will."

"What am I going to do if this keeps up?" My chin quivers as the question hangs in the air.

Rea crouches down with empathy in her eyes. "You'll fight. You'll fight with every ounce you have to come back to us the way you are now. It'll be hard. It'll take all the courage you can find, but you have it. You have Liam, Aarabelle, and you have me."

"Liam's missing, Rea. I may lose him and this baby."

"I wish I could take this for you. I won't fill you up with bullshit, but know I'm not going anywhere."

I need to take my mind off of all this. None of it can be controlled. I can't make Liam come back, or this baby happen, but I can control how I handle it. Once again, I'm being tested. "One day I'm going to be able to be the rock in our friendship."

"You are," she kisses my cheek. "Now, is there anything I can do?"

"Can you clean the house for me?" I ask Rea.

It may seem like an odd request, but she nods. Reanell picks up the toys and starts to get some things organized. We make idle chit chat about nothing, and I see through her ruse. I know she wants to keep me busy and talking, that way my mind doesn't go in a million directions.

Like how my boyfriend is missing. I could lose a baby that said boyfriend doesn't know about. My ex-husband is spouting love and other bullshit. And Liam's mother could be dying at any moment and he won't make it home.

"I need to call Liam's dad and get an update," I say reaching for my phone.

"Here," she hands it to me. "Please, lean on me. I know this entire situation sucks, but I'm here."

"I love you for it too." I try to smile but it fails.

I hover over the keypad afraid to call and give an already horrific situation more bad news. He called me for help and here I am about to tell him that the other reason he stays strong is in trouble as well.

"Hello?" he answers.

"Hi, Mr. Dempsey . . . it's Natalie."

"Have you heard from Liam?" he asks straight away. I can hear the exhaustion in his voice. I've been there.

"No, not yet. He's still on a mission and they're not able to compromise it by sending a message."

I tell him a half-truth, but I don't have it in me to break his heart. I don't know all the facts either, so making him suffer for maybe no reason would do more harm than good.

"Oh." The disappointment is evident. "I don't know how much time we have. I hoped he'd be on his way by now. Will you call me if anything changes?"

"Of course," I say immediately. "I'm doing everything possible. I want him home for you just as bad as anyone. I have everyone I know doing whatever they can as well." I hope to reassure him. We talk a little about his wife's condition and how it happened. I wish I could do more for him, but we're both a mess. Once I hang up, I will the phone to ring. He has to be okay. Liam has my heart and my soul. He needs to call me. He needs to come home, and I need him to know about our baby.

"Lee," Rea draws my attention back to her. "Mason knows what he's doing. I have to have faith in him."

Before I can say anything, I hear a knock at the door.

All the blood rushes from my face and fear chokes me.

"Hey, it could be UPS," Rea says and puts her hand on my arm.

"I can't answer."

"Natalie," she chides.

"I've answered that door before. I know what comes on the other side. You've never had to be me. You have no fucking clue what this is like. The fear. The terror that eats at me with him gone. I'm pregnant—again. He's in a hostile area with no coms. Don't you dare judge me," I spit the words like razors to cut her.

Yes, she's my best friend, but she doesn't get it. It's the crippling fear of déjà vu that eats at me. But I have to move. I don't get a choice. I have to answer that door.

Knock. Knock. Knock.

I lift myself and count the steps to the door. My mind starts to check off all the things that I'll need to do.

My heart rate accelerates with each step, but I keep moving. I remind myself that I'm strong, resilient, and have my babies to think of.

I've done this once. I lived. I have to be strong for his child.

I open the door but no one is there. There's a package on

the ground.

The phone rings, and I close the door without even grabbing it. I rush over to the phone.

"Hello?" I don't even look at the caller ID. I'm just grateful there's no one at my door in a uniform.

"Lee," Liam's voice is thick and scratchy. Tears fall immediately. My hand clutches my chest and a sob escapes.

"Liam," I say his name and sink down.

"It's okay, it's okay, I got the AmCross. I'm getting on a plane in a few hours."

"I'm so . . . I can't even talk," I admit. "I was so scared."

"I know. I'll talk when I get to Virginia. Is she . . . ?" he asks hesitantly.

"She's not doing well. You need to get home, and we'll head to Ohio."

"I love you, Lee."

I smile with the taste of tears on my lips. It's bittersweet, his return. It's not the happy reunion we dreamed of. It'll be getting off the plane and heading to another. We need to get to his mother as fast as we can.

"I love you. So much. Please don't scare me again," I request.

He lets out a deep sigh. "I gotta go. I'll see you soon."

"Yes, you will."

The call disconnects and I sit there trying to muddle through my emotions. Relief, joy, sorrow, and fear all come flooding at the same time. It's so many things to try to process at once.

Reanell sinks down next to me and pulls me into her arms. I lose it. I sob as she rubs my back without saying a word. It's cathartic and draws new worries with each one I let go. I worry about the baby, Liam, Aarabelle, Aaron, Liam's mother and father, but more than anything, I worry he has to go back.

"I'VE GOT HER," Aaron tries to reassure me—again. "I've been here almost every day and Paige will be here two of the days. I would never hurt her."

"I know that," I say exasperated. "I just want to make sure you're sure."

"It's either I watch our daughter or the babysitter does. So I'd like to have this time with her. I missed so much of her life."

Aaron has been great with Aarabelle, and he's been trying so hard. Paige said she'd stay at my house to make sure Aaron didn't need help. I've just never left her for so long before.

"Okay, thank you."

He walks over and holds my shoulders. His light brown eyes stare me down. "I may wish we could've worked things out, but Liam was my best friend, he needs you, and I may be a fuck up, but I don't want to watch him burn in hell. I hate that of all the people it was you two." His hands drop. "I hate that he's what you need and I'm not, but I did this to you. I deserted you when you needed me most and Liam loves you." Aaron looks down at my stomach and closes his eyes. "He can give you things I couldn't."

"We'll find a way for all of us. I know this is hard on you, and I don't want to hurt you. I never wanted to."

"One day, and for Aarabelle, we will."

I look at her eating her breakfast and I nod. I'd sell my soul if it were for her happiness. Aarabelle is the one thing keeping all of us grounded. That little girl has saved us all. I walk over and kiss her cheek.

"I'll miss you. Mommy has to go get Liam." She smiles and looks away, oblivious.

"Go, Lee." Aaron grabs my bag and heads toward the door.

I went to the doctor yesterday and she said everything was fine. She told me to go but to take it easy. At this point, there's nothing we can do to stop a miscarriage, but she wants me to rest as much as I can. Considering we're heading to a hospital, at least I'll be close to medical attention.

Now to tell Liam and pray he's happy about it.

"Thanks again," I say to Aaron as I open the car door.

"Give him my condolences. He was really close with his parents. Also, tell Aidan I'm sorry for his loss. I know how much it . . ." he trails off. "Drive safe and I've got Aara."

"I'll tell him," I lean in and embrace him. He flinches and glances at my stomach once again. It's awkward, but Aaron is still my oldest friend.

My hands drop, and I rush out the house. Once I get in the car, I smile and head to see the love of my life.

chapter twenty-four

WAITING FOR THIS plane to land is more painful than shoving bamboo splints in my nails. Each time I hear the engines, my heart speeds up. I think it could be the one and then it's not and my stomach drops. I sit in the most uncomfortable chair at the Navy airfield. Mason called ahead and got me access to be able to pick Liam up.

My phone bings with a text.

Liam: You'll know I'm close when this finally goes through. I'm on the plane and counting down the seconds until I see you.

I smile and realize he's within cell phone range.

Liam: My entire body is aware I'm going to have you in my arms soon.

Liam: I love you more than my own life.

Liam: I hope you know how much it means to me that you're coming to Ohio with me.

They keep coming in, and each one causes my smile to grow.

Liam: I'm hoping security doesn't care that I'm going to maul you.

The blush paints my cheeks as I picture him attacking me. Not that I'm far off wanting the same.

Liam: God, seeing your face is going to be the only good thing about this trip. I miss you so much.

I close my eyes and try to respond but another one comes in.

Liam: Look up.

My eyes lift, and he stands before me. He drops his bags and the loud thump echoes in the terminal. I get on my feet and rush toward him. He's here.

Liam's arms open as I approach. I close the gap between us with a smile and wrap my arms around him. As soon as our bodies connect, I feel whole.

"Hi, sweetheart," his deep voice grounds me, and I look into his blue eyes. His lips lower and he kisses me.

My mouth molds to his as his arms keep me flush against him. All the fear disappears like a puff of smoke, and I know I'll survive no matter what. If I lose this baby, I know we'll make it through. Liam won't turn his back on me and seek out another. He's the man who will hold me and love me regardless. We're reunited and all is right in the world. There may be a lot of hell waiting for us, but we're together. He's alive and I'm in his arms.

He breaks the kiss and stares into my eyes. "I missed the shit out of you."

I laugh, "I missed you too." He pulls back a little as I bite my lip. He's going to see, and I want to tell him before he does. "Liam, I have to tell you something," I blurt out.

His face falls, "I didn't make it in time . . ."

"No," I stop him before he thinks he lost his mother. I practiced and rehearsed this all day, but now I'm choking on the words. I take his hand in mine and place it on my stomach. "I'm pregnant."

He looks up with wide eyes, and his breath catches. "You're . . . ?" he stumbles on the words. "We're . . . ?"

I nod with unshed tears forming.

"A baby?"

I sigh while touching his cheek. "I'm pregnant with a baby. Your baby."

He takes me into his arms again with such tenderness. "I wish I could say something, but you have no idea how I feel right now," Liam says against my hair. "Are you sure?"

"Yeah, I'm sure."

His eyes return to my stomach as his hand rubs the small bump. "Lee, I didn't think you could."

"I didn't either . . . apparently, you and I worked." I don't know how to explain it other than a miracle.

Liam smiles before he kisses my nose. "I love you so much. I love Aarabelle, and I'm going to love this baby just as much."

Right there. Those words solidify everything. He not only included Aara, he said her first. Once again, he proves why he has my heart. He didn't choose to love his own child any more or any differently. Liam is the man who will be a father to both my children, because to him, Aara is his as well.

"I want you to be happy, but I need to be honest," I say and we sit. "I had a huge scare. You know some of what I went through to have Aarabelle, and the fact that I've carried this long is promising. I cramped pretty bad the other day and have been trying to stay off my feet . . ."

Liam cuts me off. "You're not going with me then."

"Stop. I got the clearance from the doctor to go."

"Natalie, you and the baby come first. I want you with me, more than you know, but I'm not going to argue."

"You're not going to boss me around either," I snap.

Liam smiles at my small outburst. "I'm not?"

"No, you're not." I cross my arms.

He cups my face and his smirk only irritates me. "I'm so in love with you."

Well, that doesn't make me hate him. "You're confusing me."

"I'm loving you. And loving that my super sperm knocked you up."

I roll my eyes and fight my smile. "You've been home five minutes and I've already cried, yelled, gotten mad, and smiled. You're something else."

"I'm yours," he replies.

"And I'm yours."

"Yeah, sweetheart. You sure are. Okay, so tell me what the doctor said," he requests.

I go over all the rules, how far along I am, and more about the scare. His emotions play across his face like a movie. The one thing that remains clear is how happy he is and how much love he has for me. I've never seen a man look at me like he does. Liam sees through me and even with every flaw showing, he only loves me more. What we share is rare and precious, just like the child we've made.

He hoists the bag on his back with a grin. "Got it," Liam puffs up. He stands with sheer determination across his face. Then, he bows down and lifts me into his arms.

"What are you doing?" I ask practically yelling.

"You said to stay off your feet. So, you're staying off your feet." He somehow manages to shrug while holding me.

"Liam!" I laugh but wrap my arms around his neck. "I could get used to this, but you know if we make it through this, I'll just get bigger."

"I'll make sure I keep hitting the gym," he smiles.

He walks with me to the car and frowns when he sees I brought my car.

"Oh, stop it. I hate driving your car."

"When is our flight?" he asks opening the door.

"We should head to the airport now. I tried to space it in case you were late, but I think we should get there sooner than later," I explain getting in my seat and he nods. "Why?"

"I wanted to see Aara if we had time."

I don't think he could be any more perfect. My heart swells, and I lean up as he fusses over me and grab his face. He looks at me with wonder and then I pull him close. Our lips touch and his hand threads in my hair. I'm whole again. No matter what happens from here, we'll save each other. If I lose this baby, if his mother passes, if the world around us collapses, we'll make it.

My mouth opens and Liam's tongue clashes with mine. He licks and pushes me back into my seat. I let him take the lead as I hold his lips against mine. I want to kiss him forever, but we have to go. I push him back, but when his blue eyes hone in on me, I pull him to me again.

Liam smiles against my mouth and gives me a small peck. "You're so cute when you want me."

"I've missed your smart ass," I laugh and he kisses me once more before closing the door.

We head to the airport and the sweet mood of reunion morphs into the fear of what we're heading to. During the drive, I explain to Liam the information I have and he calls his father while we wait for the plane to board. Liam slips into his mask but keeps his hands on me in some way. His hands never leave my skin other than when he has no choice.

Early in the flight to Cincinnati, Liam and I talk briefly about what he's missed with Aaron and Aarabelle.

"Are you going to tell me why no one could get in touch with you?" I ask. It's been driving me insane, but I wasn't sure whether to bring it up.

"It was a clusterfuck." He looks away.

"Is that all I get?" I ask softly. There's a line between significant other and SEAL. He and I have to establish it and this is one of those defining moments. It's not a matter of trust and I know this. It's a matter of protection.

Aaron wouldn't tell me much other than it was no day at the beach. I knew that was his way of saying the discussion was over. Only once did he ever go in depth about a mission, and it was when they lost their three friends. He came home and lost it. I held him in my arms as he sobbed. That funeral was the most horrific day. All three caskets draped in our nation's colors. The tears flowed relentlessly through the entire ceremony.

"I wish I could tell you, but it's a lot. There wasn't one fucking thing that went right. Not one. It was as if there was someone sabotaging every move we made." He runs his hands down his face. "I swear, Lee, I work with some really smart guys, but they were all dumb that day."

I nod and hope he'll go on.

"They forgot batteries, rounds, a clip, I mean either that or someone was swiping shit before we left. But then we'd get it straight and all set and then something would break. We got to this one area to do some intel and none of our radios would work. I couldn't communicate with anyone. The guys were pinned down in one area of the village, and I stayed hidden until Quinn made visual. I figured the coast was clear, but it wasn't. As soon as we figured out we were being trailed, we split off again. The radio wasn't working, and I couldn't risk using the sat phone."

Liam grips my hand and looks away. His head rests against the seat as I wait.

"We're lucky. It was straight luck that we were able to get out of that one, but we had to double back a different route to make sure nothing led us back to the rest of the team. There were hostiles watching our every move. I wasn't able to get the intel we needed because of what a mess everything was. As soon as we got to a safer place, I got the message, and we high-tailed it home."

"I was so worried."

"I can imagine. But you'd have never known if this wasn't happening."

I let out a deep sigh and look down at our joined hands. "That doesn't comfort me either. I know you're at risk, but I'm pregnant again. I don't want to raise two babies as a single mom."

Liam lifts our hands then kisses the top of my hand. "I can't promise you anything in regards to this, Lee. You know that. I know it sucks worrying about me when I'm gone, but I can only promise that I love you and I'm doing everything I can."

He's right and I know that I have to be strong. I don't doubt our love. I know what we have is special but it's also fragile. We live in a world where they are trained to think they're invincible. They take chances everyday people don't take.

"You mean so much to me," I explain.

"Relax, I'm here now. We've got a long few days ahead of us."

I lay my head against his shoulder and inhale his scent. The sandalwood and cologne takes me back to where it all started. The way he held me and calmed me. I allow that feeling to wash over me again.

He doesn't say anything, but I know it's because his mind is lost on his mother. He lifts the seat divider and tucks me against his chest. My hand rests on his heart, and he keeps his on my belly. The exhaustion and overload of emotions takes over and we both fall asleep.

"Hey," Liam's voice breaks through my sleep-induced fog. "Come on, sweetheart."

He nudges me a little and I get up. "I haven't slept that good in a long time." I smile, and he looks at my stomach.

He puts his bags down and grabs my hips. I watch in awe as his head lowers and he kisses my belly. "Hi." Tears well in my eyes. "I'm going to be your Daddy."

A woman behind Liam stands with her hand over her chest. My fingers touch his dark brown hair and gently move of their own accord. He amazes me with the amount of care and tenderness he has. He's killed people, interrogated terrorists, climbed mountains, and who knows what, but with me . . . he's different.

Liam's head lifts and he kisses me, grabs the bags, and smiles.

"Why do you have to be so perfect?"

"Because I was made for you."

"There you go again." I smile and shake my head.

"You like me this way."

"I guess so," I shrug my shoulders and start to turn, but Liam grabs my hand. "What's wrong?"

"I don't know that I can say goodbye to her," he admits. "I didn't even see her before I left. I mean, what kind of piece of shit doesn't say goodbye to his own mom before deployment?"

The guilt rises because instead of Liam going home to see his family, we went away.

"I'll be with you the entire time," I try to reassure him. This will be hard on him and his father. I know what loss feels like, and I can only hope I give them a tiny amount of comfort.

We grab a cab then head toward the hospital. Liam is filled with nervous energy as his leg bounces and he keeps grabbing his neck. I've been there and I'm relying on my own memories to help get him through this. I remember the things I hated, but then in my situation, I also didn't know it was coming. I was distraught, but I try to imagine how it would be to know this is happening. To watch someone you love die must be worse.

Liam calls his father and he instructs us where to go.

"Liam," his father says in a half cry as he sees him.

"Dad." He takes him into his arms and both men begin to

lose it.

"I can't lose her, son. I don't know a world without her." He cries on his shoulder and tears stream down my cheek. His father looks up and steps back. "You must be Natalie."

I nod and walk to him. "I am. I'm so sorry we are meeting this way." I go to shake his hand, but he embraces me immediately.

"I've heard so much about you and your daughter." He lets me go and Liam smiles.

Liam pulls me to his side then kisses my temple. He murmurs, "Go sit. It's been a lot of time on your feet."

I nod in agreement. I head over to a chair while the two men talk. He fills Liam in on more details, and Liam's head falls into his hands. They both cry with each other as they mourn the fact that she will never recover. She's on full life support and Aidan has been keeping her alive so Liam could say goodbye.

Liam heads over to me and squats down, taking my hand in his and rubbing his calloused thumb across the delicate skin. "I have to go in there," A tear falls. "I need you with me. I need to introduce you to her and tell her about our baby."

The sorrow in his eyes mirrors mine. I don't say anything, but I stand. He tugs me against his side and holds my hip. We walk slowly and I wrap my arms around his torso. I hold him while he holds me. I know he's hurting. You can feel it coming off of him. The smell of bleach and despair filters through the air.

He stops and glimpses at me as the mask I know all too well slips into place. He's shutting himself off to try to ease the pain. But I'm also aware that it doesn't stop it. You may think it does. You only hope to cloak yourself in the delusions of being fine. The pain though doesn't care. It penetrates through the open fibers, seeps through your soul, and eats at you if you let it. I won't let it consume him though. I'll fight for him to come to the light just as he did for me.

CHAPTER

TWENTY-FIVE

LIAM

I'M SUPPOSED TO be a man. A man's man, the ones who can do anything. I'm a goddamn Navy SEAL. I've been to war and seen some awful shit. I've battled through things most men can only imagine. Yet here I stand like a little bitch hesitating to open that door.

This is the woman who fucking raised me. She gave me everything. Taught me how to treat a woman, slapped me around when I did it wrong. I never really thought about what it would be like to lose a parent. They're still young and I'm not ready to lose her.

"Liam," Natalie encourages. Her thin arms stay wrapped around me as if she's holding me together. And right now—she is. I look down at her and wait for some sort of courage to arrive. But it's there in her eyes. Her strength and love are there in her face. Even with all the crap that's come between us, she's been strong.

I nod and open the door. She lies there with tubes and monitors everywhere. The steady beeping tells me that she's alive, but only thanks to the machines. A white sheet is draped over her, keeping her warm, but everything around me is ice cold.

I step toward her slowly. Her chest rises and falls, but there's no life there. All I can pray for is that she doesn't feel any pain.

"Hi, Mom," I say as I reach her bedside. "I got here as soon as I could. It's a long story, but you know how it goes." I try to stay strong, but this is my mother. The woman who apparently did diapers and didn't rip the tabs. She's the one who wiped my knee and made me a cape when I needed to be Superman. Shannon Dempsey is the strongest woman in the world. She had kids, buried one, raised another, and I never saw her break down and lose it. I swear she could run laps around the SEALs and put us all to shame.

I failed her. I wasn't here to protect her.

"Please wake up, Mom. I don't know that there's any chance, but I'm begging you, please, if you can . . . do it now. I'm sorry . . . for so many things. I don't know how to say goodbye to you like this." I need to take a second, because I'm going to lose it.

Natalie rubs her fingers down my arm, and I close my eyes. "Hi, Mrs. Dempsey. We met once, but I'm Natalie."

The woman of my dreams stands here talking to my mother while I try to keep it together. She gives me the out so I don't feel so weak.

"I remember you loved to bake. I wish I had the chance to learn from you since I literally am the worst." Natalie smiles and releases my hand. Before I can grab it back, she grips my mother's. "Thank you for giving Liam life. Thank you for raising him to be the man he is. I'll be eternally grateful to you for the joy he's brought into my life." Natalie looks over at me with tears streaming down her face. "He loves me more than I deserve. He loves my daughter and he's given me more than he'll ever understand." She turns back, and I wipe my eyes. "I can only hope to raise my children to be like the man you've raised. He really is the best man I've ever known, and I attribute that to you, so thank you."

She leans down and kisses my mother's cheek. A woman she's only met once. Then she whispers in her ear and squeezes her hand once more.

That's my undoing.

I fall to my knees and they hit the cold tile. My head falls on the side of the bed and I grip my mother's leg. "Haven't we lost enough? Hasn't my family suffered enough?" I mutter aloud.

We grew up with strict Irish-Catholic parents. Mom stayed home, but I think she worked harder than my father. He got to go to work and come home after Mom had the entire house cleaned and food on the table. Dad is a lawyer and worked his ass off to put me and Krissy in private school. He showed me that hard work was for the family, and when you want something, you don't slack off. You push harder and make your own destiny. So why can't I work to make her better?

"Talk to her, Liam," Natalie encourages while I keep my head bowed. I can't let her see me like this. "Tell her what you want to let her know. She loves you." Her soft voice calms me and I try to hold it, but it's all too fucking much. Everything crashes around me and I remember my sister. I remember her telling me the same thing. She would always tell me that Mom loved me, so I could tell her the truth.

"I'm so sorry, Mom! I'm so fucking sorry! I haven't seen you in a long time and I didn't say goodbye to you." I break apart as Natalie's hand rubs my back. "I lied to you and I didn't tell you all the things that you should've heard. I didn't tell you about how much I wished it were me and not Krissy. I didn't tell you about how much you mean to me. I should've always told you the truth. Like how I really did put gum in Krissy's hair on Easter. Or how I broke your rules about sneaking girls in the house. I took your car that day and then told you it was Krissy. I'm sorry I lied! I failed you."

"Shhh." Natalie runs her fingers through my hair as I sob, crying at my mother's bedside. "It's okay, trust me, she's not upset or mad. She loves you, Liam. And she knew it was you, you didn't lie. She knows."

I pull back and look at her as we both cry for the pain that surrounds us. There's been so much we've dealt with, but I need Natalie by my side. I only wish my mom could've seen how special she is. That she could've held our children and they would know her love. She would've doted on them, baked cookies, spoiled them until they never wanted to come home to us. She would've been the best grandmother our children ever knew.

"Mom, I want you to meet Lee officially. I told you how I felt a few months ago and you said to follow my heart. She's my heart." I look at Natalie with her glossy eyes and then I stand. I walk and pull a chair over and point to it.

She shakes her head and sits.

"Anyway, I wanted you to be the first to know we're having a baby." Natalie grips my hand. God, I love this woman. "We're going to have a kid, and I'm going to marry her. She doesn't know that yet, but I am. I'm going to love her and be the man you told me to be. I'll give her the world because she deserves it. I'll make you proud."

I hear Natalie sniff and she lets her tears fall. I get down on one knee in front of her. I didn't plan this, I don't have a ring, but I have my heart and she already owns it.

"Natalie Gilcher, I love you more than anyone could love another. My world only makes sense since you've come into it. I want to marry you, love you, adore you, give you children and anything else you want. I'll provide for you and never take you for granted. I know what life is like without you, and I only want to live in a world with you by my side. When I'm gone, my heart will remain with you. Will you allow me the honor to love you from now until the end of time?"

chapter

twenty-six

NATALIE

MY HEART RATE is through the roof and the tears won't stop long enough to see him clearly. I never in a million years expected him to propose now. I mean, we haven't been together that long, and while I know that he's the one for me in every way, I can't think.

"Liam," I say and he wipes the tears from my eyes. "Are you sure?"

I don't want him to do this out of some sense of obligation because we're having a baby. There's not a doubt that I love him and want to be his wife, but I know in grief you can do things impulsively. I want to marry him when he's sure that this is what he's ready for.

"I've never been more sure of anything. I love you, Natalie. I love you more than I can ever tell you. I want to hold you, wipe your tears, kiss you, console you, watch you smile, make love to you every day and every night. I know I don't have a ring—"

"Yes," I say before he can say another word. "Yes, I want to be your wife. I don't need a ring . . . I just need you."

Liam stands and takes me into his arms. He kisses me with

tears spilling between the two of us. He holds my face and looks at his mother who rests peacefully. "She said yes, Mom."

Liam's dad enters a few seconds later and walks to the end of the bed. "Dad, I'd like to tell you that Natalie and I are getting married and she's having our baby. I told Mom as well."

His father smiles and his lip quivers. He looks at his wife and my chest aches. You can see how badly he wants to share this moment. I extract myself from Liam's arms and walk to his father. He opens his arms and I embrace him.

"I'm so happy, but so sad at the same time," he murmurs. "She would've loved you."

I nod understanding exactly what he means. When I held Aarabelle for the first time when we thought Aaron was dead, I wasn't sure if smiling was okay. I remember feeling the utter despair of being without him in that moment but also elation that she was here. His happiness is clouded by his agony. The thing about grief is it comes in many forms and there's no right or wrong way.

"I'm sure I would've loved her as well. But her memory will be cherished. I promise our child will know the woman she was and how much she would've loved them." I vow this and I will live up to that. She was clearly loved and a wonderful woman.

We spend the next few hours in Shannon's room talking to her and telling her stories about Liam and Aarabelle. Aidan smiles and laughs when I tell him about Liam's diaper issues. He tells me stories about Liam as a kid and how he was always into some kind of trouble.

"The worst was when he got into sticking things up his nose," he chuckles and Liam groans.

"Really?"

"Oh, yeah . . . anything he could find. Shannon always wondered when he sneezed what might come out. He was always talking my Kristine into doing something too. She would get stuck and Liam would pretend he knew nothing." Aidan gets lost in his memories. "I remember one time coming home from work and Shannon was baking a cake for a neighbor. She loved to do things for the other women on the block. She was always helping someone and bringing them food . . . anyway, she was busy, and Liam and Kristine were supposed to stay in the yard. Liam told Krissy that Shannon said it was okay for her to go to their friend's house. I came home and asked her where Kristine was and she panicked. Liam of course claimed Krissy said she didn't care that she wasn't allowed to go . . ."

I look at Liam, who for the first time since we arrived has a little life in his eyes. He smiles and shakes his head. "I think you exaggerate that, Dad. I was a good boy."

He gives one throaty cough-laugh. "I think you're mistaken, son. You were always doing something to get your sister in trouble."

"And she always believed me."

"She loved you," he murmurs. "Now I'll lose both my girls." Aidan looks at his wife and sighs.

"I know the pain you're feeling. It won't ever go away. But one day it won't hurt so bad." I take his hand in mine. "It won't be so hard to breathe. It won't feel like the world is crushing you. One day that will come and it just gets a little easier each day." I give him the small amount of hope I have. "I know right now that seems like a lie, but I've walked in your shoes."

"Thank you, Natalie. My son is very lucky." His other hand covers mine. "I had a great love with Shannon. I always prayed my children would find something like I was blessed to have. I only wish she could see that Liam has."

"I wish she could too," I reply.

"THIS IS HOME." Liam extends his hand forward, and I walk through the door. After spending a few more hours at the hospital, Aidan demanded I get some rest and care for the baby he already loves.

We offered to stay in a hotel, but he would hear nothing of it, and since he refuses to leave her side there's no point in us giving him space. The house is just as I imagined based on what Liam described. It's an old, brick house with cute, white awnings. The front door is old oak and inside is immaculate. Everything is clean and homey. This is the home you want to spend Sunday dinners at.

"It's exactly like I pictured."

"What does that mean?" he grins.

"Just it's a home. I grew up on a farm in Arkansas, so I'm sure you have this idea of what it looks like. I always pictured you living on a quaint street with green lawns and plastic on the couches." I laugh and then Liam lifts me into his arms. "Put me down."

"Off your feet. I'll show you around."

"I can walk, Liam."

He leans closer and presses his lips against me. "Let me take care of you. I need to hold you."

I understand his need to care for something. When your world is falling apart, sometimes you need something to hold on to. He needs to feel grounded and in control of one aspect of his life.

"You make it really hard to say no."

"I'm counting on that."

I lightly slap his chest and he begins the tour. We find our way through the house. I admire how beautiful her taste is. She's classic with a touch of modern. The kitchen was recently redone, and you can tell that's the heart of the home. Everything is labeled and in its place. It's exactly the type of home where you'd expect Martha Stewart to come out at any moment.

Liam climbs the stairs laughing about how he's having

flashbacks of basic training carrying a log. He gets another slap for that.

"This is my room." He opens the door, and I refrain from busting out laughing. It's covered in old posters and photos.

"Wow, this is something else," I say as he still refuses to put me down.

"Zip it."

"Is this Yasmine Bleeth? Like from Baywatch?" I can't stop the hysterical giggles that follow.

"She was hot," he defends and puts me on my feet.

"Will I find old Playboys under your mattress?" I mock him and lift the side up. Before I can get it high enough to see, his hands come around the front of me.

"I'd rather look at my fiancée."

"Liam," I chide. "We're at your parents' house."

"They already told you I don't follow rules well. Besides," his gruff voice drops as his mouth glides across my ear. "You're already pregnant. I think they know."

His tongue runs the rim of my ear and I shiver. "I've missed you," I say as my hand reaches up and wraps around his neck. I hold him against me as I feel his erection press against my ass.

"I need you, Lee. I need you so fucking bad. Are we allowed?"

I nod as his hand comes around my front and presses gently against my stomach. He slowly moves his fingers up and groans as he takes my breast in his hand. "So much better . . ." I trail off as he touches me.

Liam spins me and then lifts my shirt off. He stares at me as his eyes worship me. I decide to take the lead on this. I reach behind me and remove my bra. My breasts fall heavy as his pupils dilate.

I unbutton my jeans and slide them down. He licks his lips as I hook my fingers into my black lace underwear. I begin to slide them lower but decide I need to toy with him a little. I step closer, and his eyes close and his head falls back as I cup his dick. "I think you're overdressed, my future husband."

"Say it again."

"Overdressed." I know this isn't what he wants, but I want to control his mind. I want all that he thinks about is us, even if just for a few minutes.

Liam's thumb presses on my chin and lifts my head. "Not that, sweetheart."

"My," I bring his other hand to my lips and place a kiss on his palm, "Future," another kiss but this time on his thumb, "Husband," the final kiss is on his ring finger where we will be bonded.

He moans and holds my face between his hands. A moment later, his mouth is on mine. Liam controls the kiss. Our mouths stay connected as he devours me. His control is barely hanging on by a thread. Any moment it will fray and he'll obliterate me. I push my tongue against his as we both savor each other. It's been so long. Too long since he's touched me. I pull at him and we're flush against each other. My body burns for him and moisture pools in my core.

Liam removes his hands slowly and his touch becomes a caress. The passion is still present, but it's as if he's found himself again. "Get on the bed," he commands.

As he walks to the door to close it, I sprawl out and wait for him. His eyes burn with an intensity I've never seen. Our gazes stay locked as he stalks me, and I yearn for him. Once he reaches the edge of the bed, I'm nearly panting. "What are you going to do with me now that I'm here?"

Liam unbuttons his pants and removes them along with his underwear. His cock juts out and my eyes flutter. "I'm going to show you just how attentive your future husband will be."

He kneels at the end of the bed and pulls my underwear down. "After I watched you touch yourself, all I could do was replay it in my mind each night. To see you come apart just from the sound of my voice . . . was fucking heaven. So now, I'm going to see how many times I can replay it live."

I rest on my elbows with a grin. "I'm thinking you should put your money where your mouth is . . ."

"How about my mouth goes here?" he leans down and licks my center. My head falls back and he does it again. "Or maybe here?" Liam says as his tongue circles my clit.

"Oh," I moan in sheer bliss.

"Hmm, maybe you'd like me to do this?" he questions as his tongue presses against my entrance. I quake beneath him as he continues to set a pattern. Sweat forms and I start to climb. Between the hormones, and the fact that it's Liam, I can't hold off long.

"Liam," I croak out his name as I start to head toward the precipice.

He inserts a finger then begins to suck on my clit and I fall over it. I sink into the bed as he keeps going. Liam extracts every morsel of my orgasm possible. His tongue doesn't leave my body as he trails up to my stomach. He stays there for a few moments as I come down.

"I'm going to love watching you grow with my child. There will never be anything sexier than knowing you're holding a life we created." I open my eyes as his lips turn up. "We're okay to do this?"

"Yes, I promise we're okay." I press my fingers against the scruff on his face. The feel of it is like home to me.

He hovers over me not putting any weight on me, and I fight the urge to laugh. "Liam, we can make love."

"What if I hurt the baby?"

"Hurt the baby how?"

"I mean, what if I poke it in the head?"

I begin to laugh hysterically and have to cover my mouth. "You're ridiculous."

"I'm serious! I'm well-endowed, you know . . . it could happen."

"Okay, I love you, so I'm going to pretend you're kidding."

"I'm not!"

Oh, for the love of God. He really has no clue.

"You're not going to poke the baby. First of all, the baby isn't anywhere near my canal. But secondly, it's not possible. We're fine. You and your giant penis will not cause any harm to the baby."

"Yeah, well, if it comes out dented, I'm telling the kid it's your fault."

I giggle while rolling my eyes. After we both stop laughing, I turn serious. "Deal. Now, make love to me. I need you."

He tilts closer and kisses me slowly and carefully. I feel him press inside of me and I sigh into his mouth. Everything feels more intense. Each stroke and thrust is ripping me apart in the best way.

"Fuck. You feel so incredible." Liam keeps his weight off of me but isn't gentle as he plunges deeper and deeper. But it's not far enough. I want to feel him everywhere.

"Let me get on top." I push him back and he turns us easily.

I close my eyes and sink down on his length. Liam's voice rasps as he tries to form words, but nothing is coherent. "Lee, fuck. God. You."

His hands hold my hips as he guides me to his pace. I feel the orgasm start to take shape again. It grows stronger with each brush of my clit and the feel of his cock inside me.

"I can't," I say aloud as the smell of sex and sweat fills the room.

"You can. Give me everything."

I close my eyes and Liam reaches between us and presses his thumb against my clit. I can't hold back. I come with such intensity I swear I black out. Liam grunts a few times and follows me over.

I lie against his chest listening to his heartbeat. After a few minutes of coming down from our incredible high, I go and clean myself. When I come back into his room, he's on his back staring at the ceiling.

He turns on his side as I climb in bed with him. "Hi," he says sounding forlorn.

"Hi."

"I think tomorrow is when they'll take her off the life support."

Liam wraps his arm around me and rubs my back. "I wish I had some magic words to make this easy. There's nothing that will ease this but time. And I'll be by your side every step. You'll never be alone." He kisses my forehead and I nestle into his chest. "I thought I lost you."

"It's going to take a lot more than some idiots to keep me from coming home to you."

I look up and he pushes my hair back. "It's a fear I'm always going to struggle with."

"And I'll try to ease it, but no matter what, I'll fight 'till the end."

"That's all we can do."

"Well, and love each other," Liam says, trying to lighten the mood.

"Good thing we've got that down."

"How about I make sure one more time?"

I smile and push him onto his back. "By all means . . . we should be sure."

"I THINK IT'S time. She wouldn't want this," Aidan says to the doctor. Liam and I stand on one side of her bed, waiting for what's to come.

"Okay, Mr. Dempsey. I'll give you each some time to say your goodbyes, and then we'll be back to start the process." He looks at all of us and no one speaks.

Aidan looks at his wife and then Liam. "I'll give you time first. I need a few minutes before I do this."

Liam looks lost. He gazes back and forth at his parents and my chest squeezes. Our fingers tangle and he stares at me. I'm not sure what to do, but I know that just holding his hand could help.

After a few moments, Liam lets go and heads to his mother's side.

"I can remember as a kid people talking about their moms and how they hated them. Do you know there was never a time I felt that way? I never hated you because there was never a reason for it. You were the mother people wish for. Yeah, you called me to the carpet, but I deserved it." Liam's voice is reverent as he speaks of her. "I don't think I ever told you how much you meant to me. I wish I had more time with you, Mom. I never thought you wouldn't be around. You'll never hold our baby or just be there to tell me to stop being stupid. What's Dad going to do? We're not a family without you."

Liam takes a break then walks toward the window. He discreetly tries to remove the tears that are falling. This wrecks me, watching him handle his grief. The pain that he feels I want to carry for him. Be the rock he needs and heal him like he did for me.

I walk over to him and place my hand on his back.

"I can't say goodbye to her. I can't tell her it's okay to die," he says defiantly.

"You love her and she loved you. You don't have to say good-bye."

"She's going to die the minute the machines stop."

"And she'll be surrounded by the two men in her life that she loves."

"My father is going to die alongside her, Lee. He's been with her since they were fifteen."

Their love story mimicked part of my own, but I won't say that. I want to point out that he'll be okay just as I was, but I don't. There will be a part of his father that won't ever recover. A young love that stands the test of time isn't something he'll ever find again. He might not ever love again, but he'll survive.

"Then you be the son you are. You remind him why he has to carry on. You give him the strength he'll need . . . just like you did for me. There's no one I know that's as strong as you."

"She was." Liam looks over at his mother again and heads toward her. He takes her delicate hand in his and kisses the top of it. "I'm going to miss you. I hope you find Kristine in heaven and tell her I loved her. Tell her how she'd be an aunt to two little girls. Hold her in your arms and know that you'll be in my heart. I was blessed to have you as a mother." Liam puts her hand down and leans in. He gently presses his lips to the top of her head and then let's out a deep sob.

I rush to his side and pull him into my arms. He holds me close and takes a few deep breaths.

"I'm here," is all I can say to him. There are no words that will comfort him, and I'm not stupid enough to try. I offer him my love and my heart.

Aidan walks in a few moments later and looks at his wife. "I've said my goodbyes to you, Shannon. And we will meet again, my love." He stands tall and almost ready. The Dempsey men stare at each other for a second before he speaks again. "Will you pray with me?"

We all gather around her bed and Liam's father grabs my hand. I take Liam's and they each grab Shannon's. Linked together, we stand, and Aidan begins to speak. "Today, I'll say goodbye to the only woman I've ever loved. We've lived a good life together. Had two children and learned that life isn't always fair. It isn't fair that

Shannon will be taken from us so soon. It isn't fair that she'll never see the life that will come." His words are shaky as emotion begins to take him. "But I trust that you'll hold my love in your hands. You'll take her pain away and reunite her with part of her heart that was lost. I pray you'll keep her protected until I can make it to her. I'll be there soon, my angel."

Aidan releases my hand, but Liam won't drop my other.

My stomach starts to clench and my hand automatically flies to it. Liam reacts instantly and sits me in the chair. "Please, stay off your feet."

"It was just a small cramp," I try to reassure him. It wasn't even nearly as bad as the last time. I called Dr. Contreras yesterday and she explained the cramping would be normal and try to take it easy.

The doctor enters and explains what's to come. We gather around as the doctors and nurses start the process. Liam sits in the chair with me in his lap. Aidan holds Shannon's hand and refuses to let go. They work around him and he nods as they turn off the final machine. Thankfully, they turn the sound off on the heart monitor. Aidan tilts down and whispers in her ear with tears floating in his eyes. He speaks continuously until her heart stops beating.

He kisses her lips, lays her hand down on the bed, and walks out of the room.

I stand and Liam follows his father. I look out the window and see him pull him into his arms and keep his father from sinking to the ground.

chapter

twenty-seven

WE SPENT A week in Ohio after she passed. Her will stated her wishes and she demanded no funeral. She wanted to be cremated and her ashes be spread in her homeland. Aidan booked a flight for Ireland, and Liam and I returned home. He's been quiet but seems okay. Aaron is coming over tonight and asked if they could talk. Mason and Liam had a call today and they're going to allow him to stay behind from the deployment since a few new guys checked in. Instead of sending him to finish out the month, he'll train and get everyone settled here.

Part of me thinks it was a favor, but all I can be is grateful.

"Okay, Aara, I've got ten bucks that says you can go on the potty." He sits on the floor and plays with her while I rest on the couch.

The flights were a lot for me, and even though I did my best to take it easy, I want to be more careful now that we can be.

"You know she's too young to be bought and you're about to have a whole heap of diapers in your life."

"But if we can get rid of one of them with diapers that's a win," he scoffs and goes back to Aarabelle. "Okay, princess, how does this work? Do you just tell me? Do we stick you on it?"

"Oh, Jesus." I lean up, and he pins me with his eyes.

"Don't make me tie you to the couch."

"You don't scare me."

He crawls toward me with a gleam in his eyes. "Oh?" His moves are lithe and catlike. Liam's mouth is a thin line as he approaches. "I think you like testing me."

"I think you like to be tested."

He reaches the couch and he scoops me into his arms. Quickly he places me on the floor and hovers over me. "No more tests. I think we've passed them all anyway."

I smile and thread my fingers in his hair. "I'd say we have."

Aarabelle stands and lies on top of Liam's back. "Dada, up?"

He does a push up with her hanging on his back and kisses me when he comes down. She giggles and I hold her sides so she doesn't fall. Liam goes slow and lingers when he reaches my lips.

"I think you're enjoying this," I giggle in between kisses.

"I'll enjoy it more when you're my wife."

I struggle with how fast we're moving. I want to marry him, give him a life, be his everything, but I also don't want to hurt Aaron terribly. Aaron's a good father and he's trying to be a good friend. The one thing I think both of these men need is their friendship back. Liam saved Aaron's life, and in a way, Aaron's death gave Liam something. It's messy and ugly, but my marriage wasn't what it appeared.

Aaron and I have worked to find a way to get along for Aarabelle, and Liam will be her stepfather. She'll live with us, and I want Aaron to be a part of Aara's life.

"Liam," I sigh and he stops. Aarabelle climbs into his lap when he sits. She's so attached to him. "I'm not trying to put anything off, but I don't think we need to rush."

He looks away and resignation paints his face. "I'm marrying you before you have this baby. I want to bring our child into the world with two loving and married parents. I'm not asking for anything big. All I want is you, me, and Aarabelle on the beach."

"This baby will have two loving parents whether we're married or not."

"This is going to sound really bad, but I don't ask you for much. I didn't push you to choose me because I knew you would. I don't get upset about your ex-husband hanging around the house because he's Aarabelle's father and he was my friend. I've sacrificed and lost a lot. Now, though . . . now, you are mine." Aara moves off his lap and he moves toward me. "I want this because life is short. I want this because if I have to leave again, I need to know you're set. I need this because *I* need it."

My mind spins in circles on how to respond. Before I can answer, a knock comes.

"We'll revisit this . . ." Liam says and he gets up to grab the door.

I look over and Aaron is standing there. Neither of them speaks and you can cut the tension with a knife.

Aaron steps a little closer and extends his hand. "I'm sorry about your mom."

Liam grips his hand. "I appreciate it."

"Glad to hear you're okay too. I know everyone was worried."

While this is the most awkward thing I've ever experienced, it gives me optimism. They're talking—civilly. Aarabelle peeks from behind the couch and begins to giggle.

"Hi, pumpkin!" Aaron exclaims and she runs full speed.

"It was a mess . . ." Liam begins but hesitates.

Aaron raises Aara up and kisses her, then turns to Liam. "The mission?"

I breathe a heavy sigh of relief and fight the smile that's building. Maybe we'll all get through this sooner than we thought.

Liam starts to tell Aaron about some of the stuff that went

wrong on the mission and why they went dark. A lot of it either goes over my head, or I just don't want to know. These two have been friends for a long time and to see their friendship end was hard. I know that there was a lot of hurt between us all, but I think Aaron and I have come to a point where we also know our marriage was over before he died. Neither of us were ready to face facts.

"Athair," Aarabelle says, which is pronounced "*ah her.*" It means "father" in Gaelic. We decided to start pushing that more and more over the last few weeks. We want her to have something special to call Liam, but allow Aaron to be her Daddy.

"I'm here. I'm here." Liam gives her one of his hands as she gives him a toy.

We spend about an hour just playing with Aara. We talk about work and some of the things the doctors have told Aaron. His PTSD symptoms are gradually getting better and he's starting to feel like the person he was before the deployment where they lost half their friends.

"Do you think we could step out and talk for a minute?" Liam says and my eyes snap up.

"Sure," Aaron replies reluctantly.

Liam walks over and grabs my hand. "Trust me. This has to happen."

"Please," I beg.

"I'll be right back."

They step out of the room, heading out onto the deck. Fear grips me, and my chest tightens. I press my ear to the door but can't hear anything. Minutes pass, feeling hopeful they're getting along since I don't hear anything breaking.

"What the heck are they talking about, Aarabelle?" I ask rhetorically and lie down before I get myself worked up.

She climbs on the couch with me, I nestle her into my chest. I love the moments I get her like this. Usually if Liam or Aaron are around, she's climbing on them, but when it's me and her, she's my snuggle bunny.

"Pretty soon Mommy is going to be so big you're going to have to lie with me on the bed. You're going to be a big sister," I say animatedly. Her smile lights up her face, and although she doesn't know what I'm talking about, my excitement grows. "You'll get to be spoiled even more, because if I know your uncles, they'll overcompensate."

More minutes go by, and finally Liam walks in without Aaron. Great.

"What happened?" I ask.

"We needed to talk, Lee. Man to man. He needed to know from me."

I turn my head and try to hold my anger in. "You should've talked to me."

"Natalie," he tries to capture my attention. "Look at me."

I let out a shaky breath and then turn to him.

"I did what I would want him to do. I told him the truth. The more we lie, the worse this will be. I know him. I know you're afraid to hurt him any more. And believe me, I don't want to watch him suffer either. He was my fucking friend. He's going to be a part of our lives forever." Liam looks at Aara. "He's her father. Aaron has a place in our family, and that's the reality we face. So I went to him as his friend and told him I asked you to marry me."

My throat feels like it's closing in. All of this is so overwhelming. My future husband is telling my former husband that he plans to marry me. I've decided that I'm the only one in the world who has to deal with this shit.

"He isn't happy, but he respects it. He said he knew it was coming and we talked. Will he be at our wedding? No. Will he be happy about it? I sure as fuck wouldn't be. But he knows and he won't be blindsided when it happens. We're both grown men and

I won't lie, and I sure as hell am not going to hide. This is our life and we have to find a way to live it."

"I know. It's just a lot. A baby, a marriage, you just lost your mom. I just want us to be sure. I want to build a solid marriage, not one that you or I feel like is because of something else."

It's not me who I worry about . . . it's him. He asked me to marry me as his mother was dying. I'm pregnant with a very high-risk pregnancy. And that is on the heels of him having major complications on a very dangerous deployment.

"I know this . . . you and I have been through hell. We've come out stronger, in love, together, and a family. I want to marry you and know that when I'm gone, you'll have the military backing. I'd wait twenty years if it took you that long to be ready to marry me, but that's not what you're saying. You keep saying it's me. It's not me, Lee. If you don't want to get married because you need more time . . . just tell me. But don't turn this on me, sweetheart. I'd pack the car and go today."

"It's not me I worry about. But if you mean it, then let's do it."

Liam lifts me into his lap then pulls my face to his. We kiss, and I feel the joy coming from his body. It's as if I just gave him the best gift. Only it's him who is giving me more than I can express. I really don't know how I could've gotten so lucky.

We head into the kitchen and I start to fuss about how there's nothing to eat. I swear I never had any cravings with Aarabelle, but this one, all I want is chicken and cashews. I could eat it every meal and be happy. Of course, I don't, but I try to convince Liam to order out. Aara sits in her highchair eating her tiny pieces of chicken nuggets while I groan and moan about Liam not getting his pregnant fiancée what she wants.

"I have something for you."

"You do? Is it an eggroll?"

"Oh, I got your eggroll, sweetheart. I think you'll like this better."

"Doubtful," I huff playfully.

Aarabelle and I make faces at each other while Liam taps his foot. "Are you done being a brat?"

"You did not just call me a brat!" My eyes widen, and I drop the fork.

"I did . . . now, I'm trying to be romantic, and you're killing the mood."

"Romance in the kitchen? I'm excited now." I sit up, pretending to be fully engaged. I'm tired, hungry, and feel nauseated all at the same time.

"Brat," he repeats as he gets down on one knee again. "Now do I have your attention?" Liam's smile is soft and his eyes are full of love.

I nod as he extracts a black box and then places it on my knee unopened.

"Aarabelle, I'm going to ask you if this is okay . . ." She looks at him while he grins. "Eat, cry, whine, poop, stare off or at me, or smile if you want me to marry your mommy."

I laugh and she looks at me.

"Sold!" Liam exclaims. "Natalie and Aarabelle . . . I want to be a part of your lives forever. I want to care for you, love you, and be here for you." He grabs her hand and I cover my mouth with my hand. "I'll be your Dad even though I'm not your father. You already own me and I'll do anything for you."

A tear falls as he addresses the one thing in this world that would've stopped me from being with him.

Liam's eyes shift and he touches my knee. "This was my mother's ring."

With shaky hands, I touch the box and open it slowly. Nestled in the velvet is the most beautiful antique ring. It's white gold with pave diamonds on the band and around the center stone. The large diamond is round and protected by the other diamonds. It's absolutely beautiful.

"Liam," I look up as another tear falls, "It's . . ."

"My father said he thinks she would want you to wear it. She would've loved you and he hopes we have as much love as they shared." He takes it out and slides it on my left ring finger.

"I think we'll have more," I press my lips against his. He holds my cheeks and kisses me with so much fierceness it nearly knocks me off the chair. Aarabelle starts to yell for him and bangs on the table.

"I love you too, princess." He kisses the top of her head and I melt.

He's going to make me very happy and I'm going to cherish every second I have with him.

chapter twenty-eight

"**A**RE YOU READY to see the baby?" Dr. Contreras asks as she puts the cold gel on my stomach. Liam stands next to me holding my hand.

"Yes," I nod and look up at him. His eyes are focused on the machine. It's finally time for my ultrasound and we're going to see our baby. We had to push back a few weeks with all the craziness, but I'm beyond ready.

"And we're doing the gender reveal later, so you don't want to know, correct?"

Liam groans then shifts his attention to me. "They don't have to know we know. We can pretend we don't know at this stupid party. Look, I even have a great shocked face." I glance over and he gives his best impression.

Such a dork.

I ignore him, "No, we don't want to know."

"You suck."

"You're being a baby. The party is in two weeks."

"Stupid. I'm the father. I should know before some damn baker."

"Zip it."

She laughs and puts the wand on my stomach. I swear I don't

remember being so big with Aarabelle this early. I'm either retaining a lot of water or my body figures it's already done this so might as well return to form.

The room fills with the wooshing sound of the baby's heartbeat. Liam's eyes widen, and his jaw drops as it echoes around us.

"What the hell is that?"

Dr. Contreras smiles. "That's your baby's heart. Nice and strong."

"Our baby has a heart," he says sounding clearly surprised.

I giggle, "I know."

"I didn't mean that literally."

I twist my fingers with his and listen with a full heart. It's a miracle we're standing here hearing our baby or that any of this is happening.

"See that there," the doctor says pointing. "That's the baby's heart. You can see everything looks good there."

She continues to show us small glimpses of our peanut. Each time she points a new piece out, Liam claims he sees a penis, which she obviously won't confirm. She goes through all the organs then hands us a few photos.

"I'll let you get dressed and then I'll be back to go over everything," she explains.

"Is there anything to be concerned about?"

"I just want to look at the timeline and set a plan." Her voice is reassuring, but something has me on edge.

Liam kisses the top of my head, and hands me a towel to clean off.

"I have a bad feeling," I relay my fears to him.

"Everything looks fine, Lee. I know you're worried, but from what I saw, the kid's got all the parts."

"Says the man who thought he would dent him or her with his giant penis."

"Can't help the equipment that was bestowed upon me."

I stare, waiting until he looks over so he can see my face. He's smiles then sits next to me.

"All joking aside, if there's something wrong, we'll handle it. But you've had a rough go at getting pregnant and staying pregnant . . . so, this is good. We're at twenty-three weeks now. I'm handling everything I can so you can stay off your feet. Let's just wait before we freak out."

My head falls on his shoulder, and he wraps his arm around me. There are times in my life I feel so weak. As if all anyone does is reassure me that things will be fine. It's just this baby . . . this life inside of me . . . is my chance. It's my chance to prove I wasn't broken or marred, but that I was meant to be a mother.

We sit here quietly and Dr. Contreras knocks and enters. "Okay, everything looked good. The baby's heart and all of the organs are great. I've sent the gender off to the cake people, so yes, we were able to get a clear picture of that." She smiles and then looks at the chart. "Only issue I have is your weight. You need to eat a little more. So far, you're not gaining much and you said you weren't having morning sickness. Are you eating healthy?"

"I have a kid who has no idea how to sit for two seconds so that could be why."

She nods. "I want you to make sure you're taking in enough calories for you and the baby."

"She'll eat." Liam offers his promise.

"I'll be more mindful."

Dr. Contreras smiles and shakes my hand. "Good. I'll see you in a few weeks."

She turns to Liam and he returns the gesture. "She'll eat . . . no worries."

"Thanks, caveman. Go put your club away before you hit yourself on the head," I say grabbing my coat.

The doctor laughs while leaving the room. Liam and I head to the car, I look closer at the sonogram to see if I can figure out if it's a boy or girl. It's going to kill me to wait until the gender reveal. Reanell and her stupid party. I was against it from the beginning, but somehow she tricked Liam into thinking this would be a fun idea.

Aidan returns from Ireland next week and is coming into Dulles, so he asked if he could come for a visit and meet Aarabelle. We figured we could spend the week with him and then find out the sex of the baby.

I groan, "I can't tell if I see a penis." I huff and throw myself back on the seat.

"Careful with the pushing on the seat please."

"You're kidding me?"

"Sweetheart, Robin has been good to us."

"Robin can't fit two kids in the back." I call this to his attention and the shock ripples across his face.

"That's not even funny if you're telling me what I think you're telling me."

I turn slightly so I can watch this. "You and Robin are going to need to come to some kind of understanding. You're going to need a new woman."

"Robin is mine and I am hers."

"I thought I was yours," I raise my brow.

"But . . . you . . . but . . ." Liam splutters and grips the wheel. I wouldn't ask him to sell his car, but this is almost too fun.

"It's just not practical." I shrug and turn my head so he can't see my smile.

"What if we have an every other weekend deal?"

I swear I've never seen a man so attached to a piece of metal before, but this is Liam. The man who fed my child cake and tied her diaper on with rope. He's the guy who will wax his car by hand for two hours to ensure the paint stays pristine. I really hope we have a girl, because if it's a boy, he'll be teaching him this same craziness.

"I'll think about it."

"I'll make it worth your while." Liam's voice is full of promise. I giggle and sink into the seat. I'm happy. Deliriously happy. I have the most amazing man, a beautiful little girl, and another baby on the way. Aaron is alive, and we both have a way to find peace. He and Liam have been speaking in very small doses, but it feels like things are how they were meant to be.

"YOU LOOK BEAUTIFUL," Jackson says as he kisses my cheek.

"Thanks, I'm getting huge." I feel like I keep saying the same thing. I swear, I'm going to wind up giving birth to a damn toddler.

It's finally gender reveal day. I've had to fight the urge to call the bakery pretending I'm Reanell and need the color of the cake. It's been killing me not knowing. I've debated killing her for talking me into this. She claims I owe her since Mason is deployed and she has no other means of fun.

"Nonsense." Jackson steps inside before I see Catherine behind him.

"Cat!" I scream and embrace her. "You didn't say you were coming."

"I wouldn't miss it. I had to come to New York for a meeting, so I planned it so I could be here."

"How's wedding planning?"

"Going . . . we're not in a rush. What about you? Jackson said you and Liam . . ."

I show her the ring and she gasps. "Wow, that's breathtaking."

"It was his mother's ring."

"It's beautiful. Any guesses on the baby?" She smiles as her shoulders scrunch up.

"I think it's a girl. Liam swears it's a girl too."

We've argued for two weeks about the sex. Before I can explain, I feel a hand on my lower back.

"It's a girl," Liam's husky voice says from behind me.

"I really think you should change to thinking it's a boy," I say for the tenth time today.

"Not a chance, sweetheart. If you want someone to be wrong, it's going to be you." Liam's hand snakes down and squeezes my butt.

I slap him and scoff, "He's impossible."

"Wait," Catherine says confused. "You want him to think opposite?"

"Yes, that way he's wrong, and I can gloat." Makes perfect sense to me.

"I thought Jackson and I were competitive." Catherine laughs as someone else knocks on the door.

"Excuse me," I say and walk to see who's here.

"Now," Reanell says as soon as the door opens. She has the cake in her hand, and I have to remember I need to keep it together. "Before you do something stupid like tackle me . . ." She waits until I look at her eyes. "You will behave, or I'll never watch your kids, and when Liam pisses you off, I'll tell him things to fuel his argument."

"Some friend you are."

"God, you're a peach when you're pregnant," she laughs and eyes me as she moves past me.

"Good enough to eat," Liam says hushed against my ear.

"Change your choice!" I yell and rush after him. I wrap my arms around his back and he sighs.

When we're like this, nothing can hurt me. He blankets the

fears that threaten to smother me. With him there is peace.

Liam turns then his arms cross against my back. He holds me as his blue eyes prick with wonder. "You are trouble." He slants down and kisses me. "Good thing I like trouble." Another kiss to my lips.

"Let's go cut our cake . . ." I try to lure him.

"Have you been cramping at all?" Liam asks seriously.

I've had a few sparingly, but nothing like the last time. I've been taking it easy and trying to stay off my feet. Of course, Aarabelle doesn't fully get that, so Paige has been brought on as a full-time nanny for a work-from-home mom. She helps with so much more than I could expect, and she's very attached to Aara.

"No, Dad. I've been good. I promise I'll be careful."

"There's my wife!" Mark comes in with his booming voice. "How's our sparkly baby coming along?"

"You're so dumb." I laugh and hit his arm.

"Hands off my woman, Twilight," Liam warns with a hint of playfulness in his voice.

"Or what?"

"I'll kick your ass."

"Bring it. I'm twice your age and twice your size." He winks at me and taunts Liam. "When the doctors told us the great news, we were thrilled . . . then we realized we'd have to tell you."

"Oh, for the love of God." I push Mark, and they both burst out laughing.

"Did you see her face?" Mark says between guffaws.

"Dude, we had her good."

"Assholes," I mutter and walk away.

Quinn arrives late as usual, and we all grab seats and catch up. This is more like a barbeque than anything else. Aarabelle is, of course, on Liam's lap most of the day and occasionally she and Jackson play a little. Knowing how Jackson also lost a child breaks my heart. His daughter or son would've been almost four I think. He will really be such an amazing dad one day.

Aidan and I spend a good amount of time talking. He's already head over heels in love with Aarabelle. She delivers him toys as she shares her half-eaten cookies. He never blinks an eye, just takes a bite and asks if he can have her call him *Seanathair,* which means "grandfather" in Gaelic.

Of course, this will take a long time to teach her, but it means a lot to him. It also will help cause less confusion for the new baby as well. It gives the men the same name for both children.

"Okay, I'm going to eat the damn cake myself if we don't get to it now," Liam says and claps his hands.

Everyone laughs as Reanell glares at him. "One call and I'll have your ass back on a plane," she toys with him.

"That is, of course, if Commander's wife says it's okay to cut the cake."

We all laugh at Liam's quick rephrasing, and Rea smiles.

"Let's go find out what the bun in the oven is."

We head over to the table where there are two small egg shaped cakes. Both white, and once we cut them open, we'll know.

"Okay, the way this works is only one of you cuts the cake and the other announces the sex," Rea explains.

"Why are there two?" I ask.

"Maybe there are two babies," she jokes. Or at least she better be joking.

"Not even funny."

Rea smiles, "I got two because the one wouldn't feed this herd. Let's be real here, Mark could eat that cake on his own."

Mark scoffs, "I'm not the one named Muffin Top. Let us not forget who's the fat kid with the cake here."

"Funny," Jackson replies, and we all bust out laughing.

"Liam, why don't you cut the egg, and Lee can let us know

what it is!" She bounces with excitement.

Liam's eyes focus on the cake as he grabs the knife. He places it down, my eyes look to him in confusion before hands grip my face, and he presses his lips to mine. You can hear the group laugh and make teasing noises, but all I focus on is him.

He pulls back and stares for a beat. "I love you and right now . . . I'm just happy."

"Me too. You make me this way."

We both smile at each other and Liam starts to look around the room. "Aara?" he calls out.

Within seconds, she's running across the room toward us.

"There you are. Wanna see if you're going to have a sister or brother?" She starts to reach for the cake. "Or better let's have some cake."

Liam inclines, and I think he's going for the knife instead he sticks Aarabelle's hand in the cake.

"Liam!" I start to complain, but then when her hand comes out, we both just look at each other and smile.

chapter twenty-nine

"A BOY?" LIAM and I both start laughing. Which only increases as Aarabelle presses her now blue hand on Liam's face.

"Well," his eyes shine bright. "We were both wrong."

"It's going to be a boy!" I yell out as everyone claps.

Aarabelle goes back for more of the cake, which is now everywhere. Liam's face is covered in frosting and cake. He dips his finger down while I warn him with my eyes.

"Don't do it."

"But we should match."

"Liam Dempsey, you do it, and so help you God . . ."

"You wouldn't want to make me blue."

"Something else is going to be blue."

Liam leans forward and lifts Aara between us and she gets me straight on the nose. Her hands glide down my face as she smears it everywhere. We all laugh, and I can't help but feel as if the sun is shining down upon us.

We clean up and everyone comes over to talk to us. Liam reaches around and grabs my hand. Sometimes out of nowhere he'll do this. It's as if he needs to ground himself and I'm that for him. I love that through our touch he can feel like home.

I head into the kitchen and start to put away some of the dirty dishes. I look out the window at the ocean and smile. Arms come around my stomach, and I settle back against him. He holds me against his chest, and I rest my head on his shoulder.

"I just talked to Quinn," Liam grumbles softly.

"I'm sorry," I joke.

"He gave me the keys to the house in Corolla. I can call a priest and we can go next weekend. What do you say?"

I put the plate down and shut the water off. Liam moves back so I can turn and face him. Immediately his arms find their way around me again. I wrap mine around his neck and look into the eyes of the man I love. "This weekend?"

"I don't need anything but you and Aarabelle. Quinn said he'd stand in for me and I'm sure Reanell will. Jackson and Catherine are here . . . it's your call, sweetheart."

If it were any other man, I don't know that I could so soon. If it were any other SEAL, I wouldn't be able to. But this is Liam. While we didn't find each other in the most conventional way, we found each other when we needed to. He's truly my other half.

"Looks like you're about to get hitched, Dreamboat."

"I'm going to make you the happiest woman in the world."

My fingers glide across to the scruff that's trimmed again. His strong jawline and dark brown hair scratch against my skin. "You made me fall in love with you and then you gave me a child. You loved me even when I was a mess. I think you've fulfilled that promise."

Liam lifts me gently and lowers himself. Our lips meet and I sigh. His tongue enters my mouth and pushes against mine slowly. Each slide against each other makes my body warm. I feel his fingers glide down my back as he cups my ass. Using the counter behind me he raises me up so I'm sitting. My legs naturally wrap around his waist and he continues to plunge into my mouth.

My fingers grip his hair, holding him against me, but he's just as urgent. Even though there's a house full of people, I can't push him away. I hold him close and I mold to him.

"Seriously, get a room," Reanell enters the kitchen.

I wipe my mouth and the tingle and swelling of my lips is torture. I want more.

"So," I say nonchalantly. "I'm getting married next weekend. Would you like to be my matron of honor?"

"Only if you don't call it matron. Makes me feel old."

"You are old."

"Whatever. You're pregnant."

"You're quick. So . . . will you?" I ask trying not to laugh.

Reanell rushes over and pushes Liam out of the way. She wraps her arms around me and rocks back and forth. "I would love to. You know I can't say no to you."

Mark walks in carrying a bunch of trash. "So the party is in here?"

Liam looks over with the biggest smile and I give him one right back. "Next weekend," Liam says. "We're getting married."

"You can't," Mark says deadpan.

"Why the hell not?" I ask.

"Because you're my wife and that's my baby. This is some Jerry Springer shit up in here."

Liam pushes his chest. "The wedding will be in Corolla, fuckstick." He laughs and walks out of the kitchen.

Mark heads over. "I'm happy for you, Lee. I don't know if I'll make it and I hope you understand. It's not choosing . . . it's just that if it were me . . ." he trails off and it clicks that he's talking about Aaron. "I wouldn't want to be alone."

"I don't want him to be either."

I've made peace with Aaron. Healing came despite great despair. Life may have thrown me around, but it's shown me that sometimes love can come in places we never thought to look.

"I'll let you know, but even if I'm not there, I want you to know I'm happy. I think you and Aaron made the right choice." Mark sits at the table and I join him.

"You know, all those years we were trying to make things work, there were times I wished he would leave. He was unhappy. I was unhappy, but I thought if we could just have a baby, it would make things okay. I really believed it would heal us."

Mark grabs my hand. "I think the mission we lost Brian, Devon, and Fernando altered all of our lives. Jackson was never the same, and I think Aaron carried more shit than we knew. All of us lost our friends that day and we lived. There's a level of guilt you carry through that. I dealt with mine and made peace with it. But I don't know that those two did. Aaron had you to focus on, and when a man can't do something he was made to do . . ." he trails off.

"Aaron didn't fail me, Mark. He wasn't the issue with getting pregnant, but he used that to be selfish. That's why I couldn't go backward."

"Just know that you're my friend too, and I'm not choosing sides. I didn't want you to be upset."

I stand and place my hand on Mark's. "I understand. Thank you for being a good friend. Aarabelle is lucky to have you and Jackson too."

"Well, I'm a fantastic godfather."

"The best."

We laugh and hug before he walks out. I stand here for a second and take in the fact that in a week, I'll be Mrs. Dempsey.

"SWEETHEART, I'M NOT going to tell you again," Liam warns

as he waits downstairs.

We came to Corolla the day after the party. It's been great being away just us and his father before everyone else arrives. Aidan has been enjoying the time with Liam and he's officially smitten with Aara. He offered to watch her so we could go to dinner just us tonight.

Jackson, Catherine, Reanell, Mark, and Quinn are coming tomorrow morning. Rea is bringing the cake and the reason Mark is now attending is Aaron went home to visit his mother. So instead of just attending, he got ordained. He decided that he couldn't miss it and he only felt it was fair to be the one to marry us. Liam thought it was brilliant—me, not so much.

"You know, it's not so easy when your stomach doesn't agree with zippers!" I yell down the stairs. One week and I can't zipper this damn dress. "Liam," I whine a little. "Please come zip me."

I hear him talking to himself about girls and how it's going to be great to have a little man to round out this group. "Sure, darling." The sarcasm drips from his tongue.

"You did this to me."

"Last I checked, you had to be present in order for me to have done this."

"Whatever. It's your fault."

"I have a feeling I'll be hearing that a lot."

I snort, "Yup."

"I didn't piss in your Cheerios, so be nice. And don't forget, tomorrow you'll legally be mine to do what I want with."

"Happy wife, happy life, buddy. Don't fuck it up," I joke and he laughs.

He zips the dress and his hands slide down my arms. His fingers touch the ring and he rubs the diamond. "She'll be here in a way tomorrow. My mom . . . she'll see us."

"She's always here with you." I turn in his arms and place my hand on his heart. "No matter how much you miss her, she lives here. Her memories can't ever be taken, and tomorrow you'll feel her presence."

"Yeah," he pauses and rubs his hands up and down my bare arms. It's laughable the dress I have on. Thanks to whoever made Lycra, because without the give there would be no way of squeezing in. "Do I seriously have to sleep in the other room?" Liam groans again.

His biggest issue is that he doesn't want to sleep apart. Let alone sleep in the same room as his father who snores so loud he's woken us twice.

"Yes."

"How about you sleep with Aarabelle, and I'll sleep in her room?"

"In the crib?"

He's out of his mind.

"I don't think we have bad luck coming our way. I'm pretty sure we've already surpassed it." Liam gives me his sly smile. His blue eyes gleam as he tries all of his moves.

"It's tradition."

"There's nothing traditional about us."

I laugh and lean in to kiss him. Our lips touch and his hands thread in my long hair. He tangles his fingers around my curls and holds my head to his. His tongue glides across the seam of my lips and I grant him access. The second our tongues touch, passion erupts between us. The slow, dull flame becomes an inferno and all I want to do is strip him down and let him take me.

My hands slide across his taut chest and I groan into his mouth as I feel each ripple of his skin. The heat burns through his shirt as he licks the inside of my mouth. I need to breathe, but I would sacrifice oxygen to keep kissing him. Liam reminds me of the good in the world just by being near me.

He pushes me against the bed and lays me down. "Liam," I say his name as a request. I'm not sure whether it's to keep going or to stop. I want him, but his father and Aarabelle are downstairs. "I'll be quick," he whispers before his mouth meets mine again. He's careful with his weight not to push against my swollen belly. Our tongues clash and his hands make their way up my dress. With one hand, he removes my underwear. I reach for the button of his pants and we hurriedly undress each other. There's no elegance or grace. Once I slide his pants off, I wrap my fingers around his dick. His head falls against my shoulder as I pump him slowly.

I push his shoulder and he falls onto his back. I smile as my hair creates a veil not allowing him to see my intention. Moving down his hard body with my tongue, he lets out a low groan.

In one quick movement, I take him fully into my mouth. My lips wrap around his dick and my tongue glides down the vein. "Fucking shit, Lee."

The way his voice cracks at the end makes me want to drive him to the brink like he's done to me so many times. I continue to go up and down, twisting my tongue around the tip.

"Natalie, now." Liam's voice is insistent, but I keep going. "Lee, I'm not going to last, sweetheart."

I go down one last time before leaning up. Within seconds, he pushes me onto my back and hovers over me. "Now that's a wedding present." He gives his signature smile and I don't know whether to laugh or slap him.

When he enters me, there's nothing funny about it. I'm home. Complete. Whole. And I'm his.

Liam sets a slow pace, but neither of us is going to last long. He reaches his hand between us and circles my clit. I climb higher as our eyes stay locked. All the emotion, love, desire, is on display.

There's no shield we can't break through. No secrets between us right here. We give ourselves to one another in body and in our souls. Tomorrow, he will give me his name and I will give him my hand.

I crash over the edge and my orgasm rocks me.

Liam follows behind me silently as we lie panting on the bed.

"Who needs a bachelor party? I much prefer your way of sending me off into married life," Liam laughs and my hand slaps his chest.

"Are you ready?" I ask even though I already know.

Liam shifts onto his side and his face is next to mine. "I've never been more ready for anything. Not BUDs, not a mission, or anything that I live for. You, you are what I've been waiting for my whole life. I never knew it. I didn't expect it. But we've found it and whether we were making it official or not, you would always be meant for me."

"I love you."

"I love you. I mean it, Lee. Even if you had chosen someone else . . . there would never be anyone that would come close to you. Believe me. You'll never have to worry about me straying or running from you."

I turn slightly and press my hand against his chest. "I know. You don't have to worry either. I've never loved anyone like I've loved you."

chapter

thirty

"ARABELLE'S DRESS IS hanging in the closet. I need to finish my makeup. Where the hell is my curling iron?" I rush around the room frantic as Reanell, Catherine, and Ashton sit on the bed trying not to laugh.

Catherine stands and walks over. "Sit. I'll do your hair. Just relax," she soothes and I listen.

Well, not about the relaxing part.

We spend the next hour getting ready and before I put my dress on, there's a knock at the door.

Ashton answers, and I hear her and Quinn talking, but soon she closes the door and hands me a small box.

"This is for you," she smiles and places it in my hands.

I open the lid and there sits another small box.

Then another.

And another.

Until I finally reach the final box. I open it while everyone looks over my shoulder. Inside sits a pair of diamond stud earrings.

"Oh my God," I gasp. Each one has to be a carat. They're gorgeous. I immediately put them in my ears and can't stop touching them.

Another knock on the door.

Catherine rushes over and sure enough, Jackson is on the other side. She walks over with a card and places it in my hands. "At least we didn't do makeup." She kisses my cheek and they all sit.

With shaky hands, I open the card. Before reading, I look at Aarabelle, Reanelle, Catherine, and Ashton curled in close to celebrate today. I really am blessed.

My sweetheart,

When our worlds altered, I found myself unsure. The days of not knowing whether I should walk away or find a way to make you see how I felt were agony. I struggled, but then it became easy. The world became ours and we found true, undiluted love. I can now change a diaper. I know about the aftermath of cake for meals. But mostly, I know about love. Years from now when our children are grown, we'll be able to tell them how we came to be. They'll know nothing in this world comes easy, but if it's right, you fight for it. I'll fight everything and everyone in this world for you and our family. I give you my word—I'll never forsake you. Now, come get your ass down that aisle and marry me.

I love you,

Liam

I laugh as tears stream down my face. Only he can make me do both at the same time.

"Mama cry," Aara says as she squirms off Rea's lap and comes over.

"It's okay, baby. Athair is just making Mommy happy."

"Athair!" She looks around for Liam.

"Soon. Do you want your pretty dress?" I ask her as I lift her into my arms.

"Lee," Rea comes over and takes Aarabelle. "Please no heavy lifting. You've been on your feet a lot and you'll be sitting very little all day."

I nod and absently rub my stomach.

We get Aarabelle dressed and unzip my gown from its bag. It's a simple, white dress with large, white beads down the entire back to the train. It has a deep U cut that drapes almost to my butt. It's classic and has a lot of room for my belly.

Reanell fixes my dress and double-checks my hair. She stands me in front of the mirror and Aarabelle stands in front of me. "Wow," I say aloud. "You look so pretty, peanut," I say, trying to keep my mind off the fact that I'm standing in a wedding dress.

In the mirror is a blonde with bright, blue eyes and red lips. Her hair is curled and hangs down her back with a little over the side. In her eyes, you can see how happy she is. I realize as I see myself through someone else's eyes how right this is. I follow the tulip shaped dress, and even with my bump, it's perfect.

"Ready?" Reanell asks in a hushed tone.

I glance at Aara and then to her reflection. "I am."

"Okay, let's go. Your man is waiting."

"Rea." I grab her arm. She stops and looks at me with wide eyes. "I need to make sure I tell you how much I love you and how much you mean to me."

Her smile spreads and I fight back the emotions overwhelming me. "I know our lives met by chance, but you're family to me. No matter where the Navy takes us, you'll always be in my heart."

Catherine peeks her head in, "I hate to interrupt, but it's time. Mark is taking this minister thing a little too far, by the way. Just to warn you." She laughs and dips her head back out.

"Okay, Aara," I put my hand out. Her small hand wraps around my fingers and we head out the door.

This morning was a little misty out, but the sun is shining through now. We walk down the beach, and Aara and I stand and wait. I wish I had my parents here, but they said they couldn't make it back so soon after their last visit. My father hasn't been feeling so well and the travel is hard. Plus, we sprung it on them quickly. Still, I wish my daddy were here to give me away.

"I'm going to head down, and whenever you and Aara are ready . . ." Rea smiles and kisses my cheek.

I squat as best as I can by my daughter and hold her hands in mine. "Oh, Aara. So much has happened in your short, little life, but love has never been missing. Liam will love you, and your daddy will too. You'll have twice the amount that most little girls have. I love you."

She plays with the flower on her dress and I smile. Aara looks up and I pucker for a kiss. She leans in and then I pull her close.

"You look beautiful, darling." I gasp and turn my head only to see my father standing there in his suit.

"Daddy!" I call out and he helps me stand. "You came!" I wrap my arms around him and want to cry.

He laughs in his rich voice that I'd know anywhere. "I wouldn't miss this for the world. Liam called after we spoke and bought us plane tickets. He was very adamant and was willing to come down and drive us if he had to," he laughs again and pulls me back. "Quite a guy you got there."

"He really is special."

"So are you," he taps my nose. "And so are you! Hello, my gorgeous princess." My father lifts Aara and holds her in one arm. He loops his arm and I circle my hand through. "Let's go and see that man of yours."

"Okay." My voice shakes, but I'm not nervous. It's quite the opposite. I'm eager and ready. I want to see him. I want to say our vows and start our life together.

We begin the walk and I keep my eyes down so I don't trip. When I look up, I can hardly breathe. Liam stands with Quinn and Jackson behind him. Reanell and Catherine on my side and Mark stands in between. There's an archway with white tulle and red flowers all around. A few chairs sit on the side for my parents and Aidan. But it's the look on Liam's face that fills me.

His smile is bright and tears fall from his eyes. I walk toward him and he moves forward. My father chuckles as Liam seems to stop himself.

When we reach him, the sun shines from behind him, and his blue eyes pierce through me. "Hi," I say and wipe a tear from my eyes.

"Hi," he says and using the pad of his thumb wipes the other.

Aarabelle wiggles from my father's arms. "Mama!" she yells and Liam crouches down with his arms open. She rushes to him and he scoops her up.

"No one forgot you," he laughs and holds her on his side.

I press my one hand on his chest and another on Aarabelle's back. Right here the world is right.

"Dearly, beloved," Mark begins, and I look at him for the first time.

"You're kidding me," I say laughing. "You got a robe?"

"I'm a man of the cloth, my child. Now, simmer down and let my mercy and love come down upon this marriage."

"Idiot," I hear Jackson mutter under his breath.

"We are gathered here today to witness Sparkles and Dreamboat create a new world."

Liam and I both burst out laughing and then Jackson moves forward and slaps Mark on the back of the head.

This is the perfect wedding. Surrounded by our friends who are family, in a setting where we really fell in love, solidifying our union.

"Anyway," Mark straightens himself. "We are here to see two people I care about deeply get married. Liam and Natalie asked for a traditional ceremony, but well, I don't think there's much traditional here. So let's do this how they are . . . perfect."

I look at Mark and his eyes soften. We smile and Aarabelle starts to tug on Liam's face. He's right . . . there's nothing traditional here.

"Natalie, did you want to say your vows or let me do them? I got his all worked out," Mark smirks.

"I'll say them, thanks." Liam puts Aarabelle down and she rushes over to Jackson. I swear this kid would never have to walk with the men in her life. I take Liam's hand in mine and our eyes lock. "I didn't write anything, so this may be rambly and not make sense." I take a deep breath and try to work through the jumble of words in my head. "We weren't supposed to be. It was never in my plans or a possibility. You came to me during a dark part in my life where I wasn't sure light even existed. I remember when I started to see you as more. More than a friend, and someone I wanted to be near, to touch, to hold, to comfort. You never pushed me because you knew me more than I knew myself. Somehow, you see it all and love me with everything. You and I may not have been supposed to be, but we're meant to be. My heart is yours, my love is yours, my days and all my nights are yours. I'll hold you up, stand by you, and give you everything I have." I take a deep breath and then the dam breaks. "I love you so much. I'll love you with all that I have."

Liam's thumbs rub against the tops of my hand and he smiles. "You're cute when you're rambly."

Mark clears his throat, "Liam, let's hear your vows. Better do better than that, my son."

Liam gives him a look and then looks back at me.

"Natalie, I wasn't looking for love when we found it. I was looking to help. But it was you who helped me. Your smile, your eyes, and your heart showed me what I was lacking. Each day I would find a reason to see you because you made my day worth waking up for. I learned how to change diapers," he pauses and we smile. "Get a kid dressed, but more than anything, how to be a man. Not a man who cares only for himself and his job, but a man who stands by a woman and steps up. You showed me what love is. We'll have hard times and we'll struggle, but I'll never leave your side. I'll stand and fight for you no matter what life throws at us. I'll love Aarabelle and our son the same. I'll protect you and them at any cost. There will never be a day you feel unloved by me. And if you ever should, you have permission to slap me." Liam smiles and I laugh.

My heart is full as he says his vows. And with Liam, I know his vows ring true.

Liam pulls at my hands, and I see the struggle to rein in his emotions is strong. "I give you my word, my name, and everything I have as your husband."

Liam turns his attention to Mark who looks like he's about to cry. He shakes his head, and I hear sniffles from behind me.

"Rings!" It finally clicks for Mark. "Okay. Quinn, please hand them over."

Quinn steps forward and claps Liam on the back.

"Thank you, my child."

I roll my eyes and giggle. He's so stupid. "You know you got your training online, right?"

"Yes, now hush and allow the grace of my ordination to come upon this union." He goes back to looking at his booklet.

"I swear . . ." Jackson mutters and I giggle.

Liam and I recite our promises and place the rings we picked out on each other's hands. His is a solid, tungsten ring with Celtic knots all along the middle. It's modern but the knots bring in his heritage. They also symbolize the forging of our lives and family. Mine is an eternity diamond band. He fought tooth and nail about it and how he was determined to spend his money how he wanted.

I wait for someone to tell him to kiss the bride, but he takes a third ring in his hand that's on a fine, gold chain. "Aarabelle," he squats down as she sits in the sand. I clutch my throat and try to stop from sobbing. "I know I'm not your father, but I'll be a daddy to you. Here's a ring of my promise to you. I'll protect you and kiss your knee, plus I promise to never be one of those jerk stepparents, because I'll never see you as anything but my daughter." He clasps the necklace around her neck. There's no holding back. Tears fall relentlessly, and Reanell, Catherine, Ashton, and my mother are all weeping too. "Oh, and I'll give you cake for breakfast and ice cream for lunch."

Liam stands and looks at me. He tugs me flush against him. "Loving you is the greatest honor of my life. You gave me not only you, but two children to love."

My hand rests against his beating heart. "You'll never know how much I love you." I sniffle and he once again wipes my eyes.

"Can I kiss my wife now?" he looks at Mark.

"Make it a good one," Mark smirks. "By the power bestowed on me from the website of ordained dot com, I now pronounce you husband and wife."

Liam wraps his arms tighter around my waist and dips me back. "You heard the reverend."

His lips press against mine as he cradles me back. Our lips mold to one another as I kiss my husband. The man who I know I'll spend the rest of my life with because we are a perfect match. He pulls me back up and then lifts Aarabelle. He kisses her cheek and she wraps her arms around him.

"I love you," Liam tells us both.

"I yuv you," Aara replies.

I glance at my family and friends around me and joy explodes from within. I've never been this happy or more sure of where I am. Sometimes you have to wade through the bad to find the good. Life isn't easy, but with Liam by my side, I know I don't have to carry it all on my own. Our love will heal us and lift us up.

EPILOGUE

LIAM

"IT'S TIME." NATALIE shakes me and I go to swat at her. Which then is followed by a slap on my back.

"Lee," I groan. I'm exhausted. We had a bunch of dives and training things this week. I've gotten a total of maybe ten hours of sleep all week. "Not now."

"No, wake up! It's time. Like the baby is coming."

What?

That wakes me up. I sit forward and look over as she looks unimpressed. "Okay, I'm awake now."

"I already called Aaron. He's on his way to get Aarabelle. I'm going to get my bag," she explains slowly as if I'm the two-year-old. Although, at this moment I feel a little out of my element.

She's going to have our son.

The last few months, Natalie's had a few minor complications. Her fake contractions were pretty much nonstop. I became a little crazy over this and asked the doctor several times to make it stop. The biggest scare came a few weeks ago when she couldn't feel him move. We had to go to the hospital for another ultrasound, which was great, but Lee was a mess. She cried for hours and begged him to move. I never felt more helpless.

"Okay, come on. We need to get the bag, get in the car . . ." I start to tick them off and another contraction must've hit because she grabs my shoulder and squeezes. "Shit!" I scream as her nails dig in.

"Aaron better get here soon or you're going to be delivering our son."

"The hell I am!" She's lost her mind.

"Liam, get out of bed."

Right.

Bag.

Car.

Hospital.

I can do this.

We have our bag and Aarabelle's by the hall closet. I grab them and put them by the front door. I rush back upstairs and grab Aarabelle from her crib. She's going to be a beast when I wake her. I swear she's the cutest kid in the world, but she has horns. They come out when you interrupt her sleep.

I gently lift her and pray she doesn't open her eyes. I somehow manage to keep her asleep and put her down on the couch. If she wakes up the next time, it's on Aaron.

I hear a knock and open the door.

"Hey, man."

"Hey," I sound like I just ran a marathon. "Aara's on the couch and that pink bag is hers."

Aaron laughs and then stops. "I'm not waking her," he says as it dawns on him he'll get her wrath.

"All on you, bro."

"Thanks," he smirks. It was strained for the first few weeks after the wedding between all of us, but then Aaron met Rebecca, and that seems to have eased some of the tension. They've been together these last few months and he seems really happy.

After that, he didn't look at Natalie and me as if we were hurting him all the time. He comes and gets Aarabelle regularly, and when he dropped her off last week while Natalie was out, we sat and had a beer.

It was odd but a step in the right direction.

"Liam!" Natalie yells out, and I take the stairs two at a time.

"I'm here."

"Did you forget to grab me? I'm kind of the key piece here." Her face scrunches and I rush over.

"Never. Plus, you're kinda scary right now."

"Uh huh."

We get down the stairs. Aaron has Aarabelle in his arms as she shoots daggers at him. I laugh to myself because at least it's not me.

Lee walks over to her and rubs her back. "Bye, my sweet girl. I'll see you soon." She kisses her and I see the tears welling in her eyes.

"Lee, you'll see her as soon as we have the baby."

"I know," she says as she kisses the top of her head.

"I'll bring her by when Liam calls," Aaron explains. It's weird that we can all be around each other so easily, but hey, I'll take it. I think for Aara's sake, we all try extra hard. And now that Becky's around, I don't have to watch him eye fuck my wife.

"Okay, car now before we don't make it . . ." I nudge Lee and she nods.

I grab the towel and rush out to the car. I try to be discreet and not let her see what I'm doing. There's not much chance she won't catch me, but you can't blame me for trying to protect the seats.

"Liam Dempsey!" she yells as she waddles behind me. She's such a cute, little penguin. "I'll cut you."

"Oh, I love when you talk sweet to me," I reply playfully.

"You left me back there. Your pregnant and having contractions wife . . ."

"No, I was preparing Robin so you'll be comfortable."

Her eyes narrow and she tilts her head. I'm screwed. I rush over and grab her arm and help her to the car. She sits down and I rush over to the other side. I can feel her hostility and I haven't even gotten inside.

"You're dead."

"I figured."

"Good . . . it'll make it less awkward when I kill you."

I grab her hand and kiss the top. Maybe I can soothe her by being swoony. "I love you so much, sweetheart. You're going to make me the happiest man in the world today."

"You're still dead."

Or not. She squeezes my hand with herculean strength and I try to pry it away, but she just grabs harder.

"I need my hand."

She doesn't say anything, but I can feel her eyes burning holes into the side of my face.

We arrive at the hospital and they bring her to the room. Once she's connected to a bunch of monitors, I start making calls. I call my command to let them know, and I'm granted immediate baby leave. I'm half tempted to tell them to forget it since I'm apparently now married to the devil. Her face turns some funky color and she hates me.

"Liam." Her voice is suddenly sweet, and I wonder what the hell is going on.

"Yes, sweetheart?"

"I want you to promise that whatever I say in the next few hours you will forget."

"I can do that."

"Okay, good. Because I hate you." Her face turns bright red and all her muscles tense as the contraction hits. I look at the monitor in amazement.

"Wow, that's a strong one!" I look at the lines going up and down.

"You're a fucking genius!" she says through gritted teeth.

I look at her and smile. Which probably isn't the smartest thing in the world, but she's kinda busy and I enjoy playing with fire.

"I'm going to pretend you don't want me to forget that."

The contraction passes and the nurse comes in before she can reply. I make note to buy her something pretty for saving my ass.

"You're almost nine centimeters. It's too late for an epidural. I'm going to get the doctor. You're going to have this baby very soon." I suddenly feel faint.

I rush over to Lee's side and grab her hand and kiss her forehead. "We're going to have our son soon. You're so perfect, sweetheart. So amazing and perfect."

"Liam," she says sounding exhausted. "I love you and I'm scared."

"Why?"

"What if something goes wrong?"

"I'm right here. I'll be by your side the whole time. You can do this," I try to reassure her, but she's been having dreams that there will be something wrong with the baby or the birth. I can't really argue her insanity because they're dreams and she threatens to kill me quite often.

I do like to drive her nuts. I'll give her that.

"I don't want anything to be wrong." Her lower lip trembles.

My hands hold her face and I press my forehead to hers. "If something is wrong, we'll handle it. Don't worry until there's something to worry about. I've got you."

I don't know how to help her and it kills me, but I know I have to keep it together.

She nods and sucks in a deep breath.

"Are we ready, Mrs. Dempsey?" A small thrill runs through

me each time I hear someone call her that. It reminds me that this woman is mine now. That she chose me, and I somehow convinced her to marry me.

"If he's ready to come out, then I guess we are." I squeeze her hand and then she adds on. "With no drugs."

"Drugs are overrated." Her eyes flash with hostility, and I put my hands up in mock surrender. "Of course, I don't know this . . ."

"Hate."

"You love me."

Natalie grunts and the doctor gives me a sympathetic look. Dr. Contreras checks her for what I don't know. I mean, is it like a turkey that the little plastic thing pops? This whole checking her thing baffles me.

"Okay, Natalie. I need you to give me a push."

She looks at me and they lift her legs. I don't comment because I know it'll end with me getting punched in the balls, so I just stay by her side. She groans and sweat breaks across her face, and I'm pretty sure my hand is now detached from my body. Where the hell does this hundred and twenty-five pound woman have this strength?

"Hand, hand, hand," I say as it starts to turn purple.

Fucking hell.

"My vagina is on fire as I push your giant kid out. Suck it up," Natalie says with a little too much happiness at my pain.

"Again," the doctor orders.

I don't even have a second before my fingers mash together as she squeezes them and pops a few out of joint. Well, not really, but it feels like it.

"The baby is crowning," the doctor says.

"Crowning?" I ask.

"Come see."

I head down as Natalie breathes and lays her head on the

pillow. There are some things I can't unsee, and this is one. I'm not queasy by nature, but I can never look at her pussy again and not think of this image. A giant, bald, nasty looking thing is stretching her, and I'm pretty sure I'm going to hurl.

Instead of freaking her out, I head back to her side. I'll take the broken fingers before that shit.

"Is he coming?" Lee asks.

Still unable to form words, I nod and offer her my hand.

"Liam?"

How the hell do I explain how disturbed I am? I know I need to say something, so I just let it out. "Yup, it's coming all right."

"Just a few more pushes, Lee, and you're right there." The doctor saves my ass this time because I don't know what I would've said if I had to go further than that. "Another contraction is coming."

"Okay," Lee says and then she pushes again. Her whole body is tight as she lets out a long cry.

"Do you want to see him?" the doctor asks. Is she high?

"No. I'm good."

She smiles knowingly. "Okay. One more, Lee. One more push and he'll be out," Dr. Contreras tells her and I look at Lee once more.

This is the woman who's going to bring my son into the world. The woman who gave me a family I could only dream of. We were meant to be and now we'll have another child. A son who will bear my name. This perfect, gorgeous woman who I hope to knock up at least ten more times.

"I love you, Natalie."

She huffs and puts her hand on my face. "I love you."

"Push!" the doctor yells and sheer determination covers Natalie's face.

She does what she's told and then I hear the most remarkable sound ever.

My son's first cry.

I look down as the doctors and nurses start to clean him and then they place him on my wife's chest. I stare at him in wonder. My son. A boy. Natalie cries as she holds him and touches his hands, feet, and face.

She looks up at me with tears and a smile. "He's perfect."

"He came from you; of course he would be," I reply and press my lips to hers. Then I touch my son's fingers. He's here and has all his fingers and toes. He's got the most important part too.

The doctor comes over and cuts the cord after I refuse. No, thank you. They weigh him and clean him up as I watch over him. I don't think my eyes leave him for even a moment.

Once he's wrapped in a blanket, the nurse extends her hands and places him in my arms.

I look at Natalie and then back to him. Tears fill my eyes as I hold my son for the first time. My heart just grew twice the size as I look at him, half me, half Natalie. I walk over and sit next to Lee as her hand touches his arm.

"Hi, Shane. I'm your dad."

The End

Continue on in the Salvation Series with *Defenseless,* available now.

keep up with CORINNE

THANK YOU SO MUCH for all your love and support! If you'd like to keep up with what I have going on, be sure to sign up for my newsletters. As a subscriber, you'll receive access to exclusives, lost love letters, giveaways, and lots more!

You can also follow me on BookBub, social media, and receive text alerts.

All this information including links can be found on my website: *www.corinnemichaels.com*

books by
CORINNE MICHAELS

THE SALVATION SERIES
Beloved
Beholden
Consolation
Conviction
Defenseless

THE RETURN TO ME SERIES
Say You'll Stay
Say You Want Me
Say I'm Yours
Say You Won't Let Go:
A Return to Me / Masters and Mercenaries Crossover

STANDALONE NOVELS
We Own Tonight
One Last Time

acknowledgements

MY ATTEMPT TO KEEP this short and sweet should be interesting.

My readers: I can never fully explain what it means to me that you not only took a chance on me, but that some of you have stuck with me. I know I tend to keep leaving you with these crazy cliffhangers and you still love me. The support that you give me is astonishing and humbling. I love you so much!

My beta readers: I really am the luckiest person because of you. Jennifer, Melissa, Katie, Roxana, Linda, and Mandi . . . you make me laugh, keep me on my toes, and always striving to impress you. You are some picky bitches but I wouldn't know what to do without you.

My early readers: Melissa & Alison, you guys are the first to get a full glimpse and each time I bite my nails. Thank you for dealing with my neurosis and messages. I love you to the moon!

Laurelin Paige: Without you, my world would be a dull place. Your support, friendship, and wisdom are insurmountable. You make me a better person and writer. You deal with my insecurities and constant crying but still love me and for that I'm eternally grateful. (I hope you at least pricked a damn tear at this.)

Christy Peckham: No words can explain how much your friendship means. None can come close. You make me smile daily, put up with my hilarious messages ← admit it they're funny, and still stick around.

Melissa Saneholtz & SFab Team: The word publicist doesn't seem fitting for what you do. You run my life pretty much and I couldn't imagine anyone else doing this with me. To the team . . . oh, how we laugh. I love you guys and can't thank you enough for all the support.

Stabby Birds: You guys are the best people I know. You're my sisters through and through. We laugh, cry, and bond together like nothing I've ever seen before. I love you!

My Fairy Godmothers: Laura, Lauren, and Christine . . . you are the true meaning of friendship. You were behind me each step of the way. Cheering me on, messaging me, and making me smile. I learned so much from you and love you three!

FYW: The writing world could only be so lucky to know people like you. Thank you for being who you are. #WednesdaysWeWearPink

Claire Contreras, Mia Asher, Whitney Gracia Williams, Rebecca Yarros, Mandi Beck, Kyla Linde, Kennedy Ryan, SL Scott, Lucia Franco, EK Blair, Kristy Bromberg, Pepper Winters, Elisabeth Grace, Livia Jamerlan, & Angie McKeon—thank you for making me smile, laugh, talking through one of my crazy ideas, and just being my friends. I'm truly blessed to have you in my life.

Jesey: I haven't been able to do this until now. Thank you. Because of something we dreamt of two years ago, look where we are. It's amazing to think the friendship we've had has somehow twisted our worlds to this place. I love you!

My Instagram girls: You make the absolute most beautiful things I've ever seen. EVER! I love you all so much! @tiffany.the.bibliophile , @smuttybooklover, @fixtion_fangirl, @dragonflyreads, @butthisbook, @macie.reads, @thereadingruth, @jengare, @demeriahh & so many more.

My editor: Lisa, you make editing fun and often funny. Thank you for the support and friendship through this process.

My formatter: Christine, I learned page breaks! Seriously, you are first-class in this business. Your professionalism and attention to detail are above and beyond. You work tirelessly and it doesn't go unnoticed.

My cover designer: Sarah, thank you for making two of the most beautiful covers ever.

My photographer: Lauren, thank you for capturing everything this story entails.

My proofreader: Ashley, thank you for finding all the errors and making it shine.

Lisa from The Rock Stars of Romance: THANK YOU! Your support has meant everything to the success of this series. I can't begin to thank you enough. I love your face!

Reanell: Thank you for letting me use your name and I didn't even make you a villain!

Bloggers: I don't think you guys understand what you do for the book world. It's not a job you get paid for (well, not nearly what you deserve). It's something you love and you do because of that. Thank you from the bottom of my heart.

To my husband and children, I'm so lucky to have you. You probably bear the worst part of this process. I love you three more than anything in this world. Thank you for putting up with all that you do. I know I need to put the computer and phone down more because you deserve that. Thank you for being here and supporting me day after day. Thank you for letting me cry when my feelings are hurt. Smile when something amazing happens. But mostly thank you for loving me and believing in me.

about the author

NEW YORK TIMES, USA Today, and Wall Street Journal Bestseller Corinne Michaels is the author of multiple bestselling contemporary romance novels. She's an emotional, witty, sarcastic, and fun loving mom of two beautiful children. Corinne is happily married to the man of her dreams and is a former Navy wife.

After spending months away from her husband while he was deployed, reading and writing was her escape from the loneliness. She enjoys putting her characters through intense heartbreak and finding a way to heal them through their struggles. Her stories are chock full of emotion, humor, and unrelenting love.

www.corinnemichaels.com

Made in the USA
Las Vegas, NV
03 December 2022

61035443R00162